GONE

A WOLF LAKE THRILLER

DAN PADAVONA

head of her, a tank-topped man with a hairy back draped his
rms around two young boys. Robyn turned her head so she
ouldn't gag. The man hadn't used enough deodorant, and the
mperature had risen to ninety degrees, steaming for early
ugust in upstate New York.

The teenager at the gate took their tickets, and Dylan scam-
red ahead of Robyn and raced toward a black horse with a
ghtning bolt across its side.

"Not so fast, Dylan. Stay with me."

Robyn doubted Dylan heard her over the clamor. Children
ughed and squealed as they climbed atop horses, parents
isting their kids with grunts. She reached for Dylan and
lped him onto the horse. The dark-haired boy was small for
age and couldn't swing his leg high enough to reach the
ddle. Once Robyn settled Dylan atop his favorite horse, the
niliar Calliope music began, and the ride spun, working up to
risk pace that caused Robyn's eyes to cross. She wasn't the
e to get sick on theme park rides, especially on a child's
raction like the merry-go-round. But the heat had taken its
on Robyn, sapping her strength and dehydrating her body.
closed her eyes and chugged a water bottle.

Dylan's delighted screams and laughter made the trip worth-
le. The boy deserved a fun time at the park, free of worries.
would enter the first grade next month, and the full-on sprint
ard high school graduation would commence. Time flew by
fast.

After the merry-go-round, Robyn bought a bag of kettle corn
shared it with Dylan as they walked hand in hand down a
k old-time street lined with shops and restaurants. Here, the
d thinned, with most people venturing toward the east end
e park and the looping coasters. Smiling down at her son,
yn wished she could bottle this evening and save it forever.

n the distance, a few miles beyond Empire Mountain and

1

The crowded amusement park made Ro[...]
feel claustrophobic.

She twisted sideways to squeeze thro[...]
of people, never letting go of Dylan's hand. Her so[...]
old and too curious for his own good, prone to r[...]
turned her head. She'd brought the boy to E[...]
against her better judgment. The crowds thi[...]
summer, when everyone wanted to enjoy the [...]
munch candy apples before the autumn chill [...]
park closed its doors until next May. After Dylan[...]
last month, which had attracted only three ch[...]
neighborhood—Robyn's family lived in Illinois[...]
son a fun evening in the park.

Dylan tugged Robyn's hand, leading her a[...]
shop and toward the merry-go-round.

"We already rode the merry-go-round thr[...]
said, grimacing over the pleading tone of her[...]
was becoming her mother.

"Just one more time," said Dylan.

Robyn dug two tickets out of her pocket[...]

the haunted house, the sun descended over the lake, making the water appear on fire. The lights flickered on throughout the park. Soon it would be time to leave, and their day together would become a lost memory.

Inside the souvenir shop, Robyn searched for an Ally the Alligator stuffed animal. Dylan loved Ally and watched the Empire Coasters promotional cartoon every Saturday morning. This evening, he wore his favorite T-shirt, with the grinning gator on the front.

As Robyn reached for the top shelf to retrieve a stuffed animal, her skin prickled. She swung around to a shop packed with people. She swore someone was watching her, but nobody looked her way.

"What's wrong, Mommy?"

"Nothing," Robyn said, chewing her lip.

Rising onto tiptoe, she snatched the alligator and handed it to Dylan, whose eyes widened. He hugged the stuffed animal against him, happier than she'd seen him in years.

"This is the best. Ally is the coolest."

"If you say so," Robyn said, with a snicker.

She wondered why kids loved the silly alligator so much. Then again, her parents' generation had grown up adoring a mouse. Who was she to judge?

Setting a hand on Dylan's shoulder, Robyn steered the boy through the throng of shoppers until she located the checkout counter. A harried woman with bifocals and gray hair struggled to keep up with customers, the line stretching halfway through the store. With a sigh, Robyn took her place in line, keeping Dylan at her side. At least the air-conditioned interior kept them out of the heat while they waited.

The line moved quicker than Robyn expected, the woman behind the counter working with experienced efficiency. When Robyn and Dylan reached the checkout counter, the hair on the back of her neck rose. From the corner of her eye, a shadowed figure moved behind a rack of T-shirts.

"Miss?"

She turned back to the cashier, who waited for Robyn to place the stuffed animal on the counter.

"Sorry," said Robyn, drawing a confused look from Dylan.

"Is everything all right?" the woman asked.

"Yes, I . . . thought I saw someone I know."

The gray-haired woman bagged the alligator. "Anything else?"

"No, just the stuffed animal."

"Very good. That will be twenty-nine dollars."

Robyn removed the credit card from her wallet, her eyes traveling around the store, worried someone was following her. She brushed the hair off her forehead, certain the heat and the long day were playing tricks on her. Her mind traveled back to six years ago, when the stalking began in Chicago—the phone calls with nobody speaking on the other end of the line, Robyn returning home from work to find open windows and items out of place, as though someone had crept inside and rearranged her belongings. She'd phoned the police after multiple break-ins. Because nothing had been stolen, the police wrote her fears off to an overactive imagination.

But that didn't explain the notes affixed to her bedroom headboard.

You can't leave me.

The stalking ended after Robyn accepted a software engineering position in New York State and moved across the country. She'd been only twenty-one then, Dylan two months old and born out of wedlock, as Robyn's mother loved to point out. Her parents never approved of Robyn leaving Illinois. Who would support Robyn? Why raise Dylan without an extended family? Shouldn't she marry the boy she'd slept with?

The cashier cleared her throat and kicked Robyn out of her daze. Behind them, the line of shoppers waiting to pay for their items glared. Robyn handed her credit card to the cashier. As soon as they exited the souvenir shop, Dylan removed the stuffed animal and tossed the bag in the trash.

"Is that a good idea?" Robyn asked. "You don't want to get Ally dirty before you get home."

"I'll keep her safe." Dylan cradled the alligator in his arms, bringing a smile to Robyn's lips. "Thanks, Mommy. This has been the best day ever."

Robyn's throat constricted. "Anything for my favorite son."

Dylan narrowed his eyebrows. "But I'm your only son."

"That's right, and you're still my favorite."

"Whatever. You're weird." Dylan pointed at the haunted house. "Can we go there next?"

"That's not a great idea, Dylan."

"Why not?"

"That's a big kids' ride," Robyn said, eyeing the steeples of the decrepit Victorian mansion looming over the park.

A howling dog sound effect traveled from the upper floors of the haunted house.

"I'm not scared."

"I'm sure you're not, but I only have enough tickets for two more rides. Anyway, I thought you wanted to ride the flying swings."

"Yeah, the flying swings!"

Robyn swallowed, thankful she'd changed Dylan's mind. The thought of slinking around a gloomy haunted house, with costumed actors bearing fake weapons and following them through the dark, sent a shiver down her back. She swung her head around and studied the crowd. Everywhere she looked, teenagers laughed and sprinted toward thrill rides, while mothers and fathers held hands with their children or pushed them in strollers.

Nobody is following me, Robyn said to herself. *This crowd is making me paranoid.*

The howling dog pulled Robyn's attention to the haunted house. When she turned around, Dylan had disappeared.

Live-wire panic surged through her body. She swiveled and called his name. How had he slipped out of her grasp? All around Robyn, the crowd surged and towered over her, blocking her view.

"Dylan?" Robyn pushed between two men carrying milkshakes. "Dylan?"

Her voice drew concerned stares. A few people stopped what they were doing and turned in a circle, seeking the lost child. But he'd disappeared, as if a hand had reached out of the dusky sky and plucked the boy off the pavement.

"Oh, my God."

"Did you lose your boy?" asked a woman in a Yankees baseball cap.

"He was right here a second ago."

"Calm down," the woman said, clutching a young girl by the shoulder. "Maria ran off on me last spring. They never get far. The worst thing you can do is panic and leave the area. Your son is probably searching for you right now."

"I hope you're right," Robyn said, her mouth dry.

As the crowd cleared, she spotted a security guard. The mustached man's belly protruded over his belt, and the sneer marked him as someone who didn't enjoy his job. Still, he was Robyn's only hope. The mother who'd attempted to calm Robyn down disappeared with her daughter, likely thankful she hadn't lost her own child. Robyn hurried to the guard, whose badge read *Faustin*.

"Can you help me, sir? I can't find my son."

Faustin, who was busy accosting a group of teenagers for running, set his hands on his hips. "Lost your son, miss? How old is he?"

"Six."

"And how long has he been missing?"

"Less than a minute. He was right here," Robyn said, motioning with her arms. "I turned around, and he was gone."

Faustin raised a walkie-talkie to his lips. "I've got a missing six-year-old boy near the haunted house." He lifted his chin at Robyn. "Give me his name and a description."

As Robyn followed his orders, her gaze landed on a boy in a green T-shirt, giggling and wrapping his arms around a roaming Ally the Alligator a hundred feet away. Her heart jumped into her throat.

"Dylan!"

Behind Robyn, Faustin growled into his walkie-talkie. "False alarm. We found the boy."

Robyn ran to Dylan, who glanced up at his mother, not understanding why he'd scared her to death.

"I told you to never run off. What if someone grabbed you and took you away?"

"Mommy, it's Ally! Isn't she awesome?"

Though Robyn couldn't see the actor beneath the mask, she discerned the helpless look Ally returned. The character gave Dylan a gentle nudge, a signal to return to his mother. Dylan hugged Ally one last time. Robyn knelt before Dylan and grasped his arms, locking eyes with the boy.

"You're never to do that again, do you understand?"

"But I only wanted to see her."

"If you want to come back to Empire Coasters, you'll obey me from now on. I mean it, Dylan. The park is a dangerous place. Never, never run away from me again."

A tear trickled out of Dylan's eye. Though Robyn wanted to get through to her son, she hadn't intended to make him cry.

"Do we have to leave now?"

Robyn stood and blew out her frustration through her bottom lip. She surveyed the park, busy with people waiting for the nighttime fireworks display. "No, I suppose not. I promised you a fun day at the park, and your mommy always delivers."

"One more ride?"

"Sure, kiddo. You choose."

Dylan pointed at the flying swings and hopped in place.

"The flying swings it is. Let's go."

The line thinned, and Robyn reached the ticket taker in short order. She handed a ticket to the woman guarding the turnstile and kissed Dylan on the forehead.

Dylan lifted his head. "Aren't you coming, too?"

"I think I'll sit this one out if you don't mind." Between the hot temperature and her frayed nerves, Robyn couldn't stomach spinning around for the next five minutes. "Mommy will wait at the gate. When the swings stop, don't climb down from your chair. I'll come get you."

Dylan nodded.

Robyn turned to the ticket taker. "Is it okay if I help my son into his seat? I'll leave before the ride starts."

"No problem at all," she said. "And you can enter through the exit gate and help him down when the ride stops."

"Thank you."

Holding Dylan by the hand, Robyn walked her son to an open chair and lifted him. After she ensured he was strapped in, she planted another kiss on his cheek and hurried for the gate, never taking her eyes off the boy.

A metal barricade surrounded the flying swings. Robyn leaned against the barricade and snapped a picture of Dylan with her phone. Then the ride started spinning, slowly at first, before building in speed until the riders became a blur. During the first few rotations, Robyn photographed her son, who wore a permanent grin. The centrifugal force and wind whipped his hair back and jiggled his cheeks. Eventually, the chairs swung too quickly to make out faces. Robyn was no longer sure where Dylan was, only that he sat in one of the outermost chairs. She chewed the inside of her cheek, hoping the ride would stop soon.

The ride seemed to last forever until the chairs slowed. Robyn searched for the boy, but he was on the opposite side of the ride now. She craned her head, seeking her son as the next riders brushed against her, forcing her against the barricade. In front of her, an overweight boy in his early teens stumbled down from the swings with a green face and vomited. The retching boy set off a repulsed chorus. The other riders gave him a wide berth. A maintenance worker in a gold Empire Coasters uniform rushed inside to clean the mess, as looky-loos gawked and laughed at the sick boy.

Where was Dylan?

Robyn tried to squeeze through the exit, but there were too many people pushing in the opposite direction.

A bearded man grumbled, "The entrance is over there, you idiot. Can't you read the signs?"

Ignoring the man, Robyn turned sideways and slipped past the crowd. The last riders climbed down from the swings. Dylan was gone.

Robyn cupped her elbows with her hands and searched the crowd. This time, she refused to panic. After all the excitement, Dylan had forgotten to stay in his chair. Robyn turned in a circle.

"Dylan? Where did you go?" She caught the ticket taker's eye. "Have you seen my son?"

The woman shook her head with concern. "Are you sure he didn't slip by you?"

"He probably did," Robyn said, though she didn't see Dylan anywhere.

Faustin, the security guard who'd helped her earlier, waddled over. "What's going on now?"

"It's Dylan. I told him to stay on the ride until I helped him out of the chair. Now I can't find him."

"He's probably with Ally again." Faustin spoke into his walkie-talkie. "Anyone have eyes on Ally? I'm looking for the same boy that ran off a few minutes ago . . . yeah, some parents are too busy on their phones to bother with their kids . . . right, same description . . . you sure he's not with the alligator?"

Robyn covered her mouth.

"Don't worry, miss. We'll find your boy. He couldn't have gotten far."

But as Robyn ran her gaze over the packed amusement park, Dylan was nowhere to be found. Cold terror welled through her chest. This time, she wouldn't find him.

2

Dusky blues blanketed the sky and reflected against the waters of Wolf Lake. Sheriff Thomas Shepherd blinked awake in bed. He'd dozed off after a late dinner and lost track of time. Now his girlfriend, Chelsey Byrd, snuggled beside him, the blankets pulled over her shoulder.

Thomas raked a hand through his unruly, sandy hair and eased off the bed, not wanting to wake Chelsey. She'd complained of a headache since returning from work this afternoon, and with a summer flu making the rounds through the village, Thomas had urged her to rest. When the mattress squeaked, she mumbled something indiscernible beneath her breath. At the foot of the bed, Jack, the huge wolf-like dog Thomas had rescued from the state park last year, raised a curious head and followed Thomas with his eyes. Then Jack lay his snout over Chelsey's legs, keeping vigil, as though he'd read the newspaper articles about the flu outbreak. Thomas assumed Jack was a Siberian husky, though his veterinarian wasn't convinced. The staff at the animal hospital cocked eyebrows and whispered among themselves whenever Thomas brought the dog in for a checkup.

The sheriff wandered to the window of his A-frame overlooking the lake. His guest house stood between the main house and the shoreline. LeVar Hopkins, a reformed gang member studying criminal justice at the community college, lived in the guest house. One light shone from the front of the guest house, where LeVar preferred to study.

As the sky turned black and the stars sharpened, Thomas glanced over his shoulder at Chelsey. After the doctor diagnosed Thomas with Asperger's syndrome as a child, Thomas's classmates bullied him throughout school. He never dreamed he'd win a beautiful girlfriend. Yet Thomas and Chelsey fell in love as teenagers and dated until senior year, when depression struck Chelsey. Unable to deal with her emotions, Chelsey broke up with Thomas and rescinded her college scholarship. They'd planned to study criminal justice together at Cortland, but Thomas left for college alone, and Chelsey vanished from Wolf Lake without saying goodbye.

Heartbroken, Thomas didn't expect he'd ever encounter Chelsey again. But after he returned from California, where he'd worked as an LAPD detective, fate reunited Thomas with Chelsey, who'd founded Wolf Lake Consulting, a private investigation firm. After a year of dating, they realized they were still in love, and Chelsey agreed to sell her house and move in with Thomas.

Chelsey moaned and turned over. The last week had been a busy one at Wolf Lake Consulting, with Chelsey working twelve-hour days to close investigations. Thomas worried she'd run her body down and gotten herself sick.

While Chelsey slept, Thomas slipped out of the bedroom and closed the door. Downstairs, he set the kettle on the stove and poured hot water over a packet of echinacea and peppermint tea. The combination boosted immunity and cooled sore throats. He sliced a lemon and dropped half into the tea, then wrapped the other half and placed it inside the refrigerator. Inside the cupboard, he located the vitamin C tablets and jostled two out of the bottle. He swallowed one, just in case Chelsey was contagious, and set the second aside for her.

The stairs creaked beneath his weight as Thomas carried the tea upstairs, careful not to spill the hot brew and scald himself. When he opened the bedroom door, Chelsey sat up and rubbed her eyes while Jack licked her face.

"I didn't expect you'd be up," Thomas said, setting the tea on the nightstand.

"I can't believe I slept for three hours. Is that for me?"

"Peppermint and echinacea with lemon. Just the way you like it."

"You're a saint," she said, gripping the cup by the handle. She sipped the tea and winced from the heat. "This is wonderful, but I'm not sick."

"You have a headache, which is among the most common flu symptoms, along with muscle aches, fever, sore throats, coughs, and—"

Chelsey waved a hand in the air, cutting him off. Thomas pressed his lips together, knowing he was obsessing.

"I only have a headache."

"What about the muscle pain you complained about?"

"That is from stacking boxes of case files at the office."

"You should let LeVar do the heavy lifting. Make him earn his internship credit."

Chelsey smirked. "Raven and I take advantage of LeVar too much as it is."

Raven Hopkins, LeVar's sister, was Chelsey's closest friend and a fellow investigator at the firm. She lived in a state park cabin with Darren Holt, a former Syracuse police officer who'd left the force to take the ranger's position at Wolf Lake State Park.

"LeVar is a lifesaver. If you'd told me when I first moved back to Wolf Lake that I'd offer LeVar my guest house, I'd have said you were crazy."

"I held the same prejudices. He was the enforcer for the Harmon Kings gang, and every rumor in Wolf Lake suggested he'd killed rival gang members."

"Rumors," Thomas said, twisting his mouth. "The kid needed a break. The first time someone showed him a path out of gang life, he took it. And now he's an honors student, with a career in law enforcement ahead of him."

"And he's good with Scout," Chelsey said, referring to Scout Mourning, Thomas's fifteen-year-old neighbor.

A car accident had paralyzed Scout from the waist down three years ago, before spinal implants and a revolutionary operation restored the girl's ability to walk earlier this summer.

"Good with Scout? They're best friends."

Chelsey looked at Thomas from the corner of her eye. "Do you think there's something going on between them?"

Thomas did a double take. "What? You mean boyfriend and girlfriend?"

"Why not?"

"Well, there's a five-year age difference. LeVar only has two semesters remaining at the community college, and Scout is still in high school."

"They care for each other a great deal."

"As friends, sure. I mean, they listen to music and help each other with homework assignments."

"So you're saying they study together."

"Yeah."

"Remember when we told our parents we were studying together?" Chelsey grinned and made air quotes around *studying together*.

Thomas's cheeks reddened. "Uh-oh. Should I be concerned

about them spending time inside the guest house without supervision?"

"They're both trustworthy. But it wouldn't be a terrible idea to mention your concern to Naomi."

Scout's mother, Naomi, raised her daughter alone. Glen Mourning, Scout's father, blamed himself for the car accident that crippled his daughter and hadn't faced his family for the better part of two years. Since the successful operation, Glen had emerged from his shell and become a father again.

"*My* concern? You're the one who claims LeVar and Scout are fooling around. They're just friends." When Chelsey gave Thomas a pointed stare, he sighed. "Fine. I'll make sure they keep the shades open and the door unlocked whenever they're inside the guest house."

"You'll make a great father one day, Thomas."

He swallowed. "Are you sure you aren't sick?"

"I don't have the flu. But," Chelsey said, lifting the cup to her lips, "this tea is a godsend. You sure know how to make a woman happy."

The phone rang. Thomas cleared his throat and answered.

"Thomas here."

"Hate to bother you on your night off, but we've got a missing child at Empire Coasters amusement park. Possible abduction."

It was Veronica Aguilar, Thomas's lead deputy at the Nightshade County Sheriff's Department.

"Give me the details."

"The kid's name is Dylan Fournette. Six years old. The mother is Robyn Fournette. She's at the security station inside the park."

"How long has the boy been missing?"

"Forty-five minutes. The park is in lock down, Thomas. Nobody gets in or out until they find the child."

Thomas peeked at the clock. "I can be there within the hour."

"I'll let the head of security know. The guy's name is Ron Faustin, and he's a real trip. If you look up disgruntled in the dictionary, you'll find his picture."

"Will you meet me at the park?"

"Up to you. Dispatch went home with the sniffles, so I'm running point and taking calls. I'm happy to close the shop and join you."

Thomas rubbed his forehead. "No, you'd better stay. Someone needs to be in the office."

"I don't want to overstep my bounds, but we need another deputy. The overtime is dragging all of us down."

"Trust me, I'm working on it. Tell you what. Call in Lambert and mobilize the state police. I want an AMBER alert for the missing boy and checkpoints along all the major thoroughfares leaving the county."

"On it."

"I'll see you at the office afterward."

"All right, Sheriff."

Thomas changed his clothes as Jack dropped his head onto his paws, figuring out he'd be alone again tonight. "Do me a favor and call LeVar. Ask him to dog-sit Jack until I get back."

"What about me?" Chelsey asked.

"You have a headache."

"Not anymore," she said, slipping her sneakers on. "I'll come with you."

"You're sure you're not sick?"

"For the last time, I'm fine. Stop worrying about me. Besides, you could use a second set of eyes at the park. It sounds like Aguilar needs to stay at the station."

"Unfortunately."

"So hire a new deputy."

"If only it were that easy." Thomas snapped his fingers and pointed at Chelsey. "Hey, why don't you hire a new PI?"

Chelsey rolled her eyes. "As you said, if only it were that easy. You know how difficult it is to find a qualified investigator?"

"About as hard as it is to hire a new deputy. Which is why I offered the position to LeVar, except he doesn't want the job."

"And I can't hire him as an investigator until he turns twenty-five," Chelsey said, hustling down the staircase behind Thomas.

Thomas pulled his jacket out of the closet and slipped his arms through the sleeves. He checked the time and grabbed the keys to his silver Ford F-150. "Let's go. Man, I hope we find that kid walking around the park. I love happy endings."

"If he was lost, wouldn't they have found him by now?"

"Given how large the crowds are this time of year, he might be wandering around and searching for his mother." Thomas shifted his jaw. "And if he isn't in the park, the checkpoints should prevent anyone from taking him out of the county."

They stepped into the night, a million stars igniting the sky. Thomas recognized the chill in the air. It was a warning that fall was coming and winter would follow on its heels. He pulled his jacket together as they crossed the dewy yard to the driveway, where Thomas aimed the key fob and unlocked the doors.

As Chelsey climbed into the passenger seat, she finished speaking on the phone with LeVar. "He says Jack can stay with him tonight."

Thomas turned the key in the ignition. He felt as if he'd hardly slept over the last week. And now he had a lost child to recover.

3

The distant lights of Empire Coasters made it appear as though a humongous Christmas tree had fallen on its side and illuminated the countryside. Spotlights swept through the sky, beaming out of Empire Mountain and reflecting off the few clouds meandering over Nightshade County.

Thomas stomped the brakes when he motored into the parking lot. Droves of people filed past his truck and hurried toward their vehicles, trying to beat the crowd. Thomas stopped his pickup along the curb and slapped his forehead.

"Why are they letting everyone leave the park? Empire Coasters should be in lockdown."

Chelsey hopped out of the cab without answering. On the sidewalk outside the gates, a mother and father escorted a girl carrying a wad of cotton candy larger than her head. Most of the cotton candy hadn't made it past the girl's lips and plastered her cheeks instead. All around Thomas and Chelsey, people grumbled, blaming some lost kid for the stupid lockdown. One woman wearing an Empire Coasters T-shirt announced that she'd never return to this park and would take her money to Florida from now on.

Thomas stopped and held out his hands, as if he might halt the flood of people storming toward the parking lot.

"People, people. Slow down. We're searching for a lost child."

"Yeah, we know, Sheriff," a burly man holding a cup of beer slurred. "Somebody should call Superman."

The idiotic joke drew laughter. Thomas threw up his arms.

When Thomas and Chelsey neared the entry gates, a thin security guard with narrow eyes and a black beard hurried to meet them.

"Sheriff Shepherd? I'm Officer Tre Kelly. Well, I'm not a police officer or anything. But Mr. Faustin insists we refer to ourselves as officers. Empire Coasters is a massive operation. Most people don't have a clue how many people come through these gates every summer."

"Speaking of which, why are you letting everyone leave the park?"

The guard gave Thomas an apologetic look. "It was Mr. Faustin's decision, not mine. I'm on the overnight shift, so I just arrived. Follow me, and I'll take you to the security building."

Thomas met Chelsey's eyes, and she shook her head in exasperation.

They filed beneath a concrete archway. A tunnel extended to the left, while the park and its many thrill rides beckoned ahead. Kelly turned down the tunnel and led Thomas and Chelsey past the lost-and-found desk and a wall of lockers, where guests stored their belongings for an exorbitant fee. Two closed doors along the wall read *Crew and Cast Only*.

Kelly pointed to the doors and said, "That's where the actors enter and change into costume."

Chelsey tutted. "And here I thought Ally the Alligator was real. Thanks for ruining the fantasy for me."

"Sorry about that."

The corridor ended at a door, with *Empire Coasters Security* written across the front. Kelly swiped an ID card through a reader, and the door clicked open.

"Follow me," Kelly said, waving Thomas and Chelsey through.

Instead of a room, Thomas encountered a staircase leading down to another tunnel.

"So this is how security moves through the park," Thomas said, glancing around in wonder.

"The tunnel system encompasses the grounds," Kelly said over his shoulder, his voice reverberating off the walls with a hollow sound. "Our engineering team uses the tunnels, too. If the merry-go-round or flying swings break down, we send the mechanics and engineers through the tunnels, so they don't have to deal with the crowd. Empire Coasters covers one hundred acres, but if you hustle, you can cross the entire park in five minutes using the tunnels."

Thomas looked over his shoulder. If someone kidnapped Dylan Fournette, he might have used the tunnels to cross the park before Faustin ordered the lock down. Kelly led them down another corridor, making Thomas wonder where they were in relation to the entrance. Were he to guess, he'd say they were below the roller coasters. The rumble overhead confirmed his theory.

A glass entryway broke up the monotony of the endless gloom. Kelly slid his card through another reader and gained entry to the security headquarters.

A wall of monitors pulled Thomas's attention. He studied video from every attraction inside the park, including a night-vision view inside the haunted house. Two guards stared at

Thomas and Chelsey from behind a long counter. The taller guard's nameplate read Wheeler. He leered at Chelsey, undressing her with his eyes. Thomas grabbed Chelsey's elbow and escorted her away from the counter.

A mustached man with an ample belly pushed past the guards and blocked Thomas from turning down a hallway.

"Sheriff, I'm Ron Faustin, head of security at Empire Coasters. I took Ms. Fournette's report and notified your office."

Thomas set his hands on his hips. "You told my deputy you'd closed the exits."

"That was ninety minutes ago. These people have lives. I can't lock them down forever." When Thomas didn't respond, Faustin held up a hand. "Listen, if we piss too many people off, we'll lose customers, and I'll take the blame."

"A lost child takes precedence."

"Of course. But I sent everyone on my team a digital photograph of the missing boy and a description of the clothes he was wearing. Nobody matching the child's description exited the park."

"So he might still be here."

"He must be. We would have caught anyone leaving with the boy." Faustin motioned at Kelly. "I'll take it from here, officer. Patrol the east end of the park. Could be the coasters freaked the kid out and he's searching for his mother."

Kelly followed Faustin's orders and exited through the glass doorway.

"Where is the boy's mother?"

"Ms. Fournette is inside our conference room. I'll take you to her. Just for the record, parents misplace their children inside our theme park with alarming frequency. They're too busy checking messages or posting pictures to Facebook, so they don't notice when little Johnny runs off."

"Is that what happened tonight?" Chelsey asked, anchoring her hair behind her ear.

Behind the counter, Wheeler nudged his partner with his elbow and whispered something about Chelsey.

Faustin folded his arms. "Ten minutes before Dylan Fournette disappeared from the flying swings attraction, Robyn Fournette came to me in a panic because she'd lost her son."

Thomas shared a glance with Chelsey and asked, "Are you suggesting Dylan went missing twice?"

"That's exactly what I'm saying. The kid spotted Ally the Alligator posing for pictures near the merry-go-round and ran to her. God only knows what distracted the mother from paying attention to her boy. We found Dylan hugging Ally. I doubt the mother even chastised her son for misbehaving. If it were my kid, I'd have tanned his hide and taken him home. These days, you raise your voice and child services show up at your doorstep."

Ignoring Faustin's commentary on parenting in the twenty-first century, Thomas said, "Well, that's good news. Dylan has a history of running from his mother when he sees characters in the park. Perhaps he spotted another character and got lost in the crowd."

"Mark my words. Dylan Fournette didn't leave our park. My guards compared his picture against every child at the exits. No way he got past the security checkpoints. We'll find him wandering among the rides, crying his eyes out because he can't find his mommy."

"Aren't there alternative ways to escape the park?" Chelsey asked.

"Like if someone abducted the boy? No chance. A twelve-foot unscalable wall surrounds the perimeter. Unless a kidnapper brought a ladder, he couldn't make it over the wall, especially with a struggling child tucked under his arm. And if he tried," Faustin said, pointing at the wall of monitors, "we'd capture him on video. Nobody climbed over the wall. As we speak, my team is conducting a thorough sweep of the park. We'll find Dylan Fournette and return him to his mother. I only hope she chooses a different amusement park next time."

Thomas tilted his head down the hallway. "We'd like to speak with the mother now."

Faustin walked Thomas and Chelsey to a rectangular room with windows looking out on the dreary underground tunnel. LED lighting illuminated the room like fireworks on New Year's Eve. A dozen black high-back chairs surrounded a long table. A dark-haired woman sat across the table, shredding a used tissue and sniffling.

"Ms. Fournette? I'm Sheriff Thomas Shepherd with the Nightshade County Sheriff's Department, and this is Chelsey Byrd with Wolf Lake Consulting. We're here to find Dylan."

She dragged the tissue beneath her nose. "Call me Robyn, please. Will you tell these people to let me search for Dylan? I should be out in the park, not sitting by myself in this cave."

"Now, now," Faustin said. "The Empire Coasters security team is the best in the business. They're trained to find lost children. We don't want to locate Dylan and have him panic because he wants his mother, and we don't know where you are. It's better you stay here and allow us to do our jobs."

Thomas sat on the edge of the table. "Robyn, describe your son and tell us what he's wearing tonight."

"Dylan is six years old and has short hair, dark like mine. He's wearing black shorts, white Skechers sneakers, and a green T-shirt with Ally the Alligator on the front."

"Mr. Faustin told us Dylan left your side to meet Ally earlier this evening. Is it possible he did it again?"

Robyn sobbed into her hand. "I'm not sure. I told Dylan not

to climb down from the flying swings until I entered the attraction. But when I circled the swings, he was gone."

The woman's words ran together as her breath flew in and out of her chest.

"Slow down. You'll hyperventilate."

"The flying swings accommodate forty riders," Faustin interjected. "When all those people exit the ride, many of them dizzy and stumbling into each other, it becomes a confusing mess. If Dylan spotted Ally or another character outside the gates, he might have slipped past his mother by weaving through the crowd. Dylan comes up to about here," the head of security said, placing his hand over his thigh. "The smaller the boy, the easier it is to lose track of him."

"Just to be safe," said Thomas, "we issued an AMBER alert and placed state police officers on the main roads leading out of Nightshade County. For now, we'll search the park and ensure Dylan isn't lost and looking for you. The haunted house is near the flying swings, right?"

"Yes," Robyn said, accepting a fresh tissue when Chelsey passed her the box.

"Maybe the haunted house scared him and he's hiding nearby."

4

Robyn didn't trust Ron Faustin, head of security at Empire Coasters, or the sketchy staff of guards he employed. Instead of searching for Dylan, Faustin blamed Robyn for losing her son. And maybe he was right. Couldn't she have done more to keep her son safe? She chided herself for not riding the swings with Dylan. A little motion sickness wouldn't have killed her, and she'd sacrifice anything to protect the boy.

Faustin was a boisterous slob, a man who hated his job only slightly less than he despised the amusement park visitors. The head of security was putting on a show for the sheriff and trying to convince Thomas Shepherd that Faustin had the situation under control. He didn't. Faustin didn't have the slightest idea where to find Dylan, or he would have returned her son already.

As Faustin pontificated on lost children and careless parents, Robyn's gaze wandered to the windows behind her, where two guards watched outside the conference room. They looked like lost miners, minus the pickaxes and sooty faces, and the way they stared at Robyn made her skin crawl.

She'd been on edge since she'd sensed someone following

her inside the souvenir shop. The foreboding paranoia dredged up old ghosts, bringing Robyn back to the nightmarish days after college graduation, when she was certain a stalker had set his eyes on her. But the stalking ceased after she moved from Illinois to New York. No more phone calls in the dead of night, no frightening messages attached to her headboard. It was crazy to assume the man had found her six years later, and this time he'd abducted Dylan.

"Robyn?"

She jumped in her seat, not hearing the sheriff's voice until he set his hands on the table and leaned toward her. Thomas Shepherd had bluish-green, trustworthy eyes. Kind-hearted eyes, Robyn's late grandmother would have said.

"Sorry, I was thinking about Dylan. Did you ask me something?"

The sheriff removed a pen and notepad from his jacket and gave Robyn a contemplative look, as if he sensed there was more to tonight's events than she'd admitted. After her disastrous encounter with the police in Chicago, she'd stopped counting on law enforcement to protect her from the dangers hiding in the shadows. But Thomas Shepherd seemed different. She could tell him everything and feel secure for the first time in her adult life.

"I asked if Dylan's friends were at the park tonight. Is it possible he spotted someone he knows?"

"Brody Carillo," Robyn said, remembering they'd passed the boy with his family near the park entrance. "He's a year older than Dylan and lives a block from our house. They play on the same baseball team."

"Do you have his parents' phone numbers?"

Hope lit a spark in Robyn's heart. Perhaps Dylan had seen Brody and run over to say hello. "Yes, I have Bella's and Cade's numbers."

"Call the parents. Let's hope Dylan is with them."

But when Robyn phoned Bella, her heart sank. She set the phone face-down on the table and shook her head. "Bella says they left at six-thirty because Brody is sleeping at a friend's house tonight."

"They weren't inside the park when Dylan vanished?"

Robyn lowered her eyes. "No."

"Are you married, Robyn?" Chelsey, the private investigator, asked.

"I never married," Robyn said, chewing a nail.

"If you don't mind me asking, who is the father?"

"Why?"

"Sometimes a birth parent decides he wants his child back and goes to extreme measures."

"No, that's impossible." Everyone stared at Robyn. "Dylan's father is just a guy I dated in college. He wasn't ready to be a parent. We broke up six years ago, and I haven't heard from him since."

The sheriff didn't appear convinced, and neither did the investigator assisting him.

"You're positive this guy hasn't contacted you?"

"Yes."

"Even so, I need his name," the sheriff said.

"TJ Soto. We dated during my senior year at the University of Chicago."

Every eye in the room locked on Robyn. Faustin deferred to the sheriff and the private investigator to conduct the interview. Yet he leaned against the wall, wearing a condescending, judgmental smirk that reminded Robyn of her mother.

"After I got pregnant," Robyn said, continuing, "I wasn't sure where to turn. Had I asked, TJ would have offered to drive me to a clinic and paid for an abortion. But I had second thoughts and kept my baby."

"Did your decision anger TJ?"

"I never told him I kept the baby. TJ had his life ahead of him and wasn't prepared to be a parent. We knew we wouldn't stay together after graduation. TJ and I were close, but not so close that we'd considered marriage. It wasn't fair to ask him to throw away his future and father a child."

"So he doesn't know he's a father."

Robyn chewed a nail. "No."

"Where does TJ live these days?"

"I couldn't tell you. It's been six years."

"Do you have family in the area?"

"Everyone lives in Illinois, mostly around Chicago. After graduation, I accepted a software engineering position in New York and never left."

"Let's start with work. You said you're a software engineer?"

Robyn described her job and reiterated that she'd worked with the company for six years.

"Any problems at work?"

"None."

"Nobody at your office who might hold a grudge over an altercation?"

"The people I work with are quiet and keep to themselves."

Sheriff Shepherd scribbled on his notepad. "What about boyfriends? Any recent breakups?"

"I don't have time to date because of work. Heck, I barely have time to take my son anywhere. It wouldn't be right to bring a father figure into Dylan's life."

"No harassing phone calls or men following you?"

You just described my life six years ago, Robyn thought to herself.

Sheriff Shepherd asked another question as Robyn's phone hummed. Praying someone had found Dylan, she peeked at the message.

If you talk, he dies.

Robyn's pulse raced. Chelsey noticed and handed Robyn a bottle of water.

"Are you all right?" the sheriff asked.

Faustin checked his watch, as if he had a pressing engagement elsewhere.

"Yes," Robyn lied. "It's hot in here."

"Who sent you a message?" asked Chelsey.

"My, uh, mother. She wants an update on Dylan."

Robyn slipped the phone inside her pocket. A cold sweat broke along her brow, and she dabbed it with her T-shirt as the sheriff continued his questions. They knew she'd lied about the message and withheld information that might save Dylan.

The time had come. Robyn needed to tell Sheriff Shepherd the truth about her past. What if the same monster who'd stalked Robyn had tracked her to New York and kidnapped Dylan? Her mind raced, the words piling up behind her lips and begging for release. The Chicago police hadn't believed a twenty-one-year-old pregnant girl. But the Nightshade County Sheriff's Department would understand and help the adult version of Robyn, the mother who'd raised a child by herself.

"Sheriff, there's something I need to tell you," she said, a moment before the phone hummed with insistence inside her pocket.

Sheriff Shepherd dropped into the chair across from Robyn and clasped his hands on the table, waiting for her to speak. She set the phone on her thigh and spied the message beneath the table.

You're talking to the sheriff. Shut your mouth, or I'll kill Dylan.

Her flinch almost sent the phone tumbling to the floor. How did the kidnapper know she was with the sheriff? Had he seen security lead the sheriff and private investigator into the tunnels?

"Robyn?" Thomas asked.

Robyn cleared her throat. The phone buzzed again, making her tremble.

A picture of Dylan arrived. The boy's tear-filled eyes stared into the camera. A strip of duct tape covered his mouth. No, this couldn't be happening. Along his throat, a razor-sharp blade lay against Dylan's skin.

Sensing eyes on her, Robyn swiveled her head. The two guards continued to leer at her through the window. The guard named Wheeler hadn't stopped staring at Robyn since she'd arrived at the subterranean security office with Faustin.

"Robyn, you wanted to tell me something," Thomas said.

She turned her attention back to the sheriff. With a shaky hand, she wiped her nose with the tissue.

"Only that I appreciate you responding so quickly and taking the time to help me find my son."

Sheriff Shepherd narrowed his eyes, expecting more. She wanted to tell him the truth, but she wouldn't risk Dylan's life.

"Is that all?"

"That's all."

"Tell me everything that occurred before Dylan's disappearance. Did anyone bother you inside the park?"

"No, sir," Robyn said, rubbing the goosebumps off her arms as she remembered someone following them through the souvenir shop.

Months of a faceless stranger stalking her in Illinois had honed Robyn's instincts. This wasn't her imagination playing tricks on her. The nightmare had begun again. The stranger had found her in New York and wouldn't let her escape.

And this time he'd taken Dylan.

5

Inside Ron Faustin's office, Thomas closed the door and drew a breath.

"You shouldn't have released the guests before I arrived."

Faustin dropped into the chair behind his desk and removed his hat. "Don't act like I don't care about Dylan Fournette, Sheriff. I have children of my own: a twelve-year-old and a toddler. If I lost either, I wouldn't know what to do with myself."

"Yet you opened the exit gate and allowed several thousand people to leave. Any of them could have taken Dylan."

Placards adorned the walls, one framed award proclaiming Empire Coasters as the safest amusement park in New York State, though Thomas noted the award carried a date from ten years ago.

Faustin slammed an open palm against the desk and pointed an accusing finger at Thomas. "I told you. My staff had a picture of Dylan. Nobody matching Dylan's description approached the gates."

"What about the wall surrounding the park? I have a hard time believing it can't be scaled."

"It's twelve feet."

"But Empire Coasters doesn't want its guests to see an unsightly wall, so you camouflage the barrier with trees and bushes."

"And your point is?"

"Anyone who can climb a tree can scale your wall and hop over."

Faustin clasped his hands against his head in exasperation. "With a struggling child under his arm? I'd like to watch that trick." Faustin wheeled around in his chair and called up the security video feeds on his computer. "Our cameras cover the wall. If someone climbed over, we'd catch him on the other side. You might not be aware of this, Sheriff, but our theme park does big business. A single-day ride ticket runs ninety-nine dollars. If we allowed guests to climb in and out of the park, we'd go broke."

"Walk me through the timeline. How long did it take before you closed the exit gates?"

"First, I helped Ms. Fournette search for her son. As you'll recall, this was the second time he'd run off."

"You assumed she was crying wolf."

"I take all matters involving lost children seriously. After Ms. Fournette came to me, we searched for Dylan between the flying swings and merry-go-round. Then we ensured he hadn't returned to Ally."

"Where was Ally?"

"Entering the tunnels. We only place Ally inside the park for ten minutes at a time, three times per day."

Thomas scratched his chin. "But she's your most popular character."

"Exactly. The less our guests see of Ally, the more sought after she is. We want to keep every appearance special."

"So you looked with Ms. Fournette for Dylan. That took what, five minutes?"

"About."

"Then what?"

"I ordered my staff to close the gates."

"That gave the kidnapper five minutes to escort Dylan out of the park and drive off."

"You keep saying kidnapper. There's no evidence someone abducted Dylan Fournette."

"You should have continued the lockdown. The kidnapper could have disguised Dylan and sneaked him through the security checkpoint."

"Hogwash. My team is the best in the business. I believe Dylan Fournette is still in the park." Faustin pulled the cuff back on his shirtsleeve and read his watch. "Given the time, we only have two hours to find him before the park closes."

Thomas tapped his foot. "Name the places Dylan might hide inside Empire Coasters and avoid detection."

"Are you serious? Between all the shops and dark rides—"

"I don't know what a dark ride is."

"A dark ride is an indoor attraction where guests ride vehicles through a scene, like the Florida Everglades in Ally's World."

"Interesting. Dylan left his mother's side to meet Ally. It's possible he went looking for his favorite character again and found Ally's World."

Faustin blew out his mustache. "I fail to see how he'd sneak onto the ride without a ticket. But I agree it's worth checking out."

"What about the haunted house? Is that considered a dark ride?"

"Negative. There are no guided vehicles inside our haunted house."

"Right, I visited when I was younger."

"With all the updates, I doubt you'd recognize the modernized version of our haunted house. Guests walk through the dark, and the characters leap out to scare them." Faustin rolled a shiver off his shoulders. "Not my cup of tea, thank you very much."

"I ask because Dylan disappeared near the haunted house. If the house frightened him, he might have hidden. Remember, he's only six."

"You might be onto something, Sheriff." Faustin lifted his radio. "Wheeler, get your ass into the park and check the area around the haunted house, especially the graveyard. And tell Jones to conduct a thorough search of Ally's World. It's possible Dylan Fournette is hiding inside the attraction and searching for Ally." After Wheeler issued a confirmation, Faustin set the radio down. "Believe me. I'm doing everything in my power to return Dylan to his mother."

"I'll canvas the area where the boy vanished. If you're right about Dylan hiding in the park, he can't have gone far."

Faustin stood from his chair. "And we'll cover every inch of Empire Coasters, Sheriff. Keep in touch via radio. I'll let you know as soon as we find him."

Before he exited the security facility, Thomas poked his head inside the conference room, where Chelsey did her best to soothe Robyn Fournette. Chelsey noticed Thomas, who stood behind Robyn in the doorway. She shook her head, indicating she was fighting a losing battle. Thomas couldn't imagine what Robyn was going through. The woman had brought Dylan to Empire Coasters, expecting a relaxing day at the park. Instead, she'd lost the most important person in her life.

Yet the situation didn't sit right with Thomas. Robyn had become evasive during the interview, and he felt certain she'd wanted to tell him something vital to the investigation.

"Stay with Ms. Fournette," Thomas told Chelsey. "I'm heading into the park to continue the search."

"I want to help," Robyn said, rising.

"Three sets of eyes are better than one. Chelsey, take Ms. Fournette to Ally's World. It's near the Ferris wheel on the north end of the grounds. After the Ally character left the park, it's possible Dylan ran off to find her."

"Where are you going?" Chelsey asked, slipping her bag strap over her shoulder.

"I'll cover the area between the flying swings and the haunted house. If Dylan returns to find his mother, I'll see him."

With Faustin busy dictating orders from his office, and Wheeler, the guard who'd leered at Chelsey, somewhere near the haunted house, only one person remained to escort them out of the tunnels. The guard's name was Melveney, the man Wheeler had whispered to behind the desk.

"Is this necessary?" Thomas asked. "We can find our way out."

Melveney glowered at Thomas. "It's against the rules. Whether you're the county sheriff or the president, nobody is allowed inside the tunnels without our supervision."

Thomas clamped his mouth shut and followed the guard, while Chelsey wrapped an arm around Robyn's shoulder and assured her they'd find Dylan. The moment Thomas stepped out of the tunnel system with Chelsey and Robyn, the door slammed behind them. A lock clicked. They weren't getting back in without Faustin's approval.

Chelsey and Robyn split off from Thomas and headed toward the north end of the park. Thomas radioed Aguilar with an update, then investigated the park, starting at the flying swings, then making his way toward the graveyard and haunted house. Gum wrappers and crushed cups littered the ground. The scents of hot dogs and hamburgers wafted across the park, reminding Thomas of the times he'd visited Empire Coasters as a child with his uncle, who'd built the lakeside A-frame. Thomas's parents wouldn't have been caught dead inside a theme park. Mason and Lindsey Shepherd had believed amusement parks were for the unwashed masses.

In the cemetery, a hulking silhouette stalked among the mock gravestones. Thomas identified the shadowed man as Wheeler before the man shook his head at Thomas. The guard hadn't found Dylan.

A dog howled. Thomas stared up at the haunted house and pictured its many gloomy corridors. The attraction had frightened him as a boy, and over the years Empire Coasters had ramped up the intensity to lure more customers. If a child wandered inside, he'd find the experience traumatic.

The red-haired woman taking tickets wore a *Friday the 13th* T-shirt, with a shattered hockey mask on the front. She took one look at the sheriff and gasped.

"Miss, have you seen a small boy hanging around the haunted house?" Thomas showed the woman Dylan's photo.

"This is about the missing child?"

"Yes."

"I kept an eye out for him, but he hasn't come by."

"If you don't mind, I'd like to look around inside."

The woman glanced over her shoulder as two guests ventured into the haunted house and disappeared behind the cloak of darkness. Mock lightning flashed in the next room. Somebody screamed.

"You want me to close the attraction and turn on the lights?"

"Please. The boy probably didn't find a way inside, but I need to be sure."

She bit her finger in contemplation. "Management won't be happy, but I'll see what I can do. I'll close the entry gate. Can you wait until the guests exit the haunted house before I turn the lights on? We'll receive complaints and refund demands, otherwise."

"How long will that take?"

The woman lifted a shoulder. "Oh, about five minutes. You're welcome to walk through. I'll radio the actors and tell them not to bother you."

"Much obliged."

After the woman locked the gate and placed a *Closed for Maintenance* sign outside, Thomas entered the first room. A dry, stifling heat lay heavy inside the haunted house. Thunder peeled in the dark, and a sudden flash of lightning blinded him. Loud noises and lights always confused Thomas and set him on edge. He flicked on his flashlight and swept the beam across the room, feeling the walls closing in on him. A grandfather clock ticked against the wall, its pendulum swinging with a lunatic's frenzy. Blood spatter dotted the walls, and a lifelike knife tinged with red lay on a wooden table.

"Dylan Fournette? My name is Sheriff Shepherd, and I'm here to take you back to your mother."

No answer.

Another scream came from inside the haunted house. Thomas looked back but couldn't see the entrance anymore. He wondered if five minutes had passed and when the woman would turn on the house lights.

Thomas shuffled down a hallway. Cracks fissured through the walls. Cobwebs hung from the ceiling, and a mechanical black widow spider skittered past his head. As he approached the end of the corridor, he sensed someone behind him. He turned and aimed the beam, but nobody was there.

In the next room, an old woman with a skeletal face sat in a rocking chair beside a window overlooking the park. Through the dusty pane, Thomas could see the flying swings and Empire Mountain. The chair creaked as it rocked, the woman's wispy gray hair fluttering as her unblinking eyes leered at unwary park guests. Thomas recognized the *Psycho* movie reference, though the designers had been careful not to infringe on the film's copyright. It occurred to Thomas the kidnapper would have seen Dylan board the flying swings from this room. He might have waited until the ride slowed, then crossed the blacktop and snatched the child amid the confusion of guests scrambling for the exit.

Halfway across the room, a silhouette lurched off the wall. A man leaped out of the black with a machete.

Thomas reached for his gun, prompting the attacker to throw up his arms.

"Don't shoot, dude. It's not a real machete."

Thomas illuminated the man with the flashlight. Bloody gauze wrapped around his face, leaving only the eyes uncovered. The machete appeared real until the actor handed the weapon to Thomas. It felt flimsy in Thomas's hand, the blade soft and dull.

Just then, the lights flared and the sound effects ceased.

"What the hell?" the actor said, peeling the gauze from around his head. Without the bloody gauze, the twenty-something actor appeared good-looking. "Nice, I can finally breathe again."

"I asked the operator to shut down the haunted house," Thomas said. "I'm searching for the child who went missing in the park."

"Okay, but why would he come here? This is an adult attraction. Nobody under the age of thirteen gets in."

"So I take it you haven't seen him."

"No."

"Did you notice anyone hanging around inside this room, staring toward the flying swings?"

The man scoffed. "People get the hell out of this room as fast as they can. If Granny doesn't freak them out, they see me coming and run for their lives."

"How many actors work inside the haunted house?"

"Two besides me. In the final room, a big guy with a chainsaw crashes through the door and chases guests out. Great shock value, plus it dissuades people from lingering. But don't worry. The word is out that you're searching the place. Nobody will bother you." The man offered a hand. "I'm Malcolm Chaney."

The corner of Thomas's mouth quirked up. "Like the werewolf actor, Lon Chaney?"

Chaney bent his head back and laughed. "Yeah, I get that a lot. No relation, unfortunately, though I tell everyone he's my great-great-grandfather." Chaney nodded at the old woman in the chair. "Pretty convincing, yeah?"

"She appears real."

"Another reason we don't allow kids inside. What child wants to meet her in the dark? But a few slip past the ticket takers now and then." The man's eyes softened. "I hope you find the boy, Sheriff. Over the years, I've rescued my share of kids inside the haunted house. They think it's cool when they're outside, daring each other to check it out. But after they sneak in, they're scared out of their minds."

Outside the window, a blonde teenage girl in a miniskirt shot a flirtatious smile at Chaney as she passed. Chaney lifted a hand. If Thomas wasn't mistaken, Chaney had to be seven or eight years older than the teenager.

Chaney coughed into his hand. "I'd better get back into costume before they turn the lights off. Good luck with your search."

Thomas walked through every room, calling Dylan's name but receiving no answer. The boy wasn't here. Noticing Thomas, the ticket taker waved and spoke into a radio before shutting off the lights and reopening the attraction.

Thomas checked the time. The park would close in ninety minutes, and there was no sign of Dylan Fournette.

U nable to stay asleep, Robyn Fournette crawled out of bed at two in the morning and shuffled bleary-eyed down the hallway. Through the parted living room curtains, she spied the state police cruiser along the curb. Two shadowed figures filled the front seat, one sipping coffee from a cup. The sheriff's department and state police were collaborating in the search for Dylan, and they agreed someone should watch Robyn's house all night in case the kidnapper contacted her.

Robyn remained in the shadows, where the officers wouldn't see her. Without turning on the lights, she brewed coffee in the kitchen and forced herself to eat a slice of toast. Starving herself wouldn't save Dylan.

Upon returning home, Robyn had phoned her parents with the news. They wanted to fly to New York, but Robyn told them to stay in Illinois. Dylan would surface soon. He had to.

She still hadn't told anyone about the messages she'd received inside the park. The warning hung like a guillotine over her head: if she alerted the sheriff or state police, the kidnapper would murder her child.

Her heart thumped when she retrieved her phone, expecting a message from the kidnapper. No message awaited. What did he want from her? Money?

She'd written the kidnapper back, but the texts bounced back to Robyn's phone as non-deliverable messages. Though Robyn didn't work with mobile phone companies, as a software engineer, she realized it was possible to send messages from a fake account, making a trace difficult. Whoever this guy was, he was smart. She wondered about the sheriff's intuition. He'd questioned her about people at work. Robyn's coworkers possessed the intelligence to send messages from hidden accounts. But she couldn't picture any of them harming a child.

She chewed and swallowed the toast without tasting it. As she passed through the living room, her own shadow along the wall caused her to hold her breath. Wherever she went, she sensed a stranger in the dark.

Halfway down the hallway, she stopped outside an open door. Dylan's bedroom. Robyn's chest clenched as she stepped inside and found the room exactly as he'd left it. A shirt and pair of socks cluttered the corner. Otherwise, Dylan kept his room neat. He'd even made his bed. From the nightstand beside the boy's bed, Robyn lifted three comic books—all of Dylan's favorite superhero adventures—and sat on the edge of the mattress, crying. Dylan's boyish scent was still on the pillow, and every shadow in the room represented his ghost. He had to be alive. She couldn't go on without her son.

She'd become a prisoner in her own home as she'd been six years ago. The idea of another stalker sent a chill down her spine, but maybe that wasn't the case this time. When she'd received the kidnapper's messages, he'd demanded that she not speak to the authorities and threatened Dylan's life if she disobeyed. This was a man hoping for a payday. There was no reason to believe the same psycho who'd terrorized Robyn in

Illinois was back. Soon she'd receive a ransom demand and another warning not to speak to the police. Whatever the man wanted for her son's safe return, she'd pay.

So why hadn't he asked for money yet?

The sheriff and the private investigator both believed TJ had something to do with Dylan's disappearance. They were wrong. TJ didn't know about his son, and even if he did, he wouldn't snatch Dylan off an amusement park ride and sneak him out of Empire Coasters. For as long as Robyn dated TJ during college, she never remembered a more docile, even-keeled boy. But people changed. Though TJ never wanted a child, he might react unpredictably if he learned his boy was six years old and living in New York State.

Robyn stacked the comic books in a neat pile and returned to the kitchen, where she sat in the dark and rubbed her eyes. Thinking back, she remembered the college stalkings beginning after she broke up with TJ. Coincidence? After graduation, Robyn rented a two-bedroom, single-story home in a suburb outside of Chicago. By then, there was no hiding the pregnancy. Her belly showed, and she finally admitted the truth to her parents. Her mother became furious, while her father played the role of the good cop, hoping to talk sense into his daughter about the realities of parenthood. She needed to respect her career goals, and already she was tying herself to a child. Robyn's father begged her to put the baby up for adoption, and while she considered the option for the first several months, her attachment to her unborn child grew until she wanted the baby more than anything in the world.

After Dylan was born, her parents slid into their roles as grandparents, offering to babysit Dylan during the day while Robyn worked. Yet neither respected Robyn as an adult, capable of making mature decisions. It wasn't their fault. They still pictured her as the girl they'd raised, from pigtails and scabby knees to the teenager who dressed in grunge clothing and blasted Soundgarden until the neighbors complained. Robyn contemplated moving even before the stalking began. Anything to break away from her parents and prove she could make her own decisions.

She'd sought help from her mother and father after she noticed items rearranged inside her home. Her mother agreed with the police—juggling a new baby and a job had overstressed Robyn, causing her to imagine a stalker. Robyn's father took the matter more seriously, agreeing to sleep in a spare room for a few nights for Robyn's peace of mind. After three nights without incident, her father complained the guest bed mattress was killing his back. He assured Robyn he'd return if the problems resurfaced. But Robyn already knew the truth. The stalker wouldn't strike while her father slept in the house. He'd bide his time and wait until she was alone.

Which meant the stalker was watching Robyn day and night. He knew when she entertained company and when she left the house unattended.

Weary from sleep deprivation, Robyn slogged into her bedroom and pulled back the covers. She placed the phone on the mattress in case the kidnapper wrote with demands. Every second that passed without Robyn hearing from the man increased her anxiety. Was Dylan still alive? He had to be. She refused to consider the alternative.

She didn't expect to fall asleep when she placed her head on the pillow. Something scratched the back of her neck and crinkled.

Robyn swung onto her side and turned on the nightstand lamp. A piece of paper lay on the bed. With a trembling hand, she raised the note to her face.

I found you.

7

Dew dripped off the leaves, and a blanket of iridescent fog shifted the first rays of sun into a kaleidoscope of colors and wonder. LeVar Hopkins wiped the sweat off his brow and kept his legs moving, knowing the moment he slowed, his body would give in. He'd tied his dreadlocks and donned a baseball cap. A tank top showed off his muscular, tattooed arms. Behind him, Scout Mourning rasped and stumbled, the teenager struggling up the incline leading into Wolf Lake State Park.

LeVar stopped and caught Scout before she fell. The girl gave him a breathless nod as he searched her eyes, worried he was pushing her too hard. Until last winter, Scout had worn glasses that made her appear bug-eyed and studious before switching to contact lenses. He thought she looked a few years older in contacts, and though she was only fifteen, he couldn't ignore how beautiful she was becoming. She wore her brunette hair in a ponytail, along with jogging shorts and a Wu Tang Clan T-shirt. Their mutual love of hip-hop had brought Scout and LeVar together. Last month, spinal surgery restored Scout's ability to walk, and she was already jogging twice per day, determined to get into shape before the school year began. He admired her courage, but the girl possessed a foolhardy, stubborn streak.

"Maybe we should slow down and walk the next mile," he said.

She shrugged his hand off her arm and met his gaze. "Five miles without rest. You promised."

"But you're hanging by a thread, and we've only run a mile."

"I can do this, LeVar."

Before he could protest, she pushed past him and continued along the trail. He sighed and followed her up the hill, understanding she'd only try to prove him wrong if he fought her. What would Naomi and Thomas say if Scout hurt herself? And how would he live with himself if he injured the teenage girl?

At the beginning of summer, he'd never believed Scout would walk again. Since the first time he'd met her over a year ago, the teenager had been confined to a wheelchair. Now, thanks to spinal implants, she had a new lease on life. In her spare time, Scout researched cold cases as an amateur sleuth on an internet forum devoted to teenage investigators. Last spring, she'd helped Thomas catch serial killer Jeremy Hyde, and over the last year, Scout and LeVar had formed an unofficial investigation team with LeVar's sister, Raven, and state park ranger Darren Holt. Scout's and LeVar's mothers jokingly referred to their team as the Scooby Doo mystery gang, though they helped the sheriff's department apprehend criminals. Though LeVar was five years older than Scout, and Raven and Darren had years of experience solving crimes, they acknowledged Scout was the key member of the team, the glue holding everyone together. Nobody denied her talent or her sixth sense for catching killers, a skill beyond her years.

Scout's dream was to work for the FBI in the Behavioral Analysis Unit. After meeting Agent Scarlett Bell, the nation's foremost serial killer profiler, Scout's determination to join the FBI only grew. Agent Bell had taken an interest in Scout after working cases with the Nightshade County Sheriff's Department and put the teenager on the fast track to becoming a BAU profiler after college. But LeVar acknowledged Scout wouldn't survive the FBI training regimen unless she improved her physical condition. If only Scout would remember, she had several years to retrain her body.

LeVar had been the sole witness when Scout first moved her leg. They were celebrating another solved case by swimming at the state park. When LeVar carried Scout into the lake, holding her in his powerful arms, the chilly water touched Scout's foot, causing her leg to twitch. The movement was subtle, but they'd both noticed.

"Hey," she said between breaths. "Isn't this where Thomas found Jack?"

LeVar surveyed the bushes and bramble along the ridge trail. When Thomas discovered Jack between the lake shore and the state park campgrounds, the pup was malnourished and bone-thin, his coat faded and plastered with mud and grime.

"Hoping we'll find another lost dog so you can bring him home?" LeVar asked.

"Mom would kill me." She coughed and swerved off the trail. "That has to be almost two miles now, don't you think?"

"Almost. You sure you don't want to take a break? We could run a mile, rest ten minutes, then run another mile."

"No, I can do this. And so can you. Come on, LeVar. Let's see if you can keep up."

To his shock, Scout pumped her arms and legs and raced ahead. Where did the girl find her boundless energy? LeVar had grown up on the streets of Harmon as enforcer for the region's most-feared gang. He'd chased rival gangs out of their territory, busted a few lips, and blackened the eyes of his enemies, though he'd never killed anyone, as the rumors suggested. Hell, he'd never even put a rival in the hospital. Years of patrolling the neighborhood had built his endurance, so he didn't understand how Scout could outrun him. Was he getting soft, living in Thomas's guest house beside the pristine lake? He pushed harder, gaining on Scout until he raced up on her heels. She glanced over her shoulder, widened her eyes in surprise, and ran faster.

"Not so fast," he said. "It's not safe to run in the fog."

Before the warning left his mouth, a log materialized out of the mist. The obstruction lay across the trail, and Scout didn't see it until the toe of her sneaker clipped the top and she tumbled head over heels. After a full somersault, the girl landed on her back and hitched, the air driven from her lungs. Wet leaves and grass speckled her hair. Rays beaming through the trees lit her face and caused her to squint her eyes.

"Are you okay?" LeVar knelt beside her. "Scout, answer me."

She didn't respond. He dug the phone out of his armband and wondered if he should call Scout's mother or Darren, whose cabin stood a half-mile up the trail.

He touched her cheek. "Is anything broken?"

She wheezed and sucked in a breath, waving him off. "My back hit the ground. It drove the air out of my chest and I couldn't talk."

"Are you sure that's all you did? You struck the earth pretty hard."

She raised herself onto her elbows with a grimace and touched her backside.

LeVar stammered. "Oh, no. Is it your back? Please tell me it isn't your spine. You can move your legs, right?"

"It's not my back," she said, drawing her leg toward her chest. "I whacked my butt on a rock."

He grinned. "No harm, no foul. You've always been a pain in the butt."

She raked the leaves out of her hair and narrowed her eyes. "That's not funny, LeVar."

"Actually, it's hilarious." He offered his hand. "Let's take things slowly, at least until the fog lifts. Okay, Bruce Jenner?"

"Yeah, that's probably a better idea," she said, struggling to her feet.

Birds chattered from the treetops and animals scurried through the underbrush. She lowered her head as he brushed the grass off her shirt.

"What's up? You're quiet all of the sudden."

"It's nothing."

"Please. How long before you stop pretending you can hide problems from me?"

She started up the trail, walking instead of running and favoring her hip. "School starts in a few weeks."

"Isn't that a good thing?"

"It's just that . . . it's hard to explain."

"Try me."

"Everyone at school knows me as the crippled girl in the wheelchair. It's not like when I lived in Ithaca before the accident. All my old friends remember me walking and running. At Wolf Lake High, nobody knows how to treat me or what to say. They just ignore me. How will they react when I walk through the front doors for the first time?"

"I'm sure they'll react the way I would. Excited. If it were me at your school, I'd be the first to high-five you in the hallway. My prediction? You'll have a ton of new friends."

Scout kicked a stick off the path. "How should I feel about that, LeVar? The same kids who ignored the wheelchair-girl and never invited me to sleepovers or parties will be my friends. That will be awkward."

"Don't blame them, Scout. They're just teenagers, and they don't have your maturity. You're expecting too much."

"What should I do?"

"Accept them for who they are. They're insecure, and they don't understand how to act around people who aren't like them. But that doesn't make them bad. Experiences shape who we are, and this experience will shape them."

She set a hand on his shoulder. "You should be a philosopher or a motivational speaker. Why stop there? You'd make the perfect shrink." Scout nudged him with her elbow. "I'd tell you all my problems."

He raised an eyebrow. "You couldn't pay me enough."

"Ha ha, hilarious."

"You're the one who will need a shrink after you get inside the heads of a few dozen serial killers."

"I don't know about that," she said, picking a leaf off a tree as they walked. "Getting into the BAU isn't easy."

"With Agent Bell looking out for you? I'll keep it one hundred with you, *aight*? Your path is set if that's the road you want to go down. She'll ensure you choose the right school and take the best courses, then she'll help you whip your application into shape. It's good to have friends in high places, Scout."

"What about you?"

"What about me?"

"It isn't right. I have all these people pulling for me. Who's pulling for you?"

"You're a special case."

She stopped and set her hands on her hips. "Why? Because a tractor trailer lost its brakes and slammed into our car, paralyzing me?"

"That's a damn good reason to give you special treatment. You paid a steep price."

"It was just bad luck. LeVar, my parents aren't poor, and until the accident, I led a normal life—decent house in the suburbs, friends to hang out with after school, summer vacations with my parents. And look at me." She gestured at her legs. "I'm back on my feet and my paralysis is in the past. If anyone deserves a break, it's you."

LeVar exhaled through his nose and walked past her. "Why do I deserve a break? If you bring skin color into this, I'll whoop your behind."

"First," she said, hurrying to catch up, "don't touch my behind. People will talk. This isn't about race. You grew up in a single-parent household, and your mother, as much as I love her, put drugs ahead of her children."

He clenched his jaw. "She's better now. Ma doesn't do heroin anymore."

"You raised yourself and survived the streets."

"No, the streets survived me. I was the problem." LeVar picked up a stone and whipped it into the forest. "The last person who deserves preferential treatment is this guy. I mean, come on. Thomas didn't have to help me, but he offered me a safe home and got me out of Harmon. And here I am, thanking him by turning down the deputy position and aiming for an FBI spot. I haven't even graduated from community college. Who am I kidding?"

"What are you saying?"

"I'm saying I should take the offer."

"You're more than a sheriff's deputy, LeVar."

"Ain't no shame in the position, Scout. Check out Aguilar and Lambert. Either could run the county, and the deputy role is good enough for them. Why should I act like I'm better?"

"If you take the deputy position, you'll have to quit school."

He waved a hand through the air. "Nah. I could go part time. Might take me an extra year to finish, but I'd make an honest paycheck."

"No way, LeVar. I won't let you settle."

"You my ma now?"

"You belong in the FBI, not in Wolf Lake. Anyway, you can't go to school part-time and hold a deputy position. You see what Aguilar and Lambert go through. Inconsistent hours, overtime, getting called into work on their days off. What if dispatch calls you when you're scheduled to take a final exam?"

"What are you two arguing about?"

Raven's voice pulled LeVar out of his thoughts. They'd wandered onto the campgrounds, where Raven pushed a wheelbarrow of weeds and overgrowth toward the tree line and Darren sealed a window outside the ranger's cabin. At twenty-six, Raven was seven years older than her brother. Their mother, Serena, had thrown Raven out of the house at eighteen, during the dark days when drugs ruled the Hopkins household. Now Raven worked as a private investigator with her best friend, Chelsey Byrd. Darren and Raven had dated for over a year, and already Serena, who'd rehabbed and bonded with her family, was dropping hints that the two lovebirds should marry.

"I'm trying to convince LeVar to stay in school," Scout said as Darren climbed off the ladder and set down the weather sealant.

"What's this about you quitting school?" Raven asked, removing her gardening gloves.

Raven stood several inches shorter than LeVar. But when fire lit her eyes, she seemed to tower over him.

"I'm not quitting anything," LeVar said, scratching behind his ear.

"Then what's the issue?"

"The open deputy position. I'm considering accepting Thomas's offer."

Raven's mouth fell open. She glanced at Darren, who shrugged. "But you've almost earned your associate's degree. I thought you wanted to work for the Secret Service or the FBI. Darren, talk sense into this fool."

Darren glanced sheepishly at Raven.

"What? Tell me you don't support his decision."

"It's a good job," Darren said. "You can't ask for a better sheriff to work under than Thomas Shepherd, and the position comes with benefits."

"LeVar is an honors student. He can't quit now."

"Look at it this way," Darren said, folding the ladder and leaning it against the cabin. "LeVar can attend school part-time while he works. He'll get the best of both worlds—a college degree and a steady paycheck. What's the point of school? It's to get a job. Am I right? When the NBA called, LeBron James took the money. College will always be there for him, but opportunity knocks once. The county is offering LeVar a terrific job at a generous starting salary. Plus, he'll gain real-world experience while he earns his degree."

"You read my mind," LeVar told Darren. "Hey, I'd be all-in on an investigator position, but New York won't let me become a PI until I turn twenty-five."

"Oh, no," Raven said, wagging a finger at her brother. "You're not going to be a PI."

"Why not? You love your job."

"You have ten times my intellect, LeVar."

"Stop."

"Don't waste your opportunity. Reach for your dreams and stop settling for second best."

"That's what I've been trying to tell him," said Scout.

They were all staring at LeVar now. Across the campground, a family of four exited their cabin with packs strapped to their backs.

"After you earn your two-year degree, I want you in a top-notch four-year program. Virginia Commonwealth, Louisville, or Florida State."

LeVar's eyes widened. "Why so far? Seems like you're trying to get rid of me, sis."

"You won't regret it. That diploma will get you where you want to go." Raven fixed LeVar and Darren with a withering stare. "Enough of this nonsense. LeVar is staying in school. We clear?"

Darren elbowed LeVar and grinned. "Your sister is pretty hot when she's angry."

Inside the conference room at the Nightshade County Sheriff's Department, Thomas sat across the table from his deputies, Veronica Aguilar and Tristan Lambert. He spread a map, highlighting with a marker where the state police had erected checkpoints.

"Nobody saw this kid?" Aguilar asked.

At a diminutive five feet in height, Aguilar appeared child-like beside Lambert, who stood fourteen inches taller. She cropped her dark hair short, almost military-like, a style choice which drew smirks from Lambert. Lambert, the office prankster, had joined the army after school, then accepted a deputy position under the former sheriff, Stewart Gray.

"The state police checked every vehicle leaving the county," Thomas said, sipping black coffee and fighting to shake off exhaustion after working until four in the morning. When last night's search for Dylan Fournette came up empty, he returned home and slept three hours before showering and returning to the office. "Chelsey and I combed the amusement park and stayed after closing time. No sign of Dylan."

"That stuff will kill you," Aguilar said, scowling at Thomas's coffee. "I thought I'd convinced you to switch to green tea."

"Desperate times call for desperate measures."

Lambert set an ankle on his knee. "Thomas, with all the overtime we're working, isn't it time to hire another deputy?"

Thomas groaned. "If you're looking for an excuse to cry, read the four applications sitting on my desk."

"That bad?"

"You have no idea."

"Only four applied?" Aguilar asked, sipping her tea.

"Sorry to say. I expected a dozen applications, but no dice. I should post the job to one of those online recruitment sites."

"You need to try something. Get creative. Maybe hold a raffle: five bucks to enter, the winner takes the pot and gets a free job. For what it's worth, I tried to talk LeVar Hopkins into applying."

"You and me both. If I were to guess, I expect LeVar will be interested after he finishes school. Can't blame him. With the long hours and rotating shifts, how could he attend classes?" Thomas rapped his knuckles on the table. "That's neither here nor there. We need more eyes on this investigation. I'll call in Wolf Lake Consulting to help with research."

Lambert winked. "It sure helps when you're dating the founder."

"Membership has its privileges. Anyhow, I spoke with Chelsey over breakfast, and she says their caseload is light enough that they can help. That means we get Raven and LeVar, too."

"And Darren Holt. He's not an official PI, but he volunteers at the office."

"Probably so he can hang out with his main squeeze," Aguilar said, grinning. "When is Darren gonna put a ring on Raven's finger?"

"He might as well," Lambert said. "They're already living together in the ranger's cabin. Darren and I went out for beers last week. He's head over heels for that woman."

"So what's he waiting for?"

Lambert shrugged. "You know guys. We need prodding."

Aguilar rolled her eyes. "You can say that again."

A knock on the door pulled their heads up. Maggie, the orange-haired administrative assistant who'd manned the front desk since Thomas was a teenager, poked her head inside.

"There's a visitor to see you, Deputy." Lambert rose from his chair, but Maggie pointed at Aguilar. "No, she's here for Deputy Aguilar."

Aguilar's brow furrowed. "A visitor for me? I don't know anyone who'd stop by the office. It's not my mother, is it?"

"She says you attended school together."

Lifting her palms, Aguilar said, "That doesn't narrow it down. Can you give me a minute, Sheriff? I'll get rid of her so we can get back to work."

Thomas ran a hand through his hair. "We're not getting anywhere on this case. Might as well take a break. Say hello to your visitor, Aguilar. I'll call Chelsey and bring Wolf Lake Consulting up to speed."

Chelsey must have been on the line when Thomas called. He left a message with an update about the Dylan Fournette investigation and asked her to call the department. With Chelsey's resources, Wolf Lake Consulting might uncover a suspect from the mother's past. Robyn Fournette said TJ Soto was the child's father. Did TJ learn about Dylan and take matters into his own hands, abducting the boy from under Robyn's nose?

Thomas grabbed the mail off Maggie's desk as Aguilar passed him. A woman with brunette hair, choppy bangs to her eyebrows, and the biggest, whitest teeth Thomas could ever remember encountering stood in the hallway, bouncing on the balls of her feet as if she'd won the lottery.

"Veronica, I'm so excited to see you again!"

Curious, Thomas set the mail aside and leaned against the wall. Lambert walked over to join him, snickering as he patted Thomas on the shoulder and lifted his chin at the mystery woman.

"What do you figure the deal is with those two?" Lambert asked, winking.

Thomas said, "I don't have the slightest."

"Do you think they're—"

Thomas coughed into his hand, cutting Lambert off.

Aguilar stood slack-jawed, frozen as if in suspended animation. She shook her head in the way someone does when clearing the fog from her brain. "Simone Axtell, is that you? How long has it been?"

"Since college," said Simone. Her smile stretched from one ear to the next. "Fourteen years. Goodness, you look the same as you did senior year."

"I doubt that," Aguilar said, stammering.

Simone pinched her finger and thumb around Aguilar's bicep and whistled. "You're still working out."

"It's part of the job. Simone, what are you doing here?"

The woman brushed her hair back. "Touring the Finger Lakes and visiting the adorable wineries. I can understand why you moved to Upstate New York. So beautiful."

"Sounds like a fun time. How did you find me?"

"Your Facebook account. I don't want to come off as the snooping type, but I looked you up and noticed you live a half-hour from where I'm vacationing. No way I'd miss out on meeting with you. Wow, you look amazing."

"I don't have any social media accounts."

The woman snapped her fingers. "That's right. It wasn't Facebook. I read about you in the alumni newsletter."

"What alumni newsletter?"

Simone strutted forward and wrapped Aguilar in an airtight embrace. The deputy's face turned bright red as she returned an awkward hug.

"We should eat dinner after you finish work," Simone said. "What time works for you? Five or six o'clock?"

Aguilar scratched her head. "I doubt I'll get out on time today, Simone. We're searching for a missing child."

Clearing his throat, Thomas stepped away from the wall. "I don't mean to barge in, but I scheduled Lambert until eight o'clock this evening. Aguilar, if you want to spend the evening with your friend, it isn't a problem."

Aguilar shot Thomas a death glare. Beside her, Simone clapped excitedly.

"So it's settled," Simone said. "Dinner after work. Oh, we have so much to catch up on. I still can't believe it's been fourteen years."

"I'm Tristan Lambert," Lambert said, stepping past Thomas and offering his hand.

Simone wagged her eyebrows and shook Lambert's hand. "Aren't you a sight?"

"Aguilar and I hit the same gym. I admit I can't keep up with her. So you two attended college together?"

"We were roomies during senior year. Isn't that right, Veronica?"

Aguilar wore a tight-lipped smile.

Simone tutted. "Two beautiful girls, one dorm room, and a locked door. Oh, the trouble we got into."

Swallowing, Aguilar moved her gaze from Simone to Lambert, whose jaw clipped the floor. "I don't know what you're—"

"Don't worry," Simone said, touching Aguilar's arm. "I won't tell."

Lambert appeared to be enjoying himself a little too much. All he lacked was a bucket of popcorn.

Thomas said, "Lambert, call Wolf Lake Consulting and make sure they got my message."

"But I was just—"

"I'll tell you how the movie ends. Please, do me this one favor."

"Sure thing, boss."

At her desk, Maggie struggled not to grin as she arranged a stack of papers. Thomas searched for a reason to excuse himself from the conversation, but Simone would have nothing of it.

"You couldn't hire a finer deputy, Sheriff," Simone said. "But I'd be careful with this one."

"Why is that?"

"I bet she's dangerous with handcuffs."

Thomas lost his ability to speak. Mortified, Aguilar slumped against the wall and bit her hand.

"Simone, really," Aguilar said. "You haven't changed."

"It's true. I don't have a filter. But it was just a joke. I'm having fun with you, Veronica. Lighten up."

"Okay, I guess."

Simone leaned toward Aguilar and employed her best stage whisper. "Are you and that Lambert stud together?" Before Aguilar could answer, Simone giggled. "How silly of me. Someone like you wouldn't be interested in Lambert."

"What is that supposed to mean?"

Simone snorted. "It's our little secret."

"On that note," Thomas said, "I should let the two of you catch up."

As he turned, Thomas heard Simone say, "There's a

gorgeous restaurant ten miles from Wolf Lake called The Lake-front. I'll meet you there at six, yes?"

"Are you sure you don't need me to work late, Thomas?" Aguilar asked.

"Take the evening off," Thomas said. "You've worked enough overtime this week. See you first thing in the morning."

"Nice to meet you, Sheriff," Simone called from the entryway.

Thomas felt Aguilar's eyes burning holes into his back as he fled into his office.

Var rolled the charcoal grill from beside the guest house to the lake shore. His forehead dripped with sweat and seasonal allergies clogged his nose after mowing the lawn, the least he could do to repay Sheriff Thomas Shepherd—or Shep Dawg, as LeVar preferred to call him—for saving his life, giving him a free place to stay, and watching after his mother. Living in the guest house behind the A-frame was supposed to be temporary, a means to an end while LeVar searched for employment and enrolled at the community college. Then one month turned into a season, and a season turned into a year.

On the lake, boats bobbed atop the waves, and the water reflected the cloudless azure sky. Two summers ago, he caught a thug from the rival 315 Royals gang approaching a Ma and Pa corner grocery store inside Harmon Kings territory. LeVar spied the gun sticking out of the boy's back pocket. He almost died that day, but he'd been quicker than the boy. The thug intended to rob the store and shoot the elderly couple who owned the business. LeVar struck the thug from behind and tossed him into the alley, where he wrestled the gun out of the boy's hand

and knocked three teeth from his mouth. Rev, who ran the Kings that summer, would have put a bullet in the thug's head and dropped him in Royals territory to send a message—anyone who enters our area leaves in a body bag. But LeVar let the kid go with a warning: he'd hurt the boy a lot worse if he ever returned.

LeVar rubbed the smoke out of his eyes. Was he too comfortable? He didn't wish to take advantage of Thomas. If he moved and paid for his own place, he'd have a lot more privacy. He'd also lose Scout, who'd somehow become his best friend. LeVar wished Scout and Naomi would always be his neighbors, but he couldn't stay here forever. Eventually, he needed to stand on his own two feet and survive.

After the coals grayed inside the aluminum chimney, LeVar dumped them onto the lower grates and let them gray another five minutes. Too many red coals meant the fire would flare up whenever the wind gusted off the lake, singeing his food. While the coals simmered, LeVar tore the plastic wrapper off the ground bison and flattened the meat into six burgers—one for dinner and one for lunch tomorrow. He'd give the last four to Thomas, Chelsey, Naomi, and Scout.

When the coals reached the perfect shade, LeVar set the burgers on the upper grates beside salt potatoes wrapped in aluminum foil. A healthy salad would complete the meal, but since he'd forgotten to make one, he opted to stack his burgers with extra lettuce, tomato, and onion.

As he flipped the burgers and inhaled the savory scents, the sliding glass door opened on the A-frame. Thomas stepped off the back deck and crossed the lawn. Jack trotted alongside the sheriff, wearing the humongous doggy grin he always donned when he spotted LeVar. A pang of guilt twisted LeVar's heart. Not only was he taking advantage of Thomas by living here for a second summer, he'd resisted when the sheriff suggested he apply for the deputy position. Not that he didn't want the job. A former gangster with a tainted reputation needed every break handed to him. The Nightshade County Sheriff's Department offered a benefits package, including health and dental insurance and a retirement program. If he worked for twenty years . . .

He couldn't imagine himself as a deputy for twenty years. Even if he became sheriff—there was a better chance that he'd dig a hole in the backyard and strike oil—life in Wolf Lake wouldn't fulfill him forever.

But he owed Thomas. The man had given LeVar and his mother a chance after everybody turned their backs on the Hopkins family. It was time LeVar paid Thomas back for his generosity.

"Shep Dawg," LeVar said, pointing the spatula at the grill. "Two of these burgers have your name on them. Your choice."

"You don't have to give me your dinner, LeVar."

"How many bison burgers can one man eat? I grilled two for you and Chelsey. Naomi and Scout get the last pair."

Thomas slapped LeVar on the back. "You're okay, LeVar Hopkins. Isn't that right, Jack?" The dog panted and drooled, locking his eyes on the grill. "I don't speak dog, but I'm confident that's a yes. How's your mom and sister?"

"Mom is cutting down two trees, so she has a better view of the lake. Well, she ain't cutting them down. I wouldn't be anywhere near that woman with a chainsaw. Her neighbor is doing the job."

Serena Hopkins lived in Raven's old house on the west side of Wolf Lake.

"Her neighbor?" Thomas scrunched his face. "Not Buck Benson."

"Yeah, that's the guy."

"But isn't he—"

"The racist dude with the confederate flag flying on his porch?"

"We're not talking about the same guy. That's impossible. The Buck Benson I'm thinking of is Mark Benson's second cousin."

Now it was LeVar's turn to look confused. "Mark Benson, the guy who kidnapped that girl and stalked Raven after he escaped prison? No way."

"Way," Thomas said. "I'll check on that situation. Buck Benson cozying up to your mom makes me a tad queasy."

"People change. Look at how my mother turned her life around. If she can overcome heroin addiction, a grumpy back-woods guy can put aside his prejudices."

"They're friends? Wow. Your mom is a miracle worker for getting that guy to see the light."

"Speaking of change," LeVar said, covering the grill when the coals flared, "I considered your offer."

Thomas straightened his back. "The deputy position?"

"The thing is, I kinda want the job. I'd need to quit school and give up my private investigation internship, but I think I can swing it."

"I can't ask you to quit school, LeVar."

"It wouldn't be forever. The way I see it, I'll work a few months and save up enough money to buy a place. Then, after a year or two, I'll take night classes and complete my associate's degree."

"Don't move. The guest house is yours for as long as you want it."

"I know, and I appreciate everything you do for me. But I'm overstaying my welcome."

"That's not true. You help me all the time, LeVar. This place is as much yours as it is mine. That roof," he said, gesturing at the guest house, "is your handiwork. You did ninety percent of the work. I just provided instruction."

LeVar removed the grill top and plated the bison burgers. "It's still not right. This is your place. Think of the view you and Chelsey would enjoy beside the lake."

"Chelsey and I get along just fine. Listen, I won't stand in your way if you want your own house. But don't leave because you think you're a burden. You're not. I can't care for Jack twenty-four hours a day, not with the job pulling me out of bed at all hours of the night. You've saved my bacon by watching Jack on many occasions."

Jack's ears pricked up.

"You said the magic word, Shep. Bacon." LeVar scratched behind Jack's ears. "I'd miss this crazy pup if I moved." Swallowing the lump in his throat, LeVar said, "And I'd miss you."

"Then don't leave. You're family, LeVar. My home will always be your home. Now, about your education."

"Like I said, no skin off my back if I put school on hold for a year or two."

Thomas paced with his head lowered. "So you'd work full time for the department, build your savings, then return to school to finish your degree."

"Makes sense, right?"

"I don't want you sacrificing your education for a paycheck."

"I spoke with Darren about the opportunity."

"And he said?"

"He brought up a valid point. We attend school to get jobs. But if a job is already waiting for me . . ."

LeVar spread his arms wide, as a way of completing his point.

"College is about expanding your horizons and pursuing knowledge," said Thomas.

"If that were true, education would be free. But it ain't. All those Benjamins I toss at the college are an investment. If they don't pay me back with interest, what's the point?"

Thomas huffed. "Even if you narrow education down to getting a job, it has to be a lifetime career, not a temporary paycheck."

"Not following you, Dawg."

"You're destined to be more than a deputy. I'm uncomfortable with you placing a ceiling over your head."

LeVar glanced at Scout and Naomi's house. "Nah. The FBI stuff is for Scout. I can't picture myself in a suit and black sunglasses. Not my style."

"You watch too many movies. LeVar, you belong in the FBI or the secret service or anywhere more exciting than Wolf Lake." Thomas set his jaw. "I can't let you do this. Stay in school. I'll figure out the deputy position."

LeVar almost dropped the plate of burgers. "What? All summer, you've sold me on joining the team. Now you're pulling the offer back?"

"I could use a man with your talents. But I won't jeopardize your future. I'd be doing you a disservice."

"This isn't how I expected our conversation to go. Are you sure about this? I'm willing to drop everything and accept the job right now."

"No doubt I'll regret this, but I can't hand you the job under these conditions." Thomas motioned at the guest house. "Come on. I'll help you bring dinner inside. We'll eat together if you don't mind the company."

Squeezed beside each other at the tiny kitchen counter, Thomas and LeVar built their burgers on onion rolls. LeVar broke off a piece of meat and tossed it to Jack, who licked his lips, expecting more. They carried their plates to the front room and set them on the card table, which the amateur investigation team used while they worked on cases. The open side windows offered a fresh cross-breeze, and the plate-glass window displayed Wolf Lake in all its glory.

Perplexed, LeVar chewed his hamburger. He'd assumed Thomas would perform back flips when he accepted the job. Until five minutes ago, he'd prepared himself to leave school and earn real money. Now his future seemed cloudier than ever.

"How is Scout progressing with her recovery?"

"Good, I guess. She runs every day, but I haven't seen her since this morning."

"I expected she'd join you for dinner."

LeVar stopped chewing. "What?"

"Oh, nothing. I just noticed you two spend a lot of time together."

When Thomas didn't elaborate, LeVar picked up his burger again, wondering what Thomas meant. Between bites, he asked, "How is the missing persons case coming along?"

"Not well. The kid vanished without a trace, and the mother is hiding something."

"How so?"

Thomas set his food aside and peered at the water. "Last night, inside the security facility at Empire Coasters, Robyn Fournette shut down. One second, she was about to tell me something important. The next, she pretended she only wanted to thank me for helping her find Dylan."

"Tell me about her background."

"Fournette graduated from Chicago after growing up in Illinois. Her boyfriend got her pregnant during her senior year of college. He urged her to get an abortion, but she had the baby and took a software engineering position in New York."

LeVar pushed the dreadlocks off his shoulders. "So she graduated college and moved away to care for a baby by herself, leaving her friends and family. If it were me, I'd want my mother around. Fournette is running from something."

Thomas hooked his thumb and pointed it at LeVar. "You have a great mind for law enforcement. Something doesn't add up."

"Where's the father in all of this?"

"The father's name is TJ Soto. According to Fournette, they broke up after the pregnancy, and she never told him about Dylan."

"Wait. Soto doesn't realize he's a father? That's cold, Shep." LeVar gulped water from a glass and wiped his mouth. "What if Soto found out and went a little crazy?"

"And kidnapped his child."

"It's plausible."

Thomas tapped his fingers on the table. "You're not the first person to consider the possibility."

10

A guilar pinched the bridge of her nose and crossed her eyes. Sitting across the table from her former roommate, Aguilar studied the wine list as her mind raced, fighting to keep pace with Simone Axtell's recollection of her life since college.

"After I spent a year backpacking across Europe, I settled on The Cape in this amazing fishing village and commuted three times a week to Providence, where my partner and I founded a boutique perfume company, but I couldn't deal with the drive and the ridiculous accents and all the people who refused to use their *blink-ahs*, so I sold my share of the company for a healthy profit and rolled it into a micro-cap investment on the Nasdaq and rented a place in midtown Manhattan, and of course, the stock price went up every freaking day because my broker is such a genius—you should really invest your money with him, I'll text you his number—so I cashed out of my stock, and suddenly I had six times the money I'd started with after the perfume company sale, and I said to myself, 'Simone, you don't need to work your entire life. Travel. Enjoy yourself. See the world before it burns to a crisp.' And you know we're living on borrowed time, right? All those chemicals and fossil fuels we pump into the atmosphere are tearing a hole in the ozone layer, and the temperature keeps going up and up, but half the people in this country refuse to believe the numbers, and wow, as much as I love So-Cal, I wouldn't want to live anywhere near the Pacific Coast with the water level rising, and if the water doesn't get you, the fires will—have you watched the news lately? It's one inferno after another."

The woman sipped her wine and drew a breath. Before Aguilar could get a word in, Simone continued.

"But in New York, you don't have to worry about the ocean carrying your house away, and the weather is so gorgeous, except for winter, which is fine for a few weeks around Christmas. But when it's April and there's still six inches of snow on the ground, I wonder how anyone survives here. I guess it's the summer that makes it worthwhile, right? The summer, the wine, apple picking during autumn. You have the best of all worlds here, Veronica."

Aguilar, dressed up for the first time since Thomas Shepherd had escorted her to the Magnolia Dance, crossed her legs under the table and fixed her skirt. "How long are you staying in New York, Simone?"

"Oh, I haven't decided. I'm considering spending six months in San Francisco. A venture capital firm wants to work with me on a new concept I'm designing. Then there's Manhattan, how I miss it so. I still have my place near Midtown."

To Aguilar's relief, the server arrived at the table. The college-age girl wore a genuine smile that complemented the soft blues of her eyes. Her blond hair perched atop her head in a bun.

"Have you had time to look over the menus?"

"We've been here for fifteen minutes," Simone said, "so I suppose that's a yes."

The girl glanced from Aguilar to Simone. "I'm so sorry. We're packed this evening and two servers called in sick."

"Not my problem."

"Simone," Aguilar said, drawing a *what-did-I-say* scowl from her friend.

"I'm not hungry. Give me the kale salad with apple and cranberries."

"Pecans all right?" the girl asked.

"If I had a nut allergy, I'd tell you. You think I want some stranger jamming me with an EpiPen?"

"House dressing with your salad?"

"Sure, whatever."

Resting a cheek on her palm to hide the red blooming through her face, Aguilar ordered a shrimp salad.

After the girl left, Simone leaned over the table and said, "You can't be afraid to speak your mind, Veronica. People will walk all over you when given the chance."

"She wasn't walking over us."

"But she took advantage of my good nature. She didn't stop at the table to inform us of the delay. It's simple etiquette. Instead, she wasted fifteen minutes before taking our orders." Simone tapped a finger on her phone, which displayed the time. "This is no way to treat customers. I'll remember when I leave a tip."

"What's with the short fuse? You were ready to rip into that girl when she brought us our menus."

Simone glanced down and rearranged her silverware.

"Simone? What's going on?"

As Aguilar shifted her chair closer to the table, Simone's eyes glazed over.

"You're right," Simone said, removing a tissue from her purse. "This is all a show."

"What is a show?"

"The dress, the power heels, the success stories. I mean, I didn't lie about my business success. But there's something going on in my life. It's so humiliating."

"It's okay. You can tell me anything. Nobody will judge you."

Simone waved a hand in front of her face. "I suppressed the memory for so long. Veronica, when I was twelve, my father molested me."

Aguilar choked on her water and set the glass down. "Oh, Simone. I'm so sorry."

"Don't feel sorry for me. I should have dealt with the issue decades ago. But here I am, a child living in an adult's body because I never faced my father."

"Do you want to talk about it?"

Simone's tear-filled eyes drifted across the restaurant and stopped on a painting of Wolf Lake on the back wall, as if hidden memories floated within the frame.

"Yes," Simone said. "I guess I finally do."

"What happened?"

"Whenever my father drank, he made terrible decisions. One night . . . it was the weekend, a Saturday night. I remember because my mother was angry at him for staying out late. Church was first thing Sunday morning. My father didn't get mean when he drank. He wasn't that type of drunk. No, he wept over the mistakes he'd made in his life. Sometimes, I'd find him at the kitchen table with his head on his forearm, his shoulders shaking."

"If you don't mind me asking, what mistakes did your father make?"

Simone shrugged. "He had visions of grandeur and wished he'd followed countless career opportunities. Instead, he never moved from his hometown. And his own father was an alcoholic, and Dad followed in his footsteps. Because of the drinking, my parents drifted apart. I'm positive they only stayed together for my sake."

The server set the salads and bread on the table. Aguilar waited until the girl moved on.

"So your father returned home on a Saturday night."

"Yes." Simone swallowed. "I heard him scuffling around in the kitchen, cupboards opening, glass clinking inside the refrigerator. He was searching for a bottle of beer. I figured he'd drink one more bottle, then collapse in bed and sleep it off. I wished he'd just go to sleep, because I always worried he'd fall and hurt himself, you know? You can't imagine how many times I cried myself to sleep, worried that he'd wrecked the car and was dying somewhere. Whenever the phone rang, I assumed it was the police informing my mother that Dad had died."

Simone drank her water and set the empty glass on the table.

"Anyway, I was about to fall asleep when my bedroom door opened. He didn't come inside at first. Just stared at me from the hallway with tears running down his face. I said, 'What's wrong, Daddy?' He didn't answer. The mattress buckled when he sat on the edge of the bed. The way he looked at me, I knew something terrible was about to happen. He touched me, beginning with my breasts and working lower, until . . ."

Simone sobbed and shook her head.

"After, he said I could never tell Mom. It would break her heart, and she'd blame me for tempting him. As insane as it sounds, that made all the sense in the world to a frightened twelve-year-old girl growing up in a dysfunctional household."

"I wish you'd told me while we lived together."

"Nobody knew. Not my friends, my family, my mother. Just my father and me. It was our secret." Simone dug another tissue out of her purse. "So that's why my nerves are frayed. I'm a mess; I never sit still. It's one trip after another."

"This isn't your fault."

"I understand, but it doesn't make it any easier. It's so easy to bury memories." She locked eyes with Aguilar. "But I remember the good things that happened, too."

"What are you referring to?"

Simone glanced around the restaurant and leaned forward, conspiratorially. "We weren't just roommates, Veronica. We had fun times together."

"Uh, I'm still not following."

The woman rolled her eyes. "Don't pretend nothing happened. You remember. That time I woke up in your arms? Talk about an amazing night. I never guessed you had that in you."

Aguilar lowered her head and rubbed the back of her neck. She recalled a dorm party and too much drinking, something Aguilar almost never did. Simone was fall-down drunk, and Aguilar needed to carry the girl back to their room and help Simone out of her clothes. Before Simone lost consciousness, she pressed her lips against Aguilar's, a long, lingering kiss that stunned Aguilar. Assuming Simone had made a drunken mistake, Aguilar never mentioned it again. That night, she stayed awake in Simone's bed, worried the girl might vomit in her sleep and choke, before drifting off beside her friend. Technically, she'd slept with her roommate. But not in the way Simone insinuated.

"I think you're misremembering, Simone."

"Apparently, one of us is," Simone said with a wink.

Aguilar changed the subject. "Are you seeing someone about your father?"

"You mean, am I getting help?"

"Sorry for being blunt."

"I spent three months of hell in therapy, and look where it got me. Let me clue you in on a dirty secret, Veronica. Shrinks don't want you to get better. The longer you deal with your suffering, the richer they get."

"That's not true. I visited an excellent therapist after I shot and killed a man."

The blood drained from Simone's face. "You killed someone? Dear lord."

"Don't worry about him. He was a dirty cop who murdered two people. But that's not the point. I can put you in touch with my doctor. She's excellent."

Simone pushed the bangs off her forehead. "I'm still dealing with what happened with my father. You're right. If I ever want to get past all of this, I should see someone else."

"If you'd like, I can give you Dr. Mandal's number."

"Thank you, but it's best if I work with someone close to home. I won't be in the Finger Lakes much longer. Thank you. I can't believe I finally told someone. I can breathe again."

"My door is always open, Simone."

"Speaking of which, I have wonderful news." Happy again, Simone hung her purse over the chair. "Want to hear it?"

Aguilar wasn't sure she did. "Tell me."

"I was supposed to check into another resort this evening, but I canceled the reservation. Veronica, we'll be roomies again."

"What?"

"My bags are in the trunk of my car. I don't have any obligations. We can spend every minute together. How fun is that?"

"Simone, this is rather sudden."

"You don't want me in your house?"

"It's not that. You understand I work forty hours a week, plus overtime, right? And I haven't touched my guest room in two years. It's not exactly homey."

"Please, Veronica. Even if I wanted to rent another room, I'd never find one. This is the busy season. Every resort is sold out through the weekend." Simone lowered her head and sighed. "I guess I can drive back to Manhattan tonight."

Aguilar chewed her lip. She hadn't set up her house for visitors, but she couldn't turn her back on Simone, not after the admission about her father. The poor woman must be going through hell, so much so that she'd imagined making love in their dorm room. Sweat broke out across Aguilar's forehead. She swore nothing had happened between them.

"Come on, roomie. It's only for a night or two. After that, I promise I'll get out of your hair."

"You're not a burden, Simone." Aguilar tilted her head in consideration. "I guess it would be nice having company around the house for a change."

Simone clapped her hands. The couple at the neighboring table looked over and giggled to each other.

"I'll swing by the store after dinner and pick us up a little something to celebrate with."

"That's not necessary."

"Then I'll come right over. This is going to be so much fun. Just like old times."

11

C helsey helped Raven carry sandwiches and chips from the kitchen of Wolf Lake Consulting. In the main office, Darren completed a background check on Robyn Fournette. The private investigations business operated out of a converted single-story, two-bedroom house in the village center, three miles from the lake. There was a full bathroom with a tub and shower down the hall from the entryway, and Chelsey kept the refrigerator and cupboards stocked with healthy foods and snacks. The investigators spent long nights at the office, and she wanted to make her friends comfortable.

After they set the plates on Chelsey's desk, Chelsey and Raven wheeled their rolling chairs to LeVar's computer, where Darren worked. LeVar and Scout, who interned under Chelsey, weren't due at the office until tomorrow.

Instead of cozying up to Darren, Raven set her chair at the edge of the desk and allowed Chelsey to sit between them. Raven had acted grumpy all morning, hardly saying a word as she perused the case notes Thomas had sent over. Now she chewed her sandwich and fixed her eyes on the monitor, avoiding Darren. Seventeen years older than Raven, Darren had turned forty-three this year. Chelsey sensed the tension in the room, like static electricity building and waiting for some unsuspecting fool to touch a doorknob.

"What did you find, Darren?" Chelsey asked.

"Robyn Fournette seems normal. She graduated high school with honors and holds a bachelor's degree in computer science. No arrests, one speeding ticket from four years ago. She was doing fifty-nine in a fifty-five. If you ask me, it sounds like the cop had a quota to meet."

He squinted his eyes at the screen and leaned forward.

Raven tsked. "When are you going to visit the eye doctor, Darren? I told you months ago that you need readers."

"I'm fine."

Raven mouthed to Chelsey, "Blind as a bat."

Chelsey held back a snicker. "So why are you so engrossed with Robyn Fournette's background check?"

Darren rocked back in his chair. "Has it occurred to you that Fournette might be involved in her son's kidnapping?"

"Explain."

"She clammed up and stopped answering Thomas's questions. After Fournette left Empire Coasters, she drove home and refused the sheriff department's offer to put her up in a hotel."

"Maybe she prefers sleeping in her own bed. With her son missing, she must be losing her mind. I can't blame her for seeking a small vestige of normalcy."

"If she sleeps at the hotel, the authorities can keep her safe. The kidnapper might come after her next."

"Okay."

"At a hotel, the kidnapper needs to get around the police cruiser in the parking lot, then dodge the hotel staff in the lobby while hiding from security cameras on every floor."

"Seems like a stretch to make the mother a suspect because she turned down a night in the hotel," Raven said, glowering.

"Let's assume Robyn Fournette hired someone to kidnap her child," Chelsey said. "Tell me why."

Darren tapped his hand against his thigh. "Money issues?"

"Who would she demand a ransom from? It's illogical. Fournette's credit report looks fine. It's north of 800 with no outstanding debts."

"You can have a clean credit report even when you have money issues."

Chelsey clicked through the background check. "Fournette has twenty-four years remaining on her mortgage. She never misses payments. Bought a car three years ago and put 5,000 down. Two years left on the car loan. I don't see a problem."

"I admit I'm reaching. Even if she's not behind the kidnapping, she knows more than she's telling the sheriff's department."

"And what do you base your theory on?"

"Thomas's notes, plus my ex-cop sense."

"You need more than that," Raven said. "Go back to the beginning. How did the unsub abduct Dylan Fournette and escape the park?"

"Thomas confirmed it takes ten minutes to walk from the flying swings, where Dylan was last seen, to the exit gates. Five minutes if you use the tunnels."

"Only the park staff and security have access to the tunnels."

"That implies an inside job. A believable theory. Creepers work everywhere."

"Assume Ron Faustin, the head of security at Empire Coasters, closed the exits in a timely manner," Chelsey said.

"Debatable."

"No argument there, but go with it. The unsub has ten minutes to escort the child out of the park without drawing attention. Can he pass the gates before security stops guests from leaving?"

"Doubtful," said Darren. "If I kidnapped someone, I'd avoid the exit and find another way out of the park."

"Over the wall," said Raven. "Except you'd have a struggling child under your arm and twelve feet of wall to scale."

"What if he wasn't struggling?"

Raven and Chelsey looked at Darren.

"How do you stop Dylan Fournette from screaming for his mother?" Chelsey asked.

"Drugs. If he sedated the boy, all he'd need to do is carry Dylan over his shoulder."

"All the more reason not to take him through the main exit," Raven said. "An unconscious child would raise suspicion."

Chelsey tapped a pen against the chair arm. "Here's another possibility. The unsub didn't drug Dylan. He didn't need to because Dylan trusted him."

"Why would a six-year-old boy trust a stranger?"

"What if he wasn't a stranger?"

Darren locked his fingers behind his head. "That brings us back to Robyn Fournette. If she hired someone her son knew to kidnap him, he wouldn't fight back."

Raven shook her head. "This is getting too convoluted. Why bother bringing your son to Empire Coasters to stage a kidnapping? It's easier for the unsub to snatch the boy from his bed while he's asleep. Robyn would unlock the door for him, no witnesses, nothing for the police to go on."

"Except for forensic evidence. You're forgetting fingerprints, hair follicles, a neighbor's camera catching the kidnapper."

"You have all the answers today, don't you?"

"Why do you say that?"

"You're arguing with yourself, Darren. First, you imply Robyn Fournette paid someone to kidnap her son."

"No, I suggested she knows more than she's admitting."

"Then, after we take your side of the argument, you find a million reasons to shoot us down."

"Guys, stay on point," Chelsey said.

"That's my process," Darren said. "While I work through the possibilities, I punch holes in each idea until I settle on a logical answer."

Raven huffed. "Well, it's counterproductive and annoying."

"Raven, what did I—"

"For over a year, my brother busted his behind to study and turn his life around. He's closing in on a degree, and now you tell him to quit school and take the first job that comes his way."

Chelsey threw up her hands. "LeVar is quitting school? What did I miss?"

"He's not quitting if I have anything to say about it."

Darren leaned over and dropped his head with his elbows on his knees. "The sheriff offered LeVar the deputy position. He should consider it. That's all I said."

"My brother is confused enough without you putting pie-in-the-sky ideas in his head."

"Like telling him to move to Kentucky or Florida? Did you see LeVar's face when you threw those suggestions at him?"

"Those states have the best criminal justice schools. I want LeVar to aim high and get out of this area. He should transfer to a four-year school and apply to the FBI after graduation."

"Raven, I'm not taking anyone's side," Chelsey said, drawing a doubtful glare. "But LeVar has a support system here. If he moves across the country, he won't have his friends and family."

"He'll make new friends."

Darren scrubbed a hand down his face. "Look, if it will make everybody happy, I'll stay out of the debate. I just figured the job offer made sense. Thomas needs a deputy, and LeVar could replace his part-time jobs and internship with a stable career.

He'd work beside Lambert and Aguilar. They'd make a helluva team."

Raven pulled her beaded hair off her shoulders. "But if he stays . . ."

"What if he stays?" Chelsey asked after Raven fell silent.

Darren touched Raven's arm. "Raven? What's up?"

Raven hitched and wiped her eyes with the back of her hand. "I don't want LeVar anywhere near Harmon."

"Because you're worried the 315 Royals or the remaining members of the Kings will seek retribution," Chelsey said.

"Yes and no. Even if the gangs leave him alone, there are too many ghosts here. Between our mother's heroin addiction, our father walking out on us when LeVar was a baby, and LeVar's history with the Kings, I'm worried he'll make the wrong choices."

"That doesn't sound like your brother," Darren said, brushing a tear off Raven's cheek.

"A year before LeVar quit the Kings, Rev tried to convince LeVar to sell narcotics. The reason LeVar chose the Kings over the Royals was the Kings didn't involve themselves in the drug trade. But everything changed after Rev took the helm. What if LeVar had said yes?"

"He didn't."

"He could have. Lord knows the Kings would pay him a lot more than he'll make as a junior deputy."

"Your brother is too smart for that."

"I agree," Chelsey said. "And temptation will follow LeVar wherever he goes. Whether it's in college or at his first job, he'll end up in a city a lot larger than Harmon. Trust your brother to make the right decisions."

Raven sniffled. "LeVar learned from his family, and we all made the wrong decisions. Yeah, Mom threw me out of the house at eighteen. But I could have returned. She was so high, she'd never have known the difference. I stayed away, not to improve my situation but because I wanted to prove her wrong, show Mom I didn't need her or the deadbeat father who walked out on us. I abandoned my brother. If I'd returned, he never would have joined the Kings or met Rev or—"

"You did the best you could," said Darren. "Because you're intelligent and strong. And so is LeVar. I didn't push him to join the sheriff's department. My intention was to show LeVar an alternate option and why it might make sense. Nobody wants him to quit school and give up on his dreams." After several seconds of silence, he asked, "Are we cool now?"

"Someone needs to slap me," Raven said, leaning her head against Darren's shoulder. "You're right. LeVar should decide what's best for his situation. There's a fine line between being a big sister and interfering, and I crossed it."

"We'll talk to him together. How's that?"

Chelsey cleared her throat. "Now that we've determined LeVar's future for him, we have a child to find."

12

Inside the burgundy ranch house on the west side of the village, Aguilar peered through the window, tapping her foot as she wondered where Simone was. After dinner, Simone had promised to arrive within the hour, but ninety minutes had passed, and still no Simone. The first stars pierced the coming darkness. In the street, two boys threw a Nerf football and scampered to the curb every time headlights approached.

This seemed like a bad idea. Aguilar wanted to comfort her old roommate, but she wasn't a psychiatrist. Simone needed professional help to come to terms with the molestation. The off-duty deputy wracked her brain for excuses, anything she might tell Simone to make the woman change her mind about staying. As she picked up the phone to fire off a text, the twin beams of two headlights washed across the window, followed by the honk of a horn.

Aguilar strolled out to the driveway as the car turned off. Simone met Aguilar with an over-exuberant hug before she reached over to the passenger seat and removed a bottle with fancy writing and a crown on the front.

"You shouldn't have," Aguilar said.

"Relax. Just a bit of the bubbly between friends."

"But I don't like to drink."

"You're not one of those crazy straight-edge types, right?"

"Huh?"

Simone giggled. "Edgy, but certainly not straight."

"Excuse me?"

Aguilar cupped her elbows to fight off the chill. The temperature had dropped fifteen degrees since sunset. Simone popped the trunk and hoisted a massive suitcase with rollers on the bottom. Aguilar stared inside the packed trunk at a loss for words.

"Why so many bags?" Aguilar asked.

"I told you I traveled all summer. A girl has to shop, am I right?"

"If you say so. Wouldn't it be easier to rent a moving van?"

"I love your sense of humor, Veronica. You always make me laugh."

"It wasn't a . . . never mind."

Aguilar tucked two bags under one arm and dragged a black suitcase with the other. It seemed Simone had loaded each bag with wet sand and bowling balls. After three trips from the house to Simone's car, Aguilar dragged her friend's belongings inside. The problem was, the bags covered the entryway and spilled into the living room. Even if Aguilar fit Simone's baggage into the guest room, the woman wouldn't have space to sleep.

"Home sweet home," Simone said. She picked up the champagne bottle. "Where should I put this?"

"Here, I'll take it."

Simone followed Aguilar into the kitchen, admiring every inch of the room. "You've done well for yourself, Veronica. All this space just for you? What a shame."

Aguilar hesitated as she set the champagne bottle on the

counter. Since she'd accepted the deputy's position, she hadn't considered dating. Not that she didn't desire companionship, but the job was her life. Hearing those words inside her head made her cringe. Helping people solve their problems fulfilled Aguilar, and by the time her workday finished, she didn't have the energy to visit clubs and meet guys. Perhaps Simone was right and Aguilar needed to make time for herself. At thirty-five, she was running out of time if she wanted a family. Most of her friends' kids were in elementary school by now, and Aguilar couldn't recall the last time she'd gone out on a date.

"If you get hungry," Aguilar said, "I have yogurt and leftovers from last night's dinner in the fridge. Turkey, stuffing, and roasted vegetables."

"Sounds . . . delectable. But after our dinner date, I don't think I'll be able to eat for another week."

"Simone, you ordered a kale salad."

"But all that dressing. It was a lot heavier than it appeared."

The years had been kind to Simone's figure. She hadn't packed on the twenty to fifty pounds her classmates had. Was she too skinny? Aguilar wondered if Simone had an eating disorder.

"I'll show you around. Not sure if we can fit your bags and suitcases into the guest room, but I can keep a few in the living room."

"Please, I don't want to be a bother."

"You've seen the kitchen. Here's the dining room," Aguilar said, leading Simone into a room with beige painting and a small table that seated four. "To be honest, I usually eat in front of the computer so I can work. I own a tablecloth but can't remember the last time I used it. Anyhow, that's the dining room."

As Aguilar crossed the threshold, she realized Simone wasn't behind her. Beside the dining room table, Simone studied a framed photograph on the wall. Her skin paled, and her mouth moved, as though she carried on a silent conversation with herself.

"Simone? Are you coming?"

Tired of waiting, Aguilar returned and found her old roommate staring at a photo depicting a smiling Aguilar with an arm wrapped around her father's shoulders after they'd completed a 5K together. That had been ten years ago. These days, her father's achy knees and arthritic hip prevented him from running. In the picture, both grinned at the camera, their shirt collars darkened with sweat, the combined looks of relief and accomplishment booming out of the photograph.

"That's you and your dad, I take it."

"Dad got me into running when I was a kid and started me down the road to taking care of my body."

Simone nodded in response, her eyes misting again. Aguilar touched Simone's arm.

"I'm sorry about what happened to you. But my father and I have a strong relationship. This isn't the only picture in the house of me and my parents. You okay with that?"

Simone breathed. "My apologies, Veronica. I'm projecting my issues on you, and I'm a little jealous that you're so close to your dad. Heck, I can't remember the last time I spoke with mine."

"I hope the photographs don't bother you. This is my life, and I celebrate my family every day."

"I'm fine. It will take some getting used to."

"Simone, you don't want me to remove the picture, do you? Because that's not an option."

"Don't be silly. I need to deal with my issues, and that begins with acknowledging that other people have it better than me. And I'm okay with it."

"Why don't we forget about the dining room and tour the rest of the house?"

"Lead the way."

Every room drew an exaggerated reaction from Simone, as if Aguilar's modest ranch was a palatial estate in the Hamptons. Strange for a woman who'd toured the world and lived in the country's most exciting cities. Afterward, Simone plopped into a chair while Aguilar tidied the kitchen. Small talk prevented the awkward quiet moments from dragging on. It seemed Simone remembered every detail about college yet misremembered their kiss and what happened after. Or what *didn't* happen after.

When the kettle whistled, Aguilar poured each of them a cup of herbal tea.

"Would you mind if I carried my tea into the living room and turned on the television?" Simone asked, yawning. "The long day is catching up to me."

"Not at all," said Aguilar, relieved Simone hadn't brought up the kiss again. "Let me clean these dishes. Find us something fun to watch."

"Your wish is my command."

The drone of the television carried from the living room as Aguilar ran the water. She listened to a soft rock Spotify playlist, featuring Fleetwood Mac, America, and Paul Simon while she rinsed the dishes. The last dish was dripping in the rack when she heard voices. At first, she thought it was the television. The volume rose, as though an argument had ensued. Aguilar recognized Simone's voice.

She shut off the water and dried her hands on the towel before hurrying to the living room. As Aguilar turned the corner, Simone closed the front door.

"Who was at the door?"

Simone rolled her eyes. "Some woman named Chelsey. She

wanted to come in, but I told her you worked all day and needed rest. Who is this Chelsey person?"

Aguilar blinked. "Chelsey Byrd. She's a private investigator in town. You sent her away?"

"She wanted to give you this," Simone said, handing Aguilar a folder.

Aguilar opened the folder and flipped through the papers. "These are case notes. Dammit. I'd better call Chelsey before she returns to the office."

"She's not the sheriff. Why would you take orders from Chelsey whatever-her-name-is? Really, Veronica. You can't allow people to push you around. The most important part of my recovery is standing up for myself, like I did at the restaurant."

"Nobody pushes me around. As I explained earlier, we have a missing child to find and a possible kidnapping on our hands. Chelsey wouldn't drive across the village and give me these notes unless it was important."

Simone set her hands on her hips. "How do you know this person? She's not a law enforcement official. You don't answer to her."

Aguilar released a tired breath. "I work for a small sheriff's department. We partner with the private investigation firm in town and help each other solve cases."

"That's an unusual arrangement."

"Chelsey and Thomas, I mean Sheriff Shepherd, share a history together. They've dated on and off since . . . forget it, it's complicated." Aguilar tapped the folder against her thigh. "These notes might help us locate that child. I'd better tear through the folder before I lose my energy."

Simone stomped a foot and crossed her arms over her chest. "Does that mean you're working all evening? I thought we'd watch a movie and talk about old times."

"The investigation takes precedence. If it was your child, you'd want the police working day and night, right?"

"I'd understand if they slept once in a while." Simone swiped a tear from her eye. "Whatever. Go work while I'll find a movie. Please tell me you have HBO or Starz."

"I have Netflix."

"Ew. Then I suppose I'll watch *Stranger Things* for the umpteenth time."

"Hey," Aguilar said, leading Simone to the couch. "I don't need to work all evening. Give me an hour to go through Chelsey's findings and I'll join you."

Simone raised her hands in placation. "Don't let me get in your way. Solving a crime takes precedent over friendship, and I don't mind watching programs alone. That's what I do all the time."

"Simone, I—"

"No need to explain. Go work. If we don't see each other tonight, maybe we'll spend time together tomorrow after you return home. If there's time."

"You're sure you're all right?"

"I'm a big girl, Veronica. You don't have to coddle me."

"Well, okay then."

"Just promise you'll stand up for yourself from now on. They can't make you work every hour of the day. It's inhumane."

13

R obyn crawled up from sleep and rubbed her eyes. She sat up in bed and surveyed the gray morning light seeping around the blinds, terrified someone had entered her house while she slept.

She snatched the phone off the nightstand. Last evening, a picture of Dylan had arrived, along with a message that instructions would soon follow. If Robyn wanted to see her child alive, she'd await the kidnapper's demands and steer clear of law enforcement. In the picture, Dylan sat in a chair with duct tape covering his mouth. Despite her best efforts, Robyn found nothing in the photograph that would lead her to Dylan's location. The white stove in the background told her the kidnapper had taken the picture inside a kitchen. A gray tiled floor spread beneath the chair, and a blender rested on a green kitchen counter. Nothing about the kitchen appeared familiar.

Robyn edged off the bed and slipped her sweatpants and socks on. After she wrapped a bathrobe around her shoulders and tied it off, she opened the bedroom closet and pulled the string, casting light inside the dark space. Nothing appeared out of place, yet she couldn't shake the all too familiar sensation of someone spying on her. Down the hall, she poked her head inside the bathroom. Nothing out of the ordinary. Upon leaving the bathroom, she hissed. Dylan's bedroom door stood closed. She was positive she'd left it open. Closing the door was akin to admitting Dylan was gone from her life, never to return.

Robyn rushed to the living room and threw back the curtains. There was no cruiser outside the house, not surprisingly, as the state police and sheriff's department didn't have enough manpower to surveil the house day and night. The police came and went, and right now they weren't watching over her. Outside, a car with a dying muffler rattled past—Mr. Klein on his way to the office. The sheen of dew glistened so strongly beneath the rising sun that it appeared as if a freak August frost had killed the vegetation.

Too many shadows congregated beyond the living room. The dome light over the kitchen sink should have been on. Robyn left the light on every night to deter criminals and drive back the darkness. Had she switched the light off in her hazy stupor? No chance. She staggered toward the wall switch and flicked it, hoping against hope that she'd left it on and the bulb had blown. Light flooded the kitchen when she pushed the switch. Someone had shut off the light while she slept.

The stalker had been here.

Her heart pumped with the cold realization that he might still be in the house. Perhaps he'd waited until the police left before he sneaked inside.

She pulled the utensil drawer open and clutched a steak knife, the only item in reach that passed for a weapon. She kept a gun locked inside a safe in her bedroom closet, but too much space lay between the kitchen and the closet, and every creak and groan in the house convinced Robyn the stalker was right behind her.

Her hand wrapped around the handle of the knife as she

walked on silent steps toward the hallway, where she stood at the corner and listened before working up the courage to enter the corridor. Dylan's door remained closed, with her own bedroom door open. Confused, she couldn't remember if she'd shut her door behind her. Robyn's trembling hand reached for the doorknob and twisted. Dylan's door swung open and released stale air, as though the boy had vanished months ago. His bed was made as he'd left it, the random clothing items tossed on the floor, his blinds open a crack and receiving the first light of day. Yet the room wasn't the way she'd last seen it. Her eyes stopped on the nightstand, where she'd paged through his comic books.

They were gone.

The closed closet door made her skin tingle with trepidation. Was the stalker hiding in the dark, waiting for Robyn to search inside, so he could capture her, too?

She whipped around and ran for the bedroom, fingers shaking as she unlocked the combination on the safe. Grabbing the gun, she returned to Dylan's bedroom and threw the closet door open, sweeping the firearm from one side to the next as her hand reached for and grasped the pull string. The closet flooded with light. She was alone.

In the bedroom, she tossed her bathrobe onto a chair and stepped into her blue jeans, one hand still aiming the gun toward the open door. The few seconds it took to place the gun on the bed while she pulled a sweatshirt over her head lasted an eternity.

As she returned to the living room, this time armed, she remembered the interview at Empire Coasters. She trusted Sheriff Thomas Shepherd. He'd help Robyn and take her seriously. She needed to tell him everything about the stalkings six years ago and how she'd instinctively known the same man had followed her into the souvenir shop inside the amusement park.

During the interview, she'd planned to tell the sheriff before the threatening messages arrived on her phone. The kidnapper threatened to kill Dylan if she spoke to the authorities.

But the stalker couldn't watch her every minute of the day. He needed to keep Dylan hidden.

Robyn called the Nightshade County Sheriff's Department. The clock read six-thirty. It took five rings before someone answered.

"Sheriff's Department," the gruff voice on the other end said.

"Please put me through to Sheriff Shepherd. It's urgent I speak with him."

"The sheriff is due in at seven. Is this an emergency, miss?"

Robyn ended the call. Her experience with the Chicago police had taught her not to trust cops. The man who'd answered at the sheriff's department wouldn't help her. But if she drove to the station now, she'd arrive just as the sheriff pulled into the parking lot.

Indecision tugged her in multiple directions. She played a dangerous game of chicken. If the man was watching the house, he might have seen her on the phone and figured out she'd called the sheriff's department. She knew what the madman would do to Dylan if she disobeyed his orders.

She had to take the risk. If the stalker followed her, she'd spy him in the mirrors while she drove.

Steeling her nerves, Robyn grabbed the keys off the counter and hurried to the car, the morning chill piercing her flesh. From the trees, birds sang with indifference, unaware that Robyn raced to save her son. She slammed the brakes at the bottom of the driveway when the garbage truck thundered past. After the truck turned the corner, Robyn followed several car lengths behind, her eyes darting to the mirror as she checked for a vehicle she didn't recognize.

Robyn passed the car dealership and the coffee shop. This

was the route she traveled to work, her everyday experience. But there was nothing typical about this morning. She caught her haggard face and sunken eyes in the mirror. It seemed she'd aged thirty years since her son had disappeared.

She steered around two more corners. A flag flew outside the sheriff's department, the glass doors reflecting the sun and forcing Robyn to shield her eyes. What appeared to be a silver pickup pulled into the parking lot behind the building, but the glare blinded her.

Robyn stopped along the curb. As she leaped from the car, the phone buzzed inside her pocket. She didn't recognize the number. It had to be the kidnapper.

"Where's my son?"

"He's alive and well, Robyn," the caller said, his voice tickling her memory. Where had she heard it before? "I kept my promise. I advise you to keep yours."

"Give Dylan back to me. Whatever you want, I'll get it for you. Money? Is that what this is about?"

"You didn't think I'd find you, did you? Do you realize how easy it is to track a person these days? You didn't even bother to change your name."

Robyn checked the intersection before stepping off the curb. People milled inside the sheriff's office beyond the sun-washed glass doors, people who would help her save Dylan and catch the maniac who'd terrorized her since college graduation. A car approached, and Robyn covered the receiver so the kidnapper wouldn't hear.

"What do you want with my son? You don't need him. It's me you want."

"You shouldn't have disobeyed me."

"I didn't."

"Liar. You're across the street from the sheriff's department right now."

Robyn froze. She looked up and down the road, past the county sheriff's office and toward the tree-shaded residences clustering along the side streets.

"I'm not at the—"

"For once in your life, tell the truth. You're wearing blue jeans this morning, white jogging sneakers, and a gray hooded sweatshirt with Buffalo written across the front." Robyn spun and searched the shadows. "I'm right behind you and have been for years."

Robyn lifted her chin. "You won't murder a child. I'm going into the sheriff's office now. Follow me inside and introduce yourself. I'm sure the sheriff would love to meet you."

As she crossed the street, the kidnapper said, "I wouldn't do that if I were you." Another photograph arrived on her phone, this one showing Dylan inside a vehicle with the tip of a knife placed against his ear. "One more step and I'll push the knife through his brain. You'll listen to your boy screaming the moment before he dies. Is that what you want?"

She searched for his vehicle. Dozens lined the street, with countless more parked in driveways. She assumed he'd hidden his vehicle from view, but with so many cars and trucks on the road, he could be hiding in plain sight. A sickening idea roiled her stomach. What if the kidnapper worked for the sheriff's department?

"What do you want from me?"

"Right now, I want you to turn around like a good girl and walk back to your car without saying a word to anyone. Return home and await my orders."

"But my son—"

"—is still alive, despite your disobedience. Don't test me, Robyn. I get what I want. Why haven't you learned that by now?"

14

The finished basement inside Scout Mourning's house provided the teenager with the perfect workout facility. She felt self-conscious visiting a gym, afraid she might run into her classmates. Here, she was free to blast her own music, strain through a difficult exercise, and not worry about people staring at the girl who'd spent the last three years in a wheelchair.

Scout had only visited the basement a handful of times since Mom purchased the house. Because of the steep and narrow staircase, it was too much hassle to install a chairlift, and Mom wasn't strong enough to carry Scout up and down flights of stairs. Sometimes, LeVar and Thomas had helped Scout into the basement. Since the successful operation, she'd gained the freedom to move about the house at her leisure. Regaining use of her legs still seemed like a dream she'd awaken from. Now and then, she pinched her arm to convince herself she could walk again.

Sweet scents followed her down the stairs and coaxed her to cut the workout short and join her mother and Ms. Hopkins in the kitchen. Naomi Mourning ran day-to-day operations at

Shepherd Systems, the project management and software collaboration company Thomas Shepherd had inherited after his father passed away from lung cancer. Serena Hopkins had proved to be a boon to Shepherd Systems, rising to the team's top sales position within months of her arrival. The two women bonded over a shared love of baking, and their desserts appeared in local cafes, including The Broken Yolk, and drew rave reviews. If there was one woman in the world Scout admired as much as her mother, it was Ms. Hopkins, who'd survived rehab and beaten a heroin addiction that almost tore her family apart.

Laughter traveled from upstairs as Scout set the barbell on the stand and stood between two safety bars that would protect her if she lost control of the weight. A notebook lay open at her feet, filled with notes from Deputy Aguilar and Raven. Both women considered themselves gym rats and possessed powerful physiques. When asked, Aguilar and Raven had leaped at the opportunity to design workout plans for Scout. Now the teen studied the photographs of a full body squat. With twenty-five-pound plates on each side of the barbell, Scout stepped beneath the bar with her back straight, knees slightly bent, and her head facing forward. She wrapped her hands around the bar, set the barbell on her shoulders, and with a grunt, she muscled the weight upward.

Her legs trembled before she steadied her footing. Maybe she was pushing herself too hard and needed to lower the weight. No, she could do this.

She gritted her teeth and breathed out through her mouth, bending her knees until her thighs were parallel to the floor. Scout tapped her inner will and drove her legs downward, thrusting the bar higher as she straightened her back and stood. Her chest heaved, each breath burning her lungs as her heart thumped.

Scout lowered the weight again, repeating the exercise until she completed ten repetitions. Sweat soaked her T-shirt as she eased the bar onto the rack. Her legs felt like gelatin. Two more sets to go.

"You're pushing yourself too hard."

The teenager jumped, noticing her mother standing in the doorway with concern etched into her brow.

"It's only fifty pounds," Scout said, wiping her face with a towel.

"You're not counting the weight of the bar," Mom said, surprising Scout with her knowledge of weightlifting. "That's an Olympic bar. It weighs forty-four pounds, which means you're lifting—"

"Ninety-four. Yes, I know. Where did you learn so much about weightlifting?"

"This might be hard for you to believe, but I used to be young. Your father and I met at a gym when I was fresh out of college. Anyway, that weight is too much for a beginner, especially a teenager who, well, you know . . ."

"Was in a wheelchair at the beginning of summer. I get it. But Deputy Aguilar squats over two hundred pounds, and Raven bench presses a hundred fifty."

"Scout, those women have lifted weights for a decade or longer. Give yourself time. While you rest between sets, I brought you a treat."

Mom handed Scout a crispy bar set on a napkin. Red berries colored the bar, still warm to the touch. The scent made Scout's mouth water.

The teen held the bar out and said, "I probably should watch what I eat while I train."

"I agree, and that's why we're letting you test our latest recipe for protein energy bars."

"Protein energy bars? You mean these things are good for me?"

"Take a bite and tell me what you think."

Scout sniffed the bar before biting off the corner. "Are you serious? They're fantastic."

"Each bar has twelve grams of protein. This ain't your grandma's granola bar."

"You could totally stock these at gyms and health food stores."

Mom leaned against the door frame. "Are they really that good?"

"Amazing. Will you bring me another after I finish?"

"Sure. We made two dozen. I'll save a batch for Raven and Deputy Aguilar."

As Mom turned away, Scout said, "Mom, can you come inside and shut the door?"

Mom closed the door and approached Scout, lowering her voice. "What's the matter?"

Scout turned down the music and tossed the towel over the bench. "I didn't want to say anything in front of Ms. Hopkins, but have you noticed how everyone pulls for me to attend the best colleges and become some kind of super profiler with the FBI, yet no one helps LeVar?"

Mom wrung her hands. "People believe in you, Scout. After the accident—"

"Which was no worse than what LeVar went through. LeVar survived a broken home and his mother's drug addiction, and he quit the Harmon Kings to better his life. He's an honors student, he interns for Chelsey and works part time at The Broken Yolk, and he solved multiple crimes for the sheriff's department last year. That's not counting the cases he cracked at Wolf Lake Consulting. Isn't it time for someone to give LeVar a break?"

"What about Thomas? He offered LeVar the deputy position."

"I'm talking about the future, like after LeVar graduates."

Mom blew the hair off her forehead and tightened the apron around her waist. "LeVar can stand on his own two feet. But I agree he deserves the same opportunity you're receiving."

"LeVar will get angry if he finds out, but I'll bring him up the next time I speak with Scarlett Bell."

Laying a hand on Scout's shoulder, Mom kissed her cheek. "You're kindhearted and always consider others' feelings. But don't push too hard. Agent Bell doesn't know LeVar as well as she knows you. It's up to her if she wants to help."

15

D eputy Lambert rode shotgun while Thomas drove the cruiser to Robyn Fournette's house. The sheriff intended to question Fournette a second time, repeating the questions he'd asked after Dylan disappeared at Empire Coasters. The technique was straight out of the police playbook: compare the person's responses to their previous answers and catch their lies.

Pressing Fournette bothered Thomas. Fournette was a victim, and he didn't wish to badger the woman and further upset her. Yet his conviction grew that Fournette had withheld crucial information pertaining to the case, and his priority was bringing the lost boy home alive.

Lambert adjusted the visor when Thomas directed the cruiser into the sun. "What's your opinion of Simone?"

Thomas glanced at his deputy. "Who?"

"Aguilar's friend. She's hot, right?"

"Uh, I suppose."

"You caught her flirting with me at the station. Everyone did."

Thomas scratched his lip to hide his grin. "What makes you think she's into you?"

"That look she gave me. Plus, she went on and on about my physique and how I must work out at the gym."

Thomas coughed into his hand and stared out the window, observing a jogger running beside his dog. He recalled Simone mentioning Lambert's physique, but it was said in passing.

"Are you considering calling her?" Thomas asked.

The deputy removed his hat and ran a nervous hand through his buzzed haircut. "I want to, but what if she's . . . you know . . ."

"What?"

"Like Aguilar?"

"Are you speaking English, Lambert?"

"I mean Simone might be into other women, like Aguilar."

Thomas bit the inside of his cheek. "We can't have this conversation. It's inappropriate to discuss a coworker's sex life."

"It makes sense, right? You ever see Aguilar out on a date with a guy?"

"I've never seen her out with a woman."

Lambert drummed his hat against his thigh. "Damn, am I way off on Aguilar? I mean, she's cool around the office and can dish out the jokes with the best of them. But I always assumed she was . . ."

"Like I said, this is inappropriate. Drop the subject."

Lambert straightened his shoulders. "You know me, Shep. I'm open-minded. Don't want you to assume I'm prejudiced.

"Lambert, I don't have the slightest idea about my friends' sexual orientations, nor does it ever cross my mind."

"So you're saying I have a shot with Simone."

"I'm not saying . . ." Thomas sighed. "Never mind. Focus on the interview. We'll arrive at the Fournette house in five minutes."

Thomas picked up the folder lying between them and handed it to his deputy. Lambert sifted through the papers.

"This TJ Soto guy," said Lambert. "Fournette claims he's Dylan's father. We should grill her about Soto. I have the sneaking suspicion that he's involved."

"First, we aren't grilling anybody. Always remember, Fournette lost her child and isn't thinking straight. But I concur we need to look into Soto."

"If I were Fournette, I'd hound the sheriff's department day and night, demanding answers. She hasn't set foot inside the office. That's suspicious."

"If she's behind her son's kidnapping, I can't figure out her motive. It can't be money. She'd have to pay her own ransom."

"Then what? She's not telling us everything." Lambert flipped through the pages. "Shep, are you aware there's a gap in the surveillance?"

"What gap?"

"Between our department and the state police, officers watched Fournette's house for all but six hours. According to the records, there's a coverage gap between four and ten o'clock this morning."

"I'm aware. The staffing situation with the state police isn't much better than ours. If you're willing to pick up another overtime shift this week—"

Lambert held up a hand. "I'm already working seventy-two hours. Not sure how I'd pull it off. Let me juggle my schedule and work something out."

"No way. You and Aguilar are both going above and beyond. I won't ask you to work another overtime shift."

"What about the hiring process for the deputy position?"

"It's still stuck in the mud. Sorry, I'm doing my best. I thought I had a candidate lined up yesterday, but the situation didn't fit."

"Beggars can't be choosers."

"Understood, and I'll deal with it later." Thomas braked. "We're here."

The cruiser stopped in front of Robyn Fournette's house. Lambert handed Thomas the folder before climbing out of the vehicle. As Thomas approached the door, the curtain parted, and a woman's face appeared in the window. Thomas raised a hand in a hesitant wave as Fournette left the window for the door.

"Ms. Fournette, this is Deputy Lambert."

The woman peeked up and down the street. "I wish you'd told me you were coming over."

"If it's a problem, we'll return this afternoon."

"No, come in," Fournette said, standing aside. "Hurry, before the air conditioning leaves the house."

Thomas found it odd the woman worried about energy usage when her son was missing.

"This will only take a few minutes."

"Please, have a seat at the table."

Fournette gestured into the kitchen. As Lambert followed Thomas to the table, the woman looked out the window and pulled the curtains together. Her nails appeared chewed and red, her hair mussed, as though she'd just awoken. Despite her complaint about letting the warm summer air into the house, she wore a bathrobe over her jeans and a hooded sweatshirt.

Fournette sat across from Thomas. "I'd offer you coffee, but the machine died this morning."

"Not a problem. We both drank coffee at the office."

The woman glanced at her phone and slid it into her pocket. A clicking sound told Thomas she'd turned off the ringer.

"If you could please hurry, my mother said she'd call soon. She wants an update on Dylan."

"Understood." Thomas clasped his hands. "Let's begin with the amusement park."

Fournette squirmed in her chair as Thomas repeated his questions from Empire Coasters. The woman gave him the same answers.

"Tell us about the father, TJ Soto," Lambert said, leaning forward with his elbows on the table.

"What about TJ? I told the sheriff. He doesn't know he's Dylan's father."

"If he found out, would the news upset him?"

The woman shifted her chair and arranged a stack of mail on the table. "TJ was a decent man. He just wasn't prepared to father a child, and we didn't love each other enough to marry."

"Where is TJ now?"

"No idea. We haven't spoken since graduation."

Lambert looked at Thomas and wrote on his notepad.

"My mother wanted me to introduce TJ to Dylan," Fournette said, tugging on a lock of hair. "I told her it was a bad idea. There's no predicting how he will respond. Besides, without a DNA test, I can't prove Dylan is TJ's son."

"Who else could Dylan belong to?" asked Thomas, sliding his chair forward.

"Nobody, I guess. But TJ has his own life to deal with now. TJ might assume I want money if I approach him about Dylan."

"But you're certain TJ is the father?"

"I am."

"Why?"

"He's the only guy I slept with. Sometimes, when TJ and I were together, we didn't use protection. A few times he forgot, and I'd stopped taking the pill. That's when I became pregnant." Fournette ripped a tissue from the box and dried her eyes. "I was a fool. When you're young, you're invincible and don't consider what could go wrong. My life changed overnight. I determined to give my child the best life I could give. I loved my baby and accepted TJ wouldn't care for Dylan as a father should."

"And there isn't anyone who would kidnap your son?"

Fournette hesitated before uttering, "No."

"Why did you leave Illinois?"

"What kind of question is that?"

"You were a young mother searching for employment. Wouldn't it have been easier to stay in Illinois with your parents?"

"I considered the option, but when the firm offered me a job in New York, I took it. I needed the money to support Dylan."

When the woman lowered her head, Thomas tilted his chin at Lambert, a signal to press the woman about Dylan's abduction.

"Ms. Fournette," said Lambert, "have you received a ransom demand?"

"Nothing."

"Is anyone threatening you to stay away from the police?"

"No!"

The shout rang off the walls and caused Lambert to flinch. Fournette's response convinced Thomas she wasn't telling the truth.

"Kidnappers will say anything to keep the police out of the investigation," said Thomas. "If he threatened you to stay quiet, you need to tell me. We're Dylan's best hope."

"I told you, Sheriff. Nobody called with ransom demands. I don't know who took my child."

16

C helsey balanced on a stepladder and brushed her fingers over the top of the windowpane.

Eyeing her from the desk across the room, Raven asked, "What on earth are you doing, besides risking your life?"

"Don't you feel that draft? These windows are older than dirt."

"Fresh air has its merits."

"It won't when winter arrives." Chelsey climbed down from the ladder and folded her arms. "I'd better seal that window. Last week, I caught three bees in the office. I'm pretty sure they're crawling through the gap."

"You *caught* three bees? Like, are you keeping them in an aquarium?"

"I released them."

"Chelsey, that's what the fly swatter is for."

"They were honeybees, not murder hornets. Respect our wildlife friends. Guess who pollinates the flowers?"

"I don't respect bugs that sting me because they're having bad days."

Chelsey folded the ladder and leaned it against the wall. "So you don't like bees. What are you working on this afternoon?"

"Another background check for a law firm out of Utica." Raven twirled a finger in the air. "Yippee, it's my lucky day."

As Raven clacked away at her keyboard, Chelsey rolled her chair over to her partner's desk. "Can I talk to you about something?"

Raven rocked back in her chair and stretched her arms. "If this is about the argument Darren and I had, I'm sorry we fought in front of you. It was wrong to argue at work. Now that we understand each other, everything is fine. You both made me see the light. I shouldn't control LeVar's life."

"Glad to hear you and Darren made up. But I want to tell you what happened when I visited Deputy Aguilar's house last night."

"You drove to Aguilar's house?"

"Thomas asked me to drop off our findings. He wanted Aguilar up to speed when she arrived for work."

"What's the problem?"

Chelsey shook her head. "I'm not sure. This woman I didn't recognize answered the door. According to Thomas, her name is Simone Axtell. She's Aguilar's friend from college."

"So Aguilar reconnected with an old friend. Why would that concern you?"

"When I brought the folder over, Simone wouldn't let me past the door. She claimed Aguilar was resting, but I heard water running in the kitchen."

"You explained you're friends with Aguilar?"

"Absolutely, but Simone blocked the doorway."

"That's weird. Maybe Simone is being cautious because she doesn't know you. Anyone could knock on the door and pretend to be a neighbor or friend. So you didn't give the folder to Aguilar?"

"I told this Simone person that the documents were confidential and I needed to hand them to Aguilar. She snatched the folder out of my hand and closed the door in my face."

"That's rude," Raven said, crossing one leg over the other. "I sure hope Simone gave Aguilar the folder."

"She did. Thomas confirmed Aguilar received our notes."

"That's a relief."

Chelsey anchored her hair behind her ear. "I don't trust that woman. She's too overprotective. I got a distinct psycho vibe when she refused to wake Aguilar."

"Don't jump to conclusions."

"I'm trying to understand her motivation. Why didn't she allow me to speak with Thomas's deputy? I guess Simone's people skills leave something to be desired."

"Simone Axtell, you said her name is? I can run a background check if you'd like."

"We have enough on our plate. I just hope Simone isn't staying long."

Raven snapped her fingers. "I have an idea."

"Shoot."

"Thomas is hosting another barbecue this Wednesday. Aguilar usually makes an appearance. Let's tell her to invite Simone."

"So we can check her out in person. I like how you think, Raven."

"That's why you hired me."

A bell rang as the front door opened. Footsteps trailed down the hall before LeVar appeared, with his shirt untucked and his dreadlocks hidden beneath a baseball cap.

"What's wrong with you?" Raven asked, sipping from her coffee mug.

"I didn't sleep well," LeVar said, falling into a chair. "Got a lot on my mind."

"Anything I can do to help?" asked Chelsey.

"Nah. It's all good. I received unexpected news yesterday. Thought I had everything figured out, but life happens."

Raven and Chelsey shared a glance. This morning, Thomas had told Chelsey that he'd zeroed in on a candidate for the open deputy position. The news struck her as strange. She'd thought LeVar was his first choice.

"If you need to take a sick day, it's fine with me."

"I'd rather work," LeVar said, rubbing his eyes. "Keeps my mind off things."

With a yawn, LeVar slumped into his chair and jiggled the mouse to wake his computer.

Raven asked, "Did you meet with your advisor yet?"

"I have time."

Raven rolled her eyes. "LeVar, classes start in a few weeks, and you haven't finished filling out your schedule."

"Don't worry, I'll call him tomorrow."

"But I—"

Raven clamped her mouth shut when Chelsey gave her a meaningful glance.

"Sorry for pushing you," Raven said, continuing. "I'm certain you'll deal with the issue. It's only your education, right?"

Chelsey winced. "Hey, I have an idea. How about we focus on the Dylan Fournette kidnapping? LeVar, I'm making smoothies for lunch. You want one?"

LeVar removed his cap and scratched his head. "I don't want to trouble you."

"It's no trouble. Besides, I want you at full strength while we go over the case." Raven fiddled with a pen as Chelsey stood. "Why don't you help me in the kitchen?"

Raven threw up her hands. "I have this background check to finish."

"You'll get to it later. Right now, I need your help."

Chelsey held Raven's gaze until her partner realized this wasn't about making smoothies. While LeVar signed on at his computer, Chelsey led Raven to the kitchen.

"Grab the mixed berries out of the freezer," Chelsey said, removing the cap from the blender. She lowered her voice. "What was that about?"

Raven palmed her forehead. "I screwed up. Every time LeVar procrastinates, I turn into the overbearing big sister."

"The more you push him, the less he'll listen."

"True. But this advisor thing—he put it off all summer. I worry LeVar's heart isn't into his education. Then Darren put that idea into his head about quitting school to become a deputy. LeVar can't give up now."

"There's no reason to assume LeVar wants to quit school," Chelsey said, filling the blender with water. She pulled a box of baby spinach from the refrigerator and added the ingredients. "Remember, you agreed to give your brother the benefit of the doubt. Give him room to breathe while he works out his issues."

"But I'm his sister. It's my job to care for LeVar."

"You can do it without overwhelming him. Now, open the side compartment in the refrigerator. There's a fresh cutting of ginger in a container."

"Wow, ginger. You're going all out."

"It's for our smoothies. Energy without the caffeine buzz."

Chelsey grabbed the vanilla protein powder from the cupboard and started the blender. After, she portioned the smoothie into three glasses. As Chelsey and Raven arrived with lunch, LeVar studied his computer screen.

"Thanks," LeVar said when Chelsey handed him a glass. "I'm going over the notes you gave to Aguilar."

"Anything stick out?"

"Not really. I'm worried. It's been almost two days since

Dylan Fournette vanished and still no ransom demand. That suggests we're dealing with a child predator."

"If that's the case, the chances drop every hour we'll find the boy alive," Raven added, sending a sick feeling through Chelsey's chest.

The phone interrupted their conversation. LeVar answered, and after a brief discussion, he set the receiver down.

"That was Deputy Lambert. Thomas and the deputies are swamped at the office. They want us to run a background check on TJ Soto."

"That's the guy who fathered Robyn Fournette's child, right?"

"Correct," said Chelsey.

"Speaking of the amusement park, didn't Empire Coasters close two summers ago because people kept injuring themselves on their rides?"

LeVar called up a news article on the internet and pointed at the screen with his pen. "I remember. The injuries caused an uproar. That's why Empire Coasters shut down a month early and tore down the old rides, replacing them with state-of-the-art attractions. It must have worked out. I don't recall any incidents since the controversy, and they're making money hand over fist."

"Hey, guys," Raven said, turning the screen on her computer to face them. "We have a problem."

Chelsey slid her chair closer. "Are you already running the background check on TJ Soto?"

"Got it up right here. Soto doesn't live in Illinois anymore."

"Where does he live?"

"In Syracuse. Chelsey, he lives right down the highway from Robyn Fournette."

17

Thomas sat beside Aguilar in the interview room, with the conference phone in the center of the table and Chelsey's voice booming through the speaker. The revelation that TJ Soto lived in Syracuse catapulted Robyn Fournette's former boyfriend up the suspect list.

"How long has Soto lived in New York?" Thomas asked as Aguilar scribbled notes.

"He moved to Syracuse eighteen months ago," Chelsey said. "Soto works for the university as the outreach coordinator. Are you bringing him in?"

Thomas sat back and considered his options. "I have to. Even without evidence linking Soto to Dylan Fournette's abduction, I can't ignore the coincidence. The problem is, we received a message from a woman who claims she caught Dylan in a photograph while she was at Empire Coasters."

"Before or after the abduction occurred?"

"Right around the time Dylan vanished. I'm following up with the woman as soon as we finish this call."

"Thomas, I have Soto's address. While you check the picture,

I can poke around and learn what I can about Robyn Fournette's old boyfriend."

"That's a bad idea, Chelsey. My department should handle Soto. Besides, if he catches you on his property—"

"All I intend to do is note the times he comes and goes. If he isn't home, I'll peek through the windows."

"I'm uncomfortable with this."

"You don't have the manpower to stake out Soto's property. Let me find out what I can. I'll get back to you after I finish."

"Please tell me you'll be careful."

"Always. Talk to you soon."

Then Chelsey was gone, and Thomas scratched his chin, worried that he shouldn't have allowed Chelsey to investigate Soto on her own. He wanted to pick up the phone and ensure Chelsey took Raven or LeVar with her. But if he did, Thomas would admit he didn't trust Chelsey to keep herself safe.

"I don't like the sound of this," Thomas said, staring at the phone, as if doing so would will Chelsey to call back and change her mind. "What do we know about TJ Soto, other than he fathered Dylan Fournette?"

"*Might* have fathered him," said Aguilar. "Lambert told me about Robyn Fournette's interview. Fournette might be lying. What if she wants to blackmail her old boyfriend?"

"She says she didn't use protection with Soto. That makes it almost certain that Soto is the boy's father." Thomas dropped his face into his hands. "How much did I miss out on in college? I didn't date, let alone have unprotected sex. Never had time between studying and internships. Why would Robyn take a risk?"

"Students mess around when they're young and don't consider consequences. Even the smart kids."

"Right. But why didn't Robyn tell Soto the truth and let him decide if he wanted to be a father?"

"You expect too much from people in their teens and early twenties. I remember how I acted, and I hardly recognize the person I was. Kids take dumb risks and make mistakes. Thomas, not everyone spends their college career studying night and day."

"I did."

"Not surprising," she said, giving him a playful jab on the shoulder. "You want me to drive to Soto's house and check on Chelsey?"

"Syracuse isn't part of our jurisdiction. I need you to get on the horn with Ron Faustin at Empire Coasters. Find out where they are in their investigation."

"I'll get right to it."

Before Aguilar rose from her chair, Maggie knocked and opened the door.

"Deputy, your friend Simone is here to see you."

Aguilar slapped her forehead. "Sorry, Thomas. I forgot I'd promised to eat a late lunch with Simone. Want me to get rid of her?"

"Don't tell your friend to leave."

"I'll call Faustin first."

"It can wait. You worked through your lunch break, so you must be starving."

"Do you mind if we sit together in the break room? I'm too strapped for funds to hit another lakeside restaurant."

"Not at all."

Though Thomas found Simone odd, he wanted to invite the woman to Wednesday's cookout. Chelsey had messaged him and planted the idea in his head. If Simone was up to something and causing problems for Aguilar, Thomas wanted to observe the woman up close.

Thomas gathered his paperwork and set the notes on his desk. He could hear Simone's excited voice from the break room and the crinkle of paper unwrapping. From the vinegary scents down the hall, Thomas assumed Simone had purchased submarine sandwiches at the deli. As he passed Lambert's desk, the deputy tugged at Thomas's shirtsleeve.

"What do you think, Thomas? Should I ask her out?"

"Who? Simone?"

"She couldn't stay away from the department and had to see me."

"Lambert, she brought Aguilar lunch."

Lambert sent Thomas a *you-have-to-be-kidding-me* stare. "It's not a coincidence. Yesterday, she asked me if I worked out. Today, she's back at the office."

"Deputy, you need a girlfriend."

"That's what I'm saying."

Lambert tried to follow the sheriff to the break room, but Thomas held up a hand. "Easy, big guy. Maybe hang back for a few minutes and play it cool."

"Yeah, cool. Play hard to get. Girls love it when guys play hard to get."

"If you say so."

When Thomas entered the break room, Aguilar and Simone were sitting beside each other at the table, hip-to-hip. Aguilar slid her chair away, and Simone inched closer. Each dinner plate held half of a roast beef sub. Simone chattered at an alarming pace, Aguilar nodding and shooting apologetic looks at Thomas in the doorway.

Thomas cleared his throat. "Nice to see you again, Ms. Axtell."

Simone glanced up from her sandwich. "Oh, hello, Sheriff. Veronica is on break, isn't she?"

"She is. Don't worry, I won't interrupt your lunch."

"So kind of you to give Veronica five minutes."

Thomas tugged at his collar. "If you're interested, I host a barbecue every Wednesday for my friends and family. I already invited Deputy Aguilar. We'd be honored if you joined us."

"Are you serious?"

"It's not much. Burgers, steaks, ribs. But everyone has a fun time."

"What do you say?" Aguilar asked Simone.

Simone scowled. "I say you should skip the cookout and spend time with a real friend."

Aguilar's mouth fell open. "Simone? Thomas is my friend."

"What kind of friend asks you to work overtime and never promotes you?"

Thomas's cheeks flushed.

"This isn't the time or place, Simone," said Aguilar. "Please apologize."

"Fine, I'm sorry. But I'm just looking out for you. Someone has to."

Aguilar crinkled the sub wrapper into a ball and tossed it into the trash. "Stay here. We'll discuss this after."

As Thomas stood dumbfounded in the doorway, Aguilar clutched his arm and led him down the hall until they were out of earshot.

"I'm so sorry, Thomas. I don't know what got into her."

"It's not your fault. I suppose it's best if Simone doesn't attend."

"Hopefully she'll move on by then."

"How long is she staying at your house?"

Aguilar massaged her temples. "It was supposed to be for a night or two. Now it appears she's staying all week."

"If you don't want her there, tell her how you feel."

"I can't, Thomas. That ridiculous outburst is just Simone looking out for me."

"Do you need Simone looking out for you?"

"She's a dear friend, and she's going through a rough patch

in her life. I can't go into the details, but she's dealing with a traumatic upbringing. If I kick her out, there's no telling what she'll . . ."

Aguilar trailed off. Down the hall, Simone whistled to herself with impatience. Thomas touched Aguilar's arm.

"Is Simone a danger to herself?"

"No, it's not like that. She needs a therapist. Please don't tell anyone."

"If you need someone to talk to, my door is open."

18

Towel in hand, Scout Mourning wiped the sweat off her brow and fell into a chair in front of her computer. She'd run two miles along the lake road before LeVar's text arrived, telling her about TJ Soto and the Dylan Fournette case. Due to arrive at Wolf Lake Consulting for her internship in ninety minutes, Scout typed on her keyboard and pulled up every link containing Soto's name.

According to his bio on the Syracuse University website, Soto was born in Japan and moved with his family to the United States when he was four years old. He graduated with honors from the University of Chicago six years ago, where he'd studied communications and public relations. In the next tab, a newspaper link contained a photograph of Soto surrounded by a dozen elementary school children. The headline read, *Overcoming Poverty through Opportunity*. Scout scanned the article and learned Soto worked with underprivileged children.

Soto appeared to be the perfect gentleman, a man who stuck up for the impoverished. But looks were deceiving.

The phone rang while she read another article, in which Soto announced a partnership between the university and the local Boys & Girls Club. Without glancing at her phone, Scout answered.

"Hey, Scout. How is your recovery coming along?"

Scout almost dropped the phone in her excitement. Recognizing the voice of Agent Scarlett Bell, Scout closed out of her browser.

"Agent Bell, great to hear from you." Scout flinched when her voice cracked. "I feel terrific."

"Take it one step at a time. You don't need to run a marathon one month after surgery."

"No marathons in my future, thanks." Scout wondered if her mother had messaged Bell, concerned about the strenuous exercise. "How's life at Quantico?"

"Same old, same old. I still partner with Agent Gardy, God help me. He's taking me out for lunch. Apparently, there's a new taco truck down the road from our building." Bell lowered her voice to a whisper. "Save me. If I eat one more fish taco, I'll grow gills."

Scout snickered. She wanted to ask if Gardy had invited Bell on a date yet, but thought better of it. When Gardy had visited Wolf Lake with Bell, Scout noticed the way he admired his partner. There was something unspoken between them, a connection neither wished to acknowledge.

Outside the bedroom window, Thomas's dog, Jack, pawed at LeVar's front door while Scout's mother waited for the dog to finish his business. Jack loved LeVar and missed him while he was at work. Everyone cared for LeVar. But only Scout received special treatment.

"Agent Bell, there's something I need to ask. You know how you and Agent Gardy always support me and point me down the right career path?"

"Because we see your potential, yes."

"I don't want you to think I don't appreciate everything you do. But . . ."

"Go on, Scout. Ask me anything."

"It's about my friend. You remember LeVar, right?"

"I remember LeVar. He's sharp and motivated, and I like that he watches over you. You couldn't ask for a better big brother."

"LeVar graduates from community college soon. He might transfer to a four-year school. LeVar has as good a mind for law enforcement as anyone I've met. But he's torn over his next move —staying home and working with the sheriff's department or furthering his education. LeVar could work for the FBI someday. I'm positive he'd be an excellent fit, but I wish someone would talk to LeVar and help him along."

"And by someone you mean me."

Scout swallowed. Had she pushed too hard and upset Bell?

"Scout, I'd be happy to speak with LeVar."

"Thank you so much. Are there FBI training and education opportunities for LeVar? As you might remember, he had a rough background and overcame a ton in his life. There must be a program for people in LeVar's situation. Did I mention he's an honors student?"

"The FBI runs a summer intern program for honors students. It's highly competitive. For every fifty students who apply, one gets accepted. Given LeVar's situation, he'd be a strong candidate for an internship. But summer is almost over, and this year's program ends on Friday. The FBI selected the BAU for an intern spot this summer, and the girl we chose did a tremendous job. I wish you'd asked four months ago. Next year, tell LeVar to apply early and put me down as a reference."

Scout's heart fell. "I'll tell him. It's just a shame that he hasn't received the same opportunity as me."

"Don't fool yourself into believing you receive special treat-

ment out of charity. Yes, the paralysis got your foot in the door."
Bell groaned. "Sorry, poor choice of words."

Scout couldn't prevent herself from giggling. "No offense
taken."

"But we took an interest in you because of your exceptional
talent. You *earned* our attention, and you'll need to excel in
school if you want a shot at the BAU after college. As for LeVar,
I'll talk to my bosses and see if there's a creative path we can take
to get him experience. Would LeVar be willing to speak to me
about the FBI?"

"I'm sure he would, but please don't tell him I asked."

"Understood."

"Thank you for helping, Agent Bell."

"Remember, we earn our opportunities through hard work
and persistence. Keep working hard, Scout. I'm confident good
things will come to you and your friend."

19

Gray clouds swallowed the afternoon sunshine. Chelsey parked her orange Honda Civic down the road from TJ Soto's Syracuse home and removed binoculars from the glove compartment. Soto lived in an upper-middle-class suburban neighborhood, replete with green lawns and two-car garages. His street sat halfway up a ridge, from which she spied the sports dome on the Syracuse University campus and the sprawling city below.

Ivy curled up the sides of Soto's red-brick two-story. It seemed Robyn Fournette's old boyfriend was doing well for himself. Chelsey focused on the windows, which appeared dark compared to the silver light of day. She didn't notice a vehicle in the driveway.

Chelsey dialed the office. LeVar answered.

"Give me an update. Learn anything about Soto since I left?"

"Poring over his cell phone records right now," LeVar said.

Chelsey heard Raven's voice in the background. "Has he contacted Robyn Fournette?"

"Not that I've found. He made twelve calls to a K. Soto. I researched his family, and his mother's name is Kami. He mostly texts. Nothing interesting so far, but I have several hundred messages to go through."

"Appreciate it, LeVar."

Chelsey pocketed the phone and stepped onto the sidewalk. Except for a man in Bermuda shorts rinsing his SUV with a hose, everyone in the neighborhood had ventured inside. She rounded Soto's house and followed the blacktop driveway—freshly sealed—to the backyard, guarded by a tall, white privacy fence. Finding the gate locked, she strode to the garage and cupped her hands around her eyes, blocking out the light as she peered through the window. The garage was empty. Soto must have been a neat freak, for he kept the concrete floor spotless. Shelves held cleaning supplies, a toolbox, and what appeared to be a plastic container of holiday ornaments.

After checking for a way around the privacy fence—there wasn't one unless she climbed over the gate—Chelsey retraced her steps and checked each window. The first pane revealed the dining room table with a table runner in the foreground and a kitchen in the background. At the side window closest to the front of the house, Chelsey stopped and stood on tiptoe, examining the living room. The hardwood floor sparkled as though recently polished. Three LEGO bricks lay scattered beside a leather sofa.

Chelsey called the office again. Raven answered this time.

"Soto is single, right?"

"He never married," Raven confirmed. "Why?"

"Toys in the living room."

"That's weird. What would he be doing with children's toys? Wait, are you peeking through windows? Don't trespass on Soto's property. Remember, you told Thomas you'd only list the times he comes and goes and take pictures."

"Soto isn't home, so there's no point in logging anything until he arrives."

"You sure you don't want me and LeVar to join you?"

"Keep researching Soto. I'll return to the office after I'm finished."

Chelsey moved to a third window and gained another view into the living room. She didn't find any toys besides the bricks, but a child's crayon drawing lay upon the end table.

"Excuse me. What are you doing?"

Chelsey swung around to the stranger's voice. A woman with wispy auburn hair peeled off her gardening gloves and crossed the neighboring lawn.

"Sorry to bother you, ma'am. My name is Chelsey Byrd." Chelsey fished a card out of her wallet and handed it to the woman. "I'm a private investigator."

"Candice Gottlieb. I live next door. I'd shake your hand, but . . ." The woman displayed her palms, muddied despite the gloves. "I wanted to weed my garden before it rained." Gottlieb lifted her chin at Soto's house. "Is Mr. Soto in some kind of trouble?"

"No, I just had a few questions to ask him about a case I'm working on. I rang the bell, but nobody answered."

"So you peeked through his windows?" Gottlieb waved away the concern. "None of my business. I'm sure you have your reasons. He works days at the university and pulls in after five."

Chelsey checked her watch. Soto wouldn't arrive for another ninety minutes.

"Are you close with Mr. Soto?"

"He's the quiet sort. Once in a while, I'll catch him in the driveway and wave. Can't recall the last time we had a conversation."

"What about girlfriends? Is he dating anyone?"

"If he is, I haven't noticed. Don't misunderstand. He's had women over to the house, but nobody steady. Not that I stare out the window all day and check up on him. Weird that a nice-looking man who works at the university hasn't married. The problem is, he's so bashful."

"How so?"

"I'll catch him on the porch when he retrieves the morning paper and wave. He gives a quick nod and hurries into the house, like he's too embarrassed to speak to anyone. Then he draws the curtains, as if he's in the witness protection program. He's lived here for . . ." Gottlieb glanced upward and pressed an index finger against her cheek. "About a year and a half. The Morrisey family owned the place before, but they moved to Albany. Too bad. They had kids in the yard all summer, and they were the first to arrive and the last to leave at neighborhood parties. Mr. Soto, not so much. You're lucky if he shows his face."

"Has he acted strangely over the last few days?"

Gottlieb paused before answering. "Well, no. Not more than usual. Last month, I asked if I could borrow a pan. It was so dark inside his downstairs that I got the creeps. I couldn't wait to get out of there after he handed me the pan."

Chelsey remembered the LEGO blocks in the living room. "Mr. Soto doesn't have a child, does he?"

Gottlieb huffed. "That would be a fine trick, since he rarely dates."

Clouds thickened over the neighborhood, the air heavy with the coming rain. Chelsey pulled a photograph of Dylan Fournette from her case notes and showed it to Gottlieb.

"Ever see this boy at Soto's house?"

Gottlieb took the picture and squinted at it. "I don't recognize him. But now that you mention it, Mr. Soto brought a boy to the house two nights ago."

Chelsey's body pumped with adrenaline. Had TJ Soto discovered Dylan Fournette was his son and hidden the boy inside the house?

"Are you certain the boy wasn't the child in the picture?"

"I'm not sure of anything. It was dark when they arrived. When I looked out the window, I saw Mr. Soto leading a small boy by the hand up the steps."

"Is the boy staying with Mr. Soto?"

"If he is, I haven't seen him since."

"You've been very helpful," Chelsey said. When Gottlieb handed the picture back, Chelsey shook her head. "Keep it. I have a copy. Hang on to my card, too. If you see the boy next door, call me."

Gottlieb rubbed her arm. "I thought you said Mr. Soto wasn't in trouble."

"He's not. As I said, I just want to ask him a question about the case I'm investigating."

"Does it have to do with the boy?"

"Please understand I can't disclose sensitive information about the case."

Chelsey bit her tongue. She'd all but admitted she was searching for the boy in the picture.

Gottlieb's eyes followed Chelsey to her car. The first rain-drops dotted the windshield as Chelsey turned the key in the ignition.

20

In the village of Coral Lake, Thomas met with Shari Newton, the woman who claimed she'd captured Dylan Fournette in the background of a family picture. They hid beneath the porch roof as rain poured from the heavens, the cloudburst lending the neighborhood a wet pavement smell. Barefoot and wearing plaid shorts and a tank, Newton cupped a hand around the phone to cut down on the glare while Thomas studied the picture over her shoulder.

The photograph focused on Newton, her husband, and two girls in strollers as they posed in front of the merry-go-round at Empire Coasters. The people in the background appeared blurry, but there was a small child amid the crowd. Someone in an alligator costume held the boy's hand.

"That's the boy on the news," Newton said, poking the screen with her forefinger. "See the green T-shirt and black shorts? Just like the description on the news."

Thomas nodded, unconvinced. It might be Dylan. He wasn't the only child in the picture wearing a green T-shirt. Thomas suspected Ally the Alligator shirts were the park's most popular souvenir.

"Will you send me a copy of the photograph?" Thomas asked, handing Newton a card with the station's email address listed along the bottom.

Newton thumbed the address into her messaging application. Thomas questioned Newton about the missing child, but the woman didn't recall passing Dylan Fournette in the park. Until she'd recognized the boy in the background of her picture, she hadn't realized she'd come so close to him.

As Thomas dodged raindrops and slid into his cruiser, Chelsey called. The rain made hollow, metallic thumps on the roof as the sheriff wiped the phone on his pant legs.

"I just left TJ Soto's neighborhood," Chelsey said, as Thomas removed his hat and wiped the water off his forehead.

"Was he home?"

"Not yet. I met his neighbor, a woman named Candice Gottlieb. She says Soto arrives home after five on weekdays, but get this: Soto escorted a young boy into his house two nights ago, the same night Dylan Fournette disappeared. I peeked through Soto's windows. There were LEGO bricks on the living room floor and a child's drawing on the end table. Soto isn't dating anyone and doesn't have a son. What does that tell you?"

"That I need to bring Soto in for questioning. Did Gottlieb identify the boy?"

"Negative. It was too dark. Meet you at home after work?"

Thomas turned the cruiser toward the station. "I wish. Don't plan on me arriving before midnight. I'm sending Aguilar home by eight, and Lambert is burning the candle at both ends. They need a break."

"So do you, Thomas."

"No time for that, not until I interview Soto and find out if he had anything to do with the Dylan Fournette abduction."

"I have a backlog of work waiting for me at the office. If you aren't coming home anytime soon, I'll work late and sleep there."

"You sure?"

"It's for the best. I'll contact LeVar and ask him to watch Jack."

After ending the call, Thomas radioed the office and spoke to Aguilar. She would contact Soto and request he visit the station.

"Aguilar, send Lambert to Soto's neighborhood and tell him to check out the property. Lambert needs to remain discreet. He can't let Soto spot him."

"I'll tell him, Sheriff."

"If Lambert sees a young boy at Soto's house, I want to know about it."

"On it."

A copy of the TJ Soto background check lay on the sheriff's desk when he arrived at the office. An hour later, his shirt and pants were still damp when Soto walked through the entrance. Maggie's voice traveled from the front desk, where she asked the suspect to wait. Soto sat upon a chair with his hands folded in his lap, a perplexed tilt to his head. The suspect wore dress slacks and a polo shirt, his black hair neat despite the rain. He removed his bifocals and wiped them with a tissue from Maggie's desk.

"Mr. Soto?" The man rose when Thomas spoke his name. "I'm Sheriff Thomas Shepherd. Thank you for coming in on short notice."

"What's this about?"

"If you'll join me and my deputy in the conference room, I have a few questions."

Soto followed Thomas to the interview room. The suspect glanced over his shoulder, as if he feared the entryway door would lock and trap him inside the building for eternity. Aguilar waited at the table as Thomas led Soto inside. Though the Nightshade County Sheriff's Department couldn't afford a modern conference facility, the room had hosted FBI briefings and countless interviews. The long table left little available space, and the chairs crowded together like agitated cattle pushing toward a gate.

Soto took a seat opposite Thomas and Aguilar and searched the room, confused as to why he was here. His eyes refused to stay in one place.

"You graduated from the University of Chicago six years ago," Thomas said, scanning the background check. "Is that correct?"

"Right."

"And you moved to Syracuse eighteen months ago."

"I accepted a position at the university. I'm the outreach coordinator."

"Do you enjoy your work?"

"I do," Soto said, a hint of a smile working across his lips as his shoulders relaxed. "It's the auxiliary work with the community that fulfills me most."

Deputy Aguilar removed a printed article. "You work with underprivileged children."

Soto's eyes lit, recognizing the photograph from the Boys & Girls Club. "All the time. Our city leaves so many children behind. The university strives to give these kids the opportunities they deserve."

Thomas asked, "Did you perform an outreach event two evenings ago?"

"No, why?"

"Where were you between the hours of five and eight o'clock?"

The suspect paused and furrowed his brow. "I worked late

that day. The staff meeting ran until six, then I drove home and cooked dinner."

"So you weren't at the Empire Coasters amusement park."

Soto sat back in his chair. "Why would I go there?"

Thomas slid a photograph of Dylan Fournette across the table. He studied Soto's face, searching for a sign of recognition. "Do you recognize the boy in the picture?"

"Should I? Is he a child I work with? He doesn't look familiar."

"His name is Dylan Fournette, and he disappeared from Empire Coasters forty-eight hours ago."

"What does this have to do with me? Even among the children I've met, I don't know them outside of work."

Aguilar tapped a fingernail against the photograph. "Look again. The name Fournette means nothing to you?"

Soto brushed his fingers through his hair. "Not really. I dated a girl with that last name in college, but that was in Illinois." His eyes shot to Thomas. "Wait, are we talking about the same person? Robyn Fournette?"

"The child in the photo is her son," said Thomas. "When was the last time you spoke with Robyn Fournette?"

"It must have been six years ago. After the breakup, we didn't keep in touch. Seriously, she lives in New York?"

"So you haven't contacted her since."

"Why would I?"

"Your move to New York had nothing to do with Robyn Fournette?"

"Like I'm stalking my ex? I didn't even realize she lived around here." Soto stared at Aguilar and Thomas. "You think I took her kid to get even. That's ridiculous. So Robyn moved to New York, met someone and had a child. Good for her. I'm not jealous."

"Robyn didn't marry and doesn't have a boyfriend. Mr. Soto,

Ms. Fournette claims she slept with you during her senior year at college and got pregnant."

Soto shifted his back. "That never sat right with me. I cared about Robyn, but I was young and stupid. We made a mistake. I would have paid for . . . you know . . . for Robyn to take care of the issue."

"You mean get an abortion," Aguilar said.

"An abortion, right. I didn't think it was proper for Robyn to pay and go through the procedure alone. It was my fault. I was the one who forgot to bring protection. Then she broke up with me." Soto's eyes flicked to Thomas. "She had the abortion, right?"

Neither Aguilar nor Thomas responded.

Soto cupped a hand over his mouth. "Oh, my God. Are you saying she had the baby? The kid in the photograph is mine?"

The man's eyes glazed over. He teetered on the chair. Aguilar rounded the table and steadied Soto before he collapsed.

"I'll get you a cup of water," Aguilar said, as Soto braced his hands against the desk.

The blood fled Soto's face and left him shocked, his pallid complexion zombie-like. Thomas spoke in soft tones, waiting for the suspect to compose himself. Aguilar returned with a cup and placed it in front of Soto.

After a long time, Soto stared over Thomas's shoulder toward the window, where the late-day light waned. "I can't believe Robyn didn't tell me. This can't be real. I have a son?"

"How does that make you feel, Mr. Soto?" asked Thomas.

For the first time during the interview, Soto's face contorted with anger. "How would it make you feel, Sheriff? How would you react if someone said you'd fathered a child six years ago and your girlfriend hid him from you?"

"Does it anger you?"

Soto bit his lip and averted his gaze.

Aguilar said, "I bet the news makes you furious, Mr. Soto. Who can blame you? But maybe you found out before today."

"What?"

"I'm thinking you'd already learned Dylan was yours, and it upset you."

"No."

"It made you a little crazy, perhaps."

"So I followed my son to an amusement park and snatched him? Absolutely not. I don't abduct children. Do I need a lawyer?"

"Mr. Soto, I need answers." Thomas said, leaning forward. "A witness watched you bring a young boy into your house the night Dylan Fournette disappeared from Empire Coasters."

Soto leaned his head back and laughed. "Yeah, my nephew." Thomas and Aguilar stared at Soto. "My sister and her husband are in town, staying at the Hilton. I offered to take Bradley for the night so they could have time for themselves. We only see each other a few times a year. This was an opportunity to bond with my nephew. I didn't kidnap anybody."

"Your sister will confirm your story?"

"Of course." Soto removed his phone and scrolled through his contacts. His attention kept returning to Dylan's picture, as though Soto had discovered a flaw in the photograph. "Here's her number. Call Hana. She's still in Syracuse."

"I'll call her after we finish."

Dylan's photograph lay in the center of the table, angled toward Soto. The man slid the picture in front of him and narrowed his eyes, his lips moving in silence as he worked a problem out in his head.

Aguilar set her forearms on the table. "Is there a problem, Mr. Soto?"

"This boy isn't mine."

"Why do you say that?"

"Please. If you hadn't noticed, I'm Asian. The boy in the photograph isn't."

Thomas waited a moment before he pulled the picture back to him. Dylan had a blocky lower face and a retruded chin, typical of some Asian-Americans. Thomas noticed the eyes—narrow, yet not Asian. He swallowed a curse and held a poker face while he kicked himself for not spotting the obvious.

Soto pushed his chair back and stood. "I hope you find Robyn's child. Really, I hope you do. But she lied to you. Dylan Fournette isn't my boy."

21

Thomas watched TJ Soto through the window as his top suspect drove away. A hollow sense of loss overcame the sheriff, and he wavered before the windowpane, wondering if he'd ever find Dylan Fournette.

Child abductions by strangers were rare in the United States, accounting for less than fifty cases per year. After twenty-four hours, the chance of recovering the child alive dropped through the floor. By forty-eight hours, a happy ending required a miracle.

Aguilar came to Thomas's side. "Hey, don't give up. We'll get the investigation on track and find him."

"I thought Soto was our guy."

"So did I. And for the record, the facial features don't rule Soto out as the father. Dylan is a combination of his parents and possesses traits from each of them. Until a DNA test proves otherwise, I'm keeping Soto on the suspect list. He admits to working around children."

"Because he wants to help them."

"Or he has an ulterior motive."

"He's not a sex predator."

"You can't be sure of that."

"The boy at Soto's house was his nephew. The sister confirmed it."

"He's suspicious. Okay, what now?"

Thomas removed his phone and swiped to the picture Shari Newton had emailed him. "We follow up with Empire Coasters security."

Aguilar took the phone when Thomas held it out for her. "The clothes look right, but I can't recognize a face with all that blur. Are you sure this is Dylan Fournette?"

"I can't tell. Dylan was enamored with this character, Ally the Alligator, so this might be him in the picture. She has a cartoon on television."

"I've seen it."

"You watch cartoons on Saturday mornings over a bowl of cereal?"

"Don't be ridiculous," Aguilar said, scoffing. "I don't eat sugary cereals. I watch cartoons over an omelet."

"Then I'll tap your expertise when it comes to animated reptiles."

"Here's an idea. What if the person in the costume abducted our missing child? It makes sense. Dylan trusted the character and wouldn't have fought if Ally led him out of the park. Maybe that's what we're seeing in this picture. Has anyone interviewed the person beneath the mask?"

"Ron Faustin, the head of security, claims he interviewed his staff members, including the characters."

"Do you trust Faustin to conduct a thorough interview?"

"Not particularly. Let's drive to the park."

As Thomas headed for the door, Aguilar placed a hand on his chest. "Before we leave, I want to apologize again for the way Simone acted."

"No reason to apologize. It's not your fault. I'm sure Simone thinks she's protecting you."

"It is my fault. Simone is my friend, and I'm responsible for inviting her to the office and expecting her to treat people with respect."

"Your friend has a point. The staffing shortage falls on my shoulders. It isn't fair to you and Lambert. I don't expect you to work seven days a week."

"These are extreme circumstances. We have a missing boy to find, and you can't hire an unqualified applicant just to ease the staffing burden. You'll figure it out, Thomas. Lambert and I know you're working on the issue."

"I appreciate your patience. It won't be much longer, I promise."

The sun dipped below the hills as Thomas and Aguilar crossed the parking lot outside Empire Coasters. Aguilar had called ahead and confirmed Ron Faustin was available. Thomas recognized the guards who met them at the gate—Wheeler, the imposing security officer who'd leered at Chelsey, and Kelly, the man who'd led Thomas into the tunnels on the night Dylan disappeared. He found it curious that Faustin had sent two guards to meet them, as if Thomas and Aguilar posed threats.

Wheeler swiped his ID card and unlocked the door to the tunnel. The guard stared at Thomas from the corner of his eye as he led them down the stairs and into the tunnel system.

Tre Kelly shot nervous glances back at Thomas and Aguilar. "Fair warning, Sheriff. Mr. Faustin is on the warpath this evening. He screamed at a staff member after I arrived for my shift."

"What about?" Thomas asked.

"Some kid got confused while exiting the merry-go-round and bumped into the man running the ride. Before anyone reacted, the worker fell against the lever and started the merry-go-round spinning. A bunch of people fell. No injuries, but it could have been a disaster. After Mr. Faustin chewed out the worker, he threw a coffee mug against the wall and shattered it. Just be careful. He has a short fuse tonight."

"Does your boss lose his cool and fly into violent rages all the time?" Aguilar asked.

"Between tonight's incident and the missing kid, Mr. Faustin is under a ton of pressure. The media blames Empire Coasters for what happened two nights ago, and they still haven't forgotten about the rides breaking down. Empire Coasters spent a lot of money upgrading the park and bringing in modern, safe attractions. I wish they'd write about how much better the park is these days. If you guys don't find that kid, the security team will take the blame. Mr. Faustin will lose his job."

When they reached headquarters, Wheeler held the door open for Thomas and Aguilar. Even before Thomas set foot inside the office, he could hear Faustin barking on the phone. The head of security spied Thomas and Aguilar standing beside the counter and slammed the receiver down.

"You're wasting your time," Faustin said, lumbering out of his office. "Ally didn't kidnap Dylan Fournette, so get the idea out of your head."

Thomas set his hands on his hips. "Tell me who wore the Ally costume the night the boy disappeared. I'd like to talk to him about this picture."

The sheriff held up the photograph with Ally and the boy, who resembled Dylan Fournette.

"It's not a *him*," Faustin said. "It's a *her*. The girl's name is Marlee Greenwood. She's a seventeen-year-old high school student, and she doesn't abduct children."

"You have a habit of hiring teenagers to play character roles inside your park?" Aguilar asked.

"Empire Coasters fostered a relationship with the local high school's drama club. Marlee has acted since she was a child, and she wants to work for Disney after graduation."

"I'd like to speak with her all the same," said Thomas.

Faustin looked away and shook his head. "If you insist. But Marlee didn't take that child."

While Thomas and Aguilar waited, Faustin lifted his radio and ordered someone to send Marlee Greenwood to the cast member lounge.

"Officer Wheeler will show you to the lounge," said Faustin.

With a nod from Faustin, Wheeler motioned for the sheriff and his deputy to follow. They retraced their steps through the tunnel system and climbed another set of stairs, which led to a hallway filled with costumed characters—an orange-and-black tiger, a giant killer whale, and a man in his twenties wearing an eye patch and holding a faux sword.

"Are these characters on your Saturday morning shows?" Thomas asked Aguilar.

"Will you stop with the cartoon talk? I don't watch every week. I'm not an expert."

"How often do you watch?"

"I don't want to talk about it."

Thomas grinned.

Wheeler pounded on a door, which read *Cast Member Lounge*. Another costumed actor opened the door. At the table, a teenage girl with long blond hair rose from a chair, her lower lip trembling as her hands tugged at her T-shirt. Thomas recognized the girl. She'd passed the haunted house while Thomas interviewed Malcolm Chaney.

"Marlee Greenwood?" Thomas asked.

The girl's voice cracked when she said, "Yes."

"No need for concern. You're not in trouble. We only want to question you about the boy who went missing in the park."

The girl bobbed her head without speaking, her gaze fixed

to the tops of her sneakers. Aguilar motioned for Wheeler to close the door and give them privacy. Wheeler hesitated before he complied, making it clear he didn't appreciate taking orders from the sheriff's department.

"Please," Thomas said, indicating the chair.

Marlee slumped into the seat and tugged at her hair as Thomas and Aguilar sat across from the teenager.

"Let's start with your job," said Thomas. "How long have you worked at Empire Coasters?"

"J-just this summer," Marlee said, stuttering.

"I understand you wish to work for Disney after school."

The tension melted out of the girl's shoulders, and she smiled for the first time since the sheriff and his deputy had entered the room. "That's my dream. It's a long shot, but I'm going to school in Florida next year so I can apply to Disney's intern program."

"I need to ask you about this photograph." Thomas placed his phone in front of Marlee and displayed Shari Newton's photo. "This picture was taken around the time Dylan Fournette disappeared."

"That's the boy." Marlee pointed at the missing child. "I remember him. He ran away from his mother and hugged me near the merry-go-round."

"Was this the only time you saw Dylan Fournette?"

"Yes, just this once."

"What did you do after Dylan ran up to you?"

"I followed protocol. We're taught to identify the child's parent or guardian and ensure he isn't alone. I didn't see a parent, so I figured he'd broken away from his mom or dad."

"What are you taught to do after you come across a lost child?" Aguilar asked.

"Stay with the child and keep him calm until a parent

arrives. We're not supposed to speak to anyone because that breaks the magic."

"The magic?"

"The belief that the characters are real. I can't imitate the actress who plays Ally on television. If I tried, every child would know I'm not the real Ally."

"Did you speak to Dylan?"

Marlee wound her hair around her finger and gave it a tug. "I did. You won't tell anyone, right? I don't want to lose my job."

"It won't cause a problem," Thomas said in a reassuring voice. "What did you and Dylan discuss?"

"I asked him who brought him to the park. He told me his mother had. Before I asked Dylan where his mother was, she found us and told him to never leave her side again. I was happy she found the boy. If the parent doesn't arrive after thirty seconds, I'm supposed to radio security."

"How do you hold a radio when you're in costume?"

Marlee giggled. "We don't need to. When in costume, we wear wireless headsets beneath our masks. That makes it easy to contact security whenever we spot trouble."

"While you waited with Dylan, did another adult approach or pay too much attention to the boy?"

"Not that I saw."

At that moment, the door opened, and a man in his mid-twenties poked his head through the opening. Marlee smiled, her face blushing as the man crossed the lounge and headed toward a door marked *Changing Room*. Thomas remembered the man from the haunted house—Malcolm Chaney. What was a man in his mid-twenties doing flirting with a high school girl?

"And you're the only actor who played Ally that night?"

"From four o'clock until closing time. Granted, I was only in the park for an hour. Most of the time, I'm down here at the lounge, waiting for my next appearance."

Thomas and Aguilar questioned Marlee for another ten minutes before letting her return to work.

After the girl exited the room, Aguilar tapped Thomas on the shoulder. "What was the deal with Marlee and that guy in the changing room?"

"You noticed, too?"

"He must be seven or eight years older than her. At Marlee's age, that's a little creepy. That blushing smile Marlee gave him? I've seen that look before. They're sleeping together."

"Guy's name is Malcolm Chaney. When he comes out of the changing room, we'll have a chat."

22

M alcolm Chaney exited the changing room in full garb, dressed in the same costume he'd worn the day Thomas encountered him inside the haunted house—a tattered gray shirt with fake blood splotches, work boots, pants with torn cuffs, and his machete. The performer hadn't wrapped gauze around his head yet.

"Still haven't found the boy, I take it?" Malcolm asked.

Thomas clicked his notes together, annoyed by Malcolm's flippant attitude. "Not yet. We're interviewing staff who might have come into contact with Dylan Fournette."

"But we talked two nights ago. Why do you need to speak to me again?"

It was a long shot to consider Chaney a child sexual predator, but he was a twenty-five-year-old man dating a seventeen-year-old high school girl. And the room he stalked inside the haunted house offered a view of the flying swings, where Dylan Fournette had disappeared. The kidnapping might have been an inside job.

Thomas slid the boy's photograph across the table to Chaney. "You told me you hadn't seen the boy. Are you certain?"

"Guess how many kids wander past the haunted house every hour. Hundreds. I don't recognize the boy, but it's possible he was outside the window while I worked."

"Your girlfriend plays Ally. Is that correct?"

Malcolm tugged at his shirt collar. "Marlee isn't my girlfriend."

"We saw how you looked at each other," Aguilar said. "If we ask your coworkers, will anyone give us a different answer?"

Malcolm stared down at his hands. "All right, we're dating. But you can't tell anyone. The park forbids staff members from dating. Too much drama in the past, I guess. I'll get fired if management finds out."

"Your girlfriend is only seventeen," Thomas said, tapping a pen against the desk. "Is your relationship sexual?"

"That isn't your business."

"If it is sexual, we're talking about statutory rape, Mr. Chaney."

"But is it really? Come on. Teenage girls date older guys all the time. If a college senior sleeps with a freshman, does campus security arrest him?"

"You're past college age," Aguilar said. "And Marlee is still in high school. Having sexual relations with a girl that young opens you up to a statutory rape charge."

"Why are you grilling me? It's not like I forced her to sleep with me. Marlee is old enough to make her own decisions."

"Where were you when Dylan Fournette disappeared?" Thomas asked.

Chaney glowered. "In the haunted house. You saw me, so you know I'm telling the truth."

"I met you almost two hours after the boy vanished."

"Are you saying I'm some kind of sicko who goes after kids, just because I'm dating Marlee?"

"You work near the flying swings. That's where Robyn Fournette last saw her son."

"I didn't take him." Chaney turned a pleading eye to Thomas. "Please believe me. If I could help you find that boy, I would."

"Security locked down the park ten minutes after Robyn Fournette lost her child. It would be almost impossible to escort a six-year-old boy out of the park in that amount of time. We believe the kidnapper used the tunnel system or an alternative exit from the park. You have access to the tunnels and emergency exits, correct?"

"All the performers do, so that's a yes. But Empire Coasters places cameras all over the tunnels, in case a guest sneaks past. You'd have to memorize every camera location to escape the tunnels without someone spotting you."

"You've memorized the camera locations by now."

"For the last time, I didn't kidnap anyone. I'm into Marlee. You've seen her; she's hot. Why would I go after a little boy?"

"Did Marlee tell her parents about you?" asked Aguilar.

Chaney opened his mouth, then closed it, reconsidering his answer. After a moment, he muttered, "No."

Thomas and Aguilar shared a glance.

"And you can't tell them. Marlee's parents are old-fashioned. They don't want their daughter dating anyone, let alone a guy my age. If they find out, they'll freak and force her to break up with me."

"Oh, come on, Mr. Chaney. A good-looking guy like you can find a woman to date. You'll meet someone else."

"Don't blab to Marlee's folks. This is bullshit."

"Given the age difference, we don't have a choice," said Thomas.

Chaney slid the picture back to Thomas. "Then we're

through talking. I know my rights. You have nothing on me. The next time you interrogate me, I'll bring a lawyer."

"You're not under arrest. We just want information that will help us find Dylan."

Chaney shoved his chair backward and stood. "I'm finished talking to you. Harass someone else next time."

The performer bumped the table on his way to the exit. At the doorway, he swung around.

"And you'd better not tell Marlee's parents about me, Sheriff."

Thomas leaned forward. "Is that a threat?"

"Just don't tell them. That would be a huge mistake on your part."

23

Aguilar heard the water running in the kitchen sink when she unlocked her door and staggered into the entryway, exhausted after another long day at the office. Night washed over the windows, cricket songs shrilling outside. Inside the kitchen, the water stopped. Hurried footsteps announced Simone's presence before she rounded the corner.

"I wondered when you'd arrive home," said Simone, taking Aguilar's jacket.

"You don't have to hang up my coat. I can handle it."

"You're exhausted. Make yourself comfortable on the couch while I finish cleaning up."

Cleaning up? Aguilar always kept the house tidy.

"I made lasagna," Simone called over her shoulder, as Aguilar collapsed on the couch. "May I fix you a plate?"

Aguilar had to admit the kitchen smelled heavenly. "I'll get it myself. Give me a few minutes to rest."

Simone wore jogging shorts that rode high on her thighs, white ankle socks, and a T-shirt with a thorny rose on the front. She'd pulled her hair back with a tie.

"More overtime?"

Aguilar groaned. "We haven't found our missing child yet. I have a bad feeling we never will."

"Don't be a defeatist. With you on the job, I'm sure the department will crack the case."

Aguilar aimed the remote at the television and scrolled through Netflix. After she located the documentary she'd started last week, featuring detectives who track criminals, Aguilar sat back.

"Really?" Simone asked. "You come home from work and watch a show about cops? We need to get you out of the house more often."

"I enjoy documentaries. Sometimes, I get interesting ideas for solving cases."

"Not tonight." Simone picked up the remote and clicked on an episode of *Dawson's Creek*. "That's better."

"What is that nonsense? This looks like a show for teens."

"It's not for teens. *Dawson's Creek* is about relationships, love, and understanding each other."

"Ugh."

"Do you want me to turn it off?"

"No, watch your show. I need to close my eyes before I get a migraine. Today lasted forever."

As Aguilar leaned back, Simone's hands fell on her shoulders.

The deputy's eyes snapped open. "What are you doing?"

"Relax," Simone said, standing behind the couch. "I worked as a masseuse for six months after college."

"Wait, I don't want a—"

Simone's fingers kneaded Aguilar's tight shoulders, unraveling the pent-up tension. "Don't talk. Just relax and keep your eyes closed. It's all right if you fall asleep."

The more Simone worked out the knots, the more Aguilar relaxed. It was as if she'd submerged her body in a Jacuzzi.

"What made you want to become a masseuse?"

"After graduation, I bounced from one job to the next, trying to find my purpose in life. It sounded like a fun diversion."

"You're very good at giving massages. If the New York City job falls through, open your own practice."

Simone snickered, kneading Aguilar's back as the deputy tilted forward. "It's okay if you lean back. I can reach."

"You sure?"

"No problem."

Aguilar felt muscles she didn't know she possessed unwinding, a serene warmth cascading down her body. "While you're at it, we need to discuss something."

"It can wait."

"No, it can't. Simone, you can't treat my friends the way you treated the sheriff."

Simone sighed. "I can't stop thinking about it. My apologies, Veronica. I overreacted. But I did it for you. It breaks my heart when people take advantage of you."

"Thomas didn't take advantage of me. He works more overtime than Deputy Lambert and me. If it wasn't for this kidnapping case, our staffing shortage wouldn't cause an issue."

"Is that what you're calling it now? A kidnapping?"

Aguilar shrugged. "If Dylan Fournette walked away from his mother and lost himself in the crowd, someone would have found him after the park closed. I'm afraid a kidnapper took him."

"That's horrible. I can't imagine what it's like to work in law enforcement. The pressure must be unbearable. Which makes it even worse that I snapped. Let me talk to the sheriff tomorrow."

"That's a bad idea. Better to let it go."

"But it's important to apologize. I should own my mistakes."

Aguilar shifted her jaw, wishing Simone would leave Thomas alone. What if Simone lost her cool? Aguilar didn't wish to apologize to Thomas again. "I'll smooth things over, Simone. Thomas realizes you're trying to protect me. He understands."

"I'm not convinced, but I'll hold off if you prefer to do the talking. You trust the sheriff. Please be careful, my friend. Bosses take advantage of their workers all the time. It's why I want to run my own business. When you work for somebody, you make them money and forward their careers. It never works out in your favor."

At least Aguilar had convinced Simone not to bother Thomas. Still, she felt like a heel for telling Chelsey about the molestation. Earlier that afternoon when Aguilar had spoken to Chelsey, the private investigator expressed concern over Simone refusing to let her inside Aguilar's house. Chelsey didn't trust Simone, and Aguilar assumed the private investigator would look into Simone's background and find out about her father. To smooth things over, Aguilar explained Simone's situation to Chelsey and swore the private investigator to secrecy. Now Aguilar needed to repair the damage Simone had caused at work, without telling anyone else about the molestation.

"You only met Thomas once," said Aguilar. "He's a good man. I trust him as much as I do any friend or family member."

"As much as you trust me?"

"Simone—"

"You don't need to explain. We haven't seen each other since college. I'm so grateful we reconnected." Simone's hands returned to Aguilar's shoulders, nudging the deputy into a deep, relaxed state. "I kept in contact with Brit and Janelle after graduation. Why didn't you ever write?"

"I didn't know where you lived."

"Veronica, I'm easy to find. You weren't avoiding me because of what happened between us, were you?"

"Not at all. I mean . . . no. I just lost touch, I guess."

"You're positive that's all it was?"

"Why would I avoid you?"

Aguilar's eyes shifted beneath their closed lids. Simone refused to relinquish the belief that they'd slept together. As Aguilar teetered on the brink of sleep, Simone's hands slid past the deputy's shoulders and crept beneath her shirt.

Bolting awake, Aguilar grabbed Simone's wrist. "Hey, what was that about?"

She released Simone's wrist and spun around. The woman took a step backward and widened her eyes.

"Nothing, I was just giving you a massage."

"Down the front of my shirt?"

Simone stammered. "I thought you wanted me to."

"What? Why? Simone, I slept *next to you* that night, not with you. There's a difference. You were so drunk, I was afraid you'd throw up and suffocate. Nothing happened between us."

The woman turned away and bit her thumb. Tears trickled down her cheeks. "Oh, my God. What did I do? I'm so stupid."

"You made a mistake and misinterpreted our friendship. It's all right. But it's time to go."

"You want me to leave?"

"It's for the best."

Simone leaned over and cried. "I violated my best friend's trust. This isn't me."

"Hey, Simone. Nobody is angry with you. We all slip up and make rash decisions."

"This is about my father, Veronica. I haven't accepted what he did to me. Everything seems so confusing. I don't know what I'm doing half the time."

Aguilar led Simone around the couch and sat her down. "You never think about hurting yourself, do you?"

Simone didn't answer. A jolt of fear rolled through Aguilar.

"I should go," Simone said, wiping away a tear. "Give me five minutes to pack my bags. I've done enough damage."

Aguilar placed a hand against her forehead. She couldn't let Simone leave distraught. If her old friend harmed herself, Aguilar would never get over it.

"I have a better idea. How about we forget what happened and move on?"

"You won't forget," said Simone, coughing through sobs. "Nor would I expect you to. I crossed a boundary. It's just that I thought our night together meant something. I misread your signals."

"Simone, I didn't send any signals. As I told you, you're misremembering what happened. You kissed me, then you fell asleep. That's all there was to it."

"Are you sure?"

"Believe me, I remember."

Simone wiped her face with a tissue and set her elbows on her knees. "What's happening to me? It's like my life is some crazy movie, and I can't remember what's real and what's fiction."

"You'll get over this. Don't worry, you're with your old friend again."

"We were a helluva team during college, weren't we?"

"Best roommates ever."

"Those were the days." Simone nudged Aguilar with her elbow. "Do you ever wish you could be young again and go back to school?"

"Not really. Memories are fine, but I prefer to live in the present."

"But it was so much simpler then. Now, there's constant pressure to move forward and perform. Sometimes, I wish I could go to sleep and not wake up for a long time. Or ever."

"Don't say that."

"I'm not suicidal, Veronica. Just overwhelmed."

Aguilar wasn't so sure. "You need to visit a therapist."

Simone bobbed her head. "You're right. The sooner I deal with what my father did to me, the better my life will be. I should confront him. My father, I mean. Not my therapist. That would be funny, though."

Simone issued a nervous giggle that sounded unhinged.

"Your father never acknowledged the molestation?"

"Never. Damn him." Simone stood up from the couch and slapped her hands against her thighs. "That settles it. If I leave now, I can reach my parents' house before midnight. I don't care if I wake them up. It's time the truth came out."

Aguilar didn't trust the wild intensity in her friend's eyes. "Not tonight."

"But I need to do this."

"It can wait. Get your emotions in check first."

"So, what do you want me to do? I can't sleep in my car."

"I was wrong to make you leave. Please, Simone. The guest room is yours for as long as you need it."

"I'm overstaying my welcome."

"No, you aren't. I'll pour you a cup of tea. Settle into bed early tonight and wake up tomorrow with a fresh perspective."

Simone cried again and threw her arms around Aguilar's shoulders. Uncertain what to do with her hands, Aguilar patted her friend on the back.

"You're the best friend I've ever had, Veronica. I don't know how I'd get through this without you."

24

Thomas jerked awake. Cold sweat dotted his brow, his heart hammering. For a confused moment, he worried he'd caught the summer flu making its rounds through Wolf Lake. He wiped the sweat away and remembered a noise knocking him out of a dream. What was it?

He turned toward Chelsey, but she wasn't there. Still hazy with fatigue, he remembered she'd worked late at the office and slept there.

Thomas rested his back against the headboard and rubbed the weariness out of his eyes. He searched for Jack and discovered the dog wasn't in his usual spot at the end of the bed. Azure moonlight trickled through the windows as the lake sloshed against the shoreline.

"Jack?"

Thomas pushed the covers back, expecting to find the dog burrowed beneath the blankets. No dog.

He swung his legs over the side of the bed and waited until the room stopped spinning. The clock read four in the morning, and he hadn't arrived home from the sheriff's department until one. Three hours of sleep wouldn't sustain him.

The bedroom door stood open. The temperature had plummeted after dark, and with the furnace turned off, the floorboards froze his feet. He peeked through the doorway.

"Jack? Are you downstairs?"

A low growl rumbled through the gloom-shrouded hallway, spiking Thomas's adrenaline. He peered into the dark, seeking the dog. Jack sprawled across the landing, blocking the staircase, his muzzle resting on the top step, fangs bared. The dog's tail swished back and forth.

Jack never acted like this. Another growl, this one reverberating off the walls. The dog's hackles rose.

Thomas turned back to the bedroom and retrieved his service weapon, which he'd laid upon a chair after staggering into the bedroom. Was someone inside the house? Impossible. If someone had broken in, Jack would have bolted after the intruder.

As Thomas returned to the hallway with his gun, he stopped along the banister. Jack stood up, his body taut with tension. A scuffing sound came from outside. Someone was in the driveway. Thomas pictured serial killer Jeremy Hyde stalking through the downstairs before Thomas shot him last year, the glint of moonlight sharpening the murderer's blade.

A thunderous woof escaped the dog's jaws. Before Jack lunged down the staircase, a window shattered in the living room.

Thomas raced after the dog, the gun raised and angled toward the window. Broken glass covered the hardwood floor. The shadows seemed wrong, as though they concealed an evil presence.

Locating the wall switch, Thomas flicked on the lights as Jack scrambled toward the window.

"Back!" Thomas yelled, worried the dog would shred the pads of his feet on the glass shards.

Jack yelped and leaped back, favoring one leg. Thomas knelt beside the dog and stroked his fur, the service weapon aimed at where the night spilled into the living room. Slowly, he stood and rounded the pile of glass beneath the sill. With his back against the wall, he listened beside the window. Footsteps raced across the lawn.

Thomas swung around and glimpsed a car speeding away from the house, shooting down the lake road like a missile. Sensing the threat had ended, Jack's barking ceased.

"Good boy. It's over now."

The sheriff hurried to the dining-room table and picked up his phone. A quick call to dispatch revealed there were no deputies near the lake. The dispatcher promised to phone the state police for backup. No sooner did Thomas return to the window to assess the damage than his phone rang.

"Sheriff Shepherd? This is Trooper Fitzgerald. I'm parked two miles from your location."

Thomas exhaled. He'd worked cases with Trooper Fitzgerald, Darren Holt's friend. "Thanks for getting back to me so quickly."

"Your dispatcher told me a vandal broke your window and drove down the lake road."

"That's correct."

Thomas described the car as best he could. It was a muscle car with dark coloration and a loud engine. That was all he could see at night. In the background, Fitzgerald gunned his motor.

"I'm heading toward your place now."

"You'll pass him on the way. The turnoff for the highway is behind you."

"Hang tight, Sheriff. I'll get back to you in a few."

With nothing left to do, Thomas donned socks and sneakers and cleaned the mess, tossing the largest shards into the trash and sweeping the rest into a dustbin. A fist-sized rock lay on the floor at the foot of the couch. Jack observed the open window with his tail thumping against the hardwood. Now that the danger had passed, the dog seemed to think this was all a game. Jack barked, expecting Thomas to chase him around the house or throw a tennis ball. Tigger, the abandoned orange tabby Chelsey had taken in, shot out of the corner and purred atop the couch.

"No running until I check that paw," Thomas said, tying the trash bag and setting it beside the door. "That goes for you, too, Tigger. Don't excite Jack."

The sheriff placed a new bag inside the container and walked it to the kitchen. He returned with a flashlight and sat on the floor in front of Jack. It took some coaxing before Jack lifted his paw. Thomas angled the beam over the dog's wound. The cut didn't go deep. Fortunately, the glass wasn't lodged in the soft padding. Tigger hopped off the couch and pawed Jack.

"You got off lucky," Thomas said, stroking the dog's fur. "Next time, you'll know better than to run over broken glass. Now all we need to do is figure out who did this."

He straightened his spine when the deck creaked beyond the dining room. This time, Jack's hackles didn't rise. Thomas recognized LeVar and unlocked the sliding glass door.

"Shep Dawg, what happened? I heard a window shatter."

"Someone tossed a rock through the living room window."

LeVar winced. "All that glass. How bad is it?"

"Not too bad. Come in and look for yourself. Mind the floor, though. Until I run the vacuum, assume I missed a few pieces."

Thomas led LeVar into the living room, Jack trotting alongside.

"I thought I'd gotten away from this crap after I moved out of Harmon," said LeVar, standing over the rock. "Except in my neighborhood, they used heavier artillery than sticks and stones. Any idea who did this?"

"Nope. Trooper Fitzgerald must have caught the vandal by now. I should hear something soon."

"How long do you figure it will take us to replace the window?"

"You're volunteering?"

"I always got your back."

Guilt clenched Thomas's chest. "Yeah, you always do. I'm sorry for pulling back on the deputy offer. That wasn't fair. I just didn't want you to sacrifice your education."

"Up to you to make the tough decisions. That's why they pay you the big bucks. I understand."

The confusion on LeVar's face made Thomas wonder if he truly understood.

"Let's cover the window with plastic sheeting. This weekend, provided I have a day off, I'll make the repair. If you're available to help, I could use a skilled partner."

"I'll be here."

"Hold on while I—" The phone rang and cut Thomas off. "It's Fitzgerald. Gotta take this."

Thomas wandered into the kitchen and poured himself a glass of water while Fitzgerald filled him in.

"I caught the guy doing eighty in a fifty-five. Didn't take long to convince him to speak. He knows you, Thomas. The guy's name is Malcolm Chaney."

Thomas leaned against the counter. "Chaney? I interviewed him at Empire Coasters."

"Apparently, he lost his job after park management discovered he was dating an underage employee named Marlee Greenwood. Then Greenwood's parents forced the girl to break up with him. Chaney lost his cool and wanted revenge."

Aguilar had phoned Marlee's parents and ensured they

knew who their daughter was dating. They hadn't. Thomas wasn't proud that he'd ended their relationship, but Chaney had left him no choice.

"So he shattered my window with a rock?"

Fitzgerald chuckled. "And let the air out of your tires. Check your pickup for additional damage, but I think he's telling the truth. The idiot held nothing back."

"Guess I'll need to wake up earlier than normal and pump my tires."

"Need a tow to a gas station?"

"Thanks, but I have a portable air pump."

"You pressing charges for the vandalism?"

"I don't know what to do. In a way, I sorta feel bad for the guy. But I can't let him get away with breaking my window."

"I'll call you after I bring Chaney to the station."

"Got it."

After the call ended, Thomas noticed the clock. He was looking at another two hours of sleep before he needed to wake up and deal with the vandalism. Might as well stay awake and cover the window.

"Did Fitzgerald catch your man?" LeVar asked, joining Thomas in the kitchen.

"He did. Turns out it was a suspect I interviewed at Empire Coasters."

"Did the vandal kidnap Dylan Fournette?"

"Doubtful. He's just a dumb guy who likes younger girls."

When LeVar questioned the sheriff with his eyes, Thomas said, "Long story."

"It's a long night."

"That it is."

"I'll grab the plastic sheeting."

"Thanks, LeVar."

25

A t the Nightshade Rod and Gun Club, Robyn Fournette adjusted the protective shooting muffs and aimed her Glock pistol at the target. She squeezed the trigger and cursed when the bullet traveled high and to the left.

This morning, Robyn was the only shooter at the club. She hadn't visited over the last year. Before leaving her house, she'd told the state trooper at the curb she was running to the store. He offered to follow, but she told the officer it was unnecessary. On her way to the club, she backtracked down side streets until she was certain the kidnapper, who'd already broken into her house on multiple occasions, wasn't trailing her. With one eye on the mirror, she took the highway exit and circled back to the shooting range. Nobody followed.

The Illinois stalkings had taught Robyn a valuable lesson—she needed to defend herself and ensure her child's safety. Except she'd failed and lost Dylan to the same psycho who'd terrorized her six years ago.

Robyn was determined to get her child back. And when the kidnapper least expected it, she'd put a bullet between his eyes and end the nightmare. Forever this time.

If only Robyn could hit a target. What good was she to Dylan if she pulled the trigger and missed? The kidnapper would kill her and keep Dylan. What did he want with her?

As Robyn raised the pistol, a gray-haired man with a mustache and biceps that bulged beneath a form-fitting shirt approached. She recognized the gun club owner, Drew Ghitelman.

"Haven't seen you around in a long time," Ghitelman said, striding over to Robyn. "How long has it been? A year or more?"

"Something like that." Robyn lowered the pistol and set it on the stand. "I'm a little out of practice."

Ghitelman, a retired police officer from the Rochester area, checked over the Glock and set it aside. "Gun looks fine. Your technique is off. Your shots veer high and left."

"Have you been watching me?"

"Don't need to." Ghitelman pointed at the holes in the target. "There's your proof."

"What am I doing wrong?"

"For one, your feet aren't the proper width apart." Ghitelman pushed his sneaker against hers and forced Robyn's foot into place. "Now, keep your body steady when you pull the trigger. Take a deep breath."

Robyn felt his eyes on her back as she lined up the target. She pulled the trigger and groaned. The bullet missed up and away again, her worst effort yet.

"I'll never get this. It's like I never fired a gun before."

"Give yourself time. You need practice."

"I don't have time."

Ghitelman narrowed his eyes at Robyn. "Are you in some kind of trouble, Ms. Fournette?"

Apparently, Ghitelman didn't read the newspaper.

"No, sir."

"Then you have all the time in the world to practice. Your

technique was better on the last shot, but you didn't hold your upper body steady. You're breathing too quickly, like something is stressing you out." Ghitelman jabbed his index finger against his forehead. "Technique starts and ends here. Slow down, relax, and you'll hit your mark."

Robyn nodded, but her hands trembled when she picked up the Glock. The club owner spoke in quiet tones, inspiring her to relax.

She pulled the trigger.

The blast traveled dead center through the target. She exhaled and placed the weapon on the stand. Ghitelman slapped her on the shoulder.

"I knew you had it in you," he said. "Remember my advice. Focus on your breathing and relax. Shooting is like riding a bike. It all comes back to you."

He left her at the range and ventured inside the facility, a long rectangular building with brown siding. An American flag on a pole waved out front. Robyn practiced for another five minutes, her accuracy never as good as it had been under Ghitelman's instruction. With a huff, she gathered her belongings and returned to the car.

There was no cruiser parked in front of the house when Robyn returned home. The sheriff's department and state police came and went, usually telling her when they'd return. The trooper must have given up after Robyn didn't come back from the store.

She unlocked the front door, with a wary eye tracking every shadow along her neighbors' houses. A car she didn't recognize motored down the road, coming her way. Robyn hurried inside, locked the door, and threw the deadbolt. Pistol in hand, she flicked the curtain as the vehicle sped past without stopping.

Before Robyn gathered her thoughts, the phone rang. Another unknown caller. It had to be Dylan's kidnapper.

"Hello," she muttered.

A pause on the other end.

"Did you think you could escape me, Robyn?"

"Who are you? What do you want with me?"

"What I've always wanted from you. I want what's mine. And now I have Dylan."

"TJ?"

No response. Who else had known about Robyn's pregnancy? She couldn't picture TJ as a deranged child abductor and stalker. But people changed. If the old TJ Robyn once trusted still existed, she could talk sense into him. She could convince TJ to come to his senses and give Dylan back to her.

While the kidnapper paused, she clicked the recording application on her phone. She didn't dare to seek help from the sheriff until she learned more about the kidnapper. But when the time came, she wanted a recording of the kidnapper's voice.

"Give me my son, or I swear I'll—"

"You'll what? Don't pretend you care about your child's life. If you gave a damn about Dylan, you wouldn't have considered an abortion."

The phone trembled in Robyn's hand. "I loved my baby from the moment I found out I was pregnant."

"Why should I believe anything you say? You've lied to me for days. I specifically told you to stay away from the police and you defied my orders. The sheriff can't rescue your child. Only I can return your boy."

"Tell me Dylan is still alive."

"He is. You'll have to take my word for it."

"That's not good enough. Put Dylan on the phone, or I'll hang up and call the sheriff."

"More idle threats? Please, Robyn. You're weak and powerless. You'll do nothing."

Anger flared through Robyn. "Put Dylan on the phone, you

bastard. If you don't, I'll assume he's gone. That leaves me nothing to lose. I'll go straight to the sheriff and tell him all about you."

"You know nothing about me. Have it your way. Here's Dylan."

Robyn's heart hammered into her throat. In the background, a chair scraped across the floor. Then a ripping sound and a yelp—the kidnapper had yanked the duct tape off Dylan's mouth.

"Mommy?"

Robyn grabbed hold of the couch so she wouldn't collapse. Tears streamed down her face.

"Dylan, it's me. It's Mommy. Are you all right? Did he hurt you?"

"I'm scared. When are you coming to get me?"

"Soon, baby, soon. I promise. Dylan, listen closely. Don't speak unless I ask you a question, all right?"

"Come get me."

"I will, I will. First, Mommy needs to know where you are. Are you near a window? Just say yes or no, nothing else."

"Yes."

"That's good, Dylan. You're being so brave. Do you see someone's house outside the window?"

A moment of silence, then, "Yes."

"What color is the house?"

A rustling sound came over the receiver.

"Nice try," the kidnapper growled. "I see what you're trying to do. One more trick like that, and you'll never see your son again."

"Give Dylan back to me. Tell me what you want."

"You'll find out soon enough."

"When? I can't go on like this."

"Midnight. If you want to see your son alive, come to the

village park in Wolf Lake. No cops, no sheriff. If I so much as sniff a pig, I'll shoot Dylan."

"Where in the park?"

Click.

Robyn stared at the phone. She called the number back. A series of beeps told her the number didn't exist.

Outside the window, a state police cruiser stopped in front of the house. It occurred to Robyn that the kidnapper never contacted her when the authorities were around. Which meant he had eyes on the house.

Or the kidnapper was a cop.

But that made no sense. The man on the phone knew her from college. It must be TJ. Unless TJ had a partner in law enforcement, someone with the know-how to abduct a child in a crowded amusement park without getting caught.

She sat on the couch and rubbed her temples. The midnight meeting was a trap. If the kidnapper intended to keep his promise, he would have demanded a ransom. He had one goal in mind: capture Robyn. This was the moment he'd waited six years for.

She eyed the pistol.

This time, Robyn was ready for him.

26

Thomas pored over the TJ Soto background check again. With his office door closed, he couldn't hear conversations in the operations area. The sheriff rolled a pen around in his palm. Why was he sure he'd missed something important about TJ Soto? On the surface, Robyn Fournette's college boyfriend seemed like the perfect gentleman. He worked with the underprivileged and possessed a clean record, and his story had checked out. The boy who'd visited Soto's house was his nephew.

The phone flashed on his desk, indicating Maggie was sending him a call. He punched the light and answered.

"Sheriff, it's Drew Ghitelman over at the Nightshade Rod and Gun Club. Don't know if you remember me. We met at a luncheon for retired law enforcement last September."

"Sure, I remember you, Mr. Ghitelman. To what do I owe the pleasure?"

"Call me Drew, please."

"All right, Drew."

"This is coming out of left field, and I might be overreacting.

But I'm worried about a club member, a woman who showed up at the range this morning."

"I'm listening."

Ghitelman spoke with an inconsistent tempo, speeding up and slowing down, reflecting his uncertainty. "She used to shoot at the club every week. Over the years, she came less frequently. This morning was the first time I've seen her since last summer. I'm worried someone is giving her trouble."

"Any idea who?"

"Your guess is as good as mine. Sheriff, I watched her shoot in the past. She's skilled. Today, even after I corrected her form, she couldn't keep her body still. Something scared the hell out of her."

"That's not a lot to go on."

"Yeah, I agree. If I was on the force and someone wandered in off the streets with a story like mine, I'd tell him not to come back until he knew more. I explained that her skill would improve with repetition and she had time to practice. She muttered that she didn't have time. That struck me as odd."

"Without more information, I'm unsure what I can do. If she has a concern, tell her to call the department. Are you willing to share her name?"

"Sure, if you keep this on the down low. The woman's name is Fournette. Robyn Fournette."

Thomas fell back in his chair. "Robyn Fournette, as in the woman from the kidnapping case?"

"Kidnapping case? What did I miss?"

"Drew, Robyn Fournette's son, Dylan, disappeared at the amusement park three nights ago."

"Oh, man. I'm sorry, Sheriff. Between work and fishing, I can't recall the last time I watched the news. Are you sure we're talking about the same woman?"

"Mid-twenties, dark hair, about my height."

"That's her. Damn. Now I feel like a fool. I can't imagine what she's going through. If someone took my kid, I'd stop at nothing to get him back. Do you suppose she's taking matters into her own hands?"

"That's what I'm afraid of." Thomas grabbed a blank sheet of paper. "Tell me everything about Robyn Fournette. How long has she attended the Rod and Gun Club?"

"Hold on." Ghitelman typed on his keyboard. "Six years."

Fournette had moved to Nightshade County six years ago. Most graduates fresh out of college found other activities besides joining the local shooting range when they moved to a new area.

"Did she tell you why she wanted to join the club?"

"I never look a gift horse in the mouth. She wanted to be a member and her background checked out. I needed enough members to stay afloat and didn't ask questions."

Thomas wondered what had made Fournette nervous enough to join the Nightshade Rod and Gun Club.

"Can you describe her demeanor six years ago? Has it changed over the years?"

"She seemed skittish when she arrived. I chalked that up to Fournette being one of the few women in the club. Plus the age difference. Most of my members are middle-aged or older. It took her several months to settle down. Her accuracy improved the more she practiced, and she didn't act nervous anymore."

"Did she ever mention anything about college or her past?"

"Only that she attended school in Illinois. Do you suppose she intends to shoot the guy who kidnapped her child?"

"I hope not. Drew, if Fournette returns to the club, I want you to call me."

"Will do, Sheriff."

Thomas set the receiver down and followed the hallway to his lead deputy's desk. He found Aguilar half-working, half-sleeping, the computer mouse held by a limp hand. Her head bobbed before she jerked awake. Aguilar blinked.

"Sorry, Thomas. I promise I won't fall asleep on the job again."

"It's me who should apologize. You work too many overtime shifts, and that's on me. How much sleep did you get last night?"

"Not enough," Aguilar said, peeling off a yawn.

"What happened? I kicked you out of the office before sunset because I wanted you to rest."

"Something happened with Simone. I can't talk about it."

"All right, but I'm here if you want to."

Aguilar sipped from a thermos of green tea. "I'm awake now. What did you want to talk to me about?"

"I just got off the phone with Drew Ghitelman from the shooting range."

After Thomas recounted the conversation, Aguilar said, "Robyn Fournette joined the club after she left Illinois. That can't be a coincidence. Perhaps she left Chicago because someone frightened her."

"What would make you join a gun club after graduating college?"

"Thomas, I was born with cop in my blood. I'm not the best example."

"Humor me."

Aguilar rocked back in her chair and balanced a booted foot against the edge of her desk. "I'd take up shooting if someone threatened me."

"Like a stalker?"

"Sure. You think TJ Soto found out about Dylan and went after Robyn?"

"That's one possibility."

"Soto moved to Syracuse four years after Fournette arrived in New York. Why did he wait so long?"

"Maybe it took him a few years to find her," Thomas said, scratching his chin. "I don't trust Soto. He seemed adamant that he wasn't Dylan's father, but my instinct tells me he's involved."

"And now Fournette intends to shoot Dylan's kidnapper and get her child back. Why didn't she come to us first?"

"The kidnapper ordered her not to speak to the police. That's the best explanation I can think of."

"So, he threatened to hurt her son," said Aguilar. "Yet he hasn't demanded a ransom for Dylan's return."

"Not that we know of. Fournette wouldn't tell us if she's worried the kidnapper will find out." Seated beside Aguilar, Thomas set an ankle on his knee. "Get me Fournette's phone records. I want every text and call that arrived on her phone over the last seventy-two hours."

"You got it."

"We need eyes on her."

"Lambert is watching the house now."

"Perfect. But even with the state police helping, we can't surveil Fournette's place twenty-four hours a day."

Aguilar lifted her chin at Thomas. "You think the kidnapper already set up a meeting."

"And Fournette will shoot him to save her son."

"I'll follow her tonight."

"You're working too much overtime. I'll handle tonight's surveillance. Go home and spend time with your friend."

Aguilar glanced away. "You sure you don't want me to work the overnight shift?"

"Not in any rush to hang out with Simone, I take it."

The deputy wore a tight-lipped smile. "There are a lot of . . . issues that Simone needs to deal with. I can't talk about what happened to her, but it wasn't pretty. I'll help her any way I can."

"Sounds like Simone needs professional help."

"She does."

"Aguilar, I don't want to overstep my bounds, but I'm concerned that you're putting too much pressure on yourself. It's impossible to keep up with work and fix your friend."

"Simone and I were close during college, and she's a good person. I can't turn my back on her."

"You believe you can handle all this pressure?"

"My job is my priority. I won't allow Simone's problems to affect my performance." Thomas raised his eyebrows. "Seriously, Thomas. I can juggle my job and Simone's issues."

"And yet if I asked you to accompany me on the overnight shift, you'd say yes."

"Are you requesting my help?"

"Nope. I'll watch Fournette tonight. Give yourself time to recuperate."

"What if Fournette leads you to the kidnapper?"

"I'll call for backup."

"What backup? By the time dispatch contacts me—"

"It's my responsibility," Thomas said. "I'll call the state police and ask them to lend a hand."

"I feel like I'm dropping the ball and letting you down."

"You've never dropped the ball, Aguilar." Thomas rose from his chair. "Help your friend."

27

At ten o'clock, the sun was a distant memory. Starlight pierced the black sky over Wolf Lake, the streets bathed in silver as Thomas concealed his pickup truck beneath a sycamore tree. Concerned Robyn Fournette would search for a cruiser, he'd chosen his own vehicle for the surveillance mission. Now all he needed to do was wait for Lambert to finish his shift.

"Tell me again what you want me to say," Lambert said over the radio.

Lambert's cruiser waited outside Fournette's house, the engine and lights off, the deputy's silhouette visible in the front seat.

"Knock on the door and ask Fournette if she wants you to stay a few more hours. Say your shift is over—which it is—but you're willing to hang out as long as she needs you to."

"What if she tells me to stay?"

"She won't."

"All right, I'll give it a shot."

Thomas surveilled the house from half a block away as Lambert stepped over the curb and followed the walkway to

Fournette's door. The deputy rang the doorbell and waited until the woman poked her head through the opening. Thomas couldn't hear their conversation. Fournette shook her head. Lambert raised a hand and waited until the woman locked the door. Thirty seconds later, the lights flared on the cruiser and Lambert pulled off the curb.

"She sent me home," Lambert said.

"Not surprised."

"You want to tell me what this is about and why you're driving the F-150?"

"I'm working on a hunch."

But it was more than a hunch. This afternoon, Aguilar had queried Robyn Fournette's phone records and discovered calls and texts from multiple unknown numbers over the last three days, beginning with a threatening message during Thomas's interview with Fournette at Empire Coasters. The kidnapper had been inside the park when the sheriff arrived, suggesting he'd stashed Dylan somewhere safe and returned. Dylan wasn't the kidnapper's target. Robyn was.

"I'm all for a gripping mystery, but would you be more specific?"

Thomas leaned over the wheel as Fournette drew the curtains. "We already know the kidnapper contacted Fournette. She won't tell us because he threatened to kill Dylan if she sought help from the police."

"If he's here, you need backup," Lambert said as his cruiser turned the corner and vanished from view.

"No cruisers. Either the kidnapper is monitoring the house right now, or Fournette is meeting him. We want him to think Fournette is alone."

"Then I'll hang back. I can be discreet."

"You've worked twelve hours already after a sixteen-hour day yesterday."

"I'm wide awake."

Thomas chewed his lip. "All right, but stay back. I'll contact you when I need backup."

TJ SOTO FOCUSED the binoculars and pulled Robyn Fournette's house into sharp clarity. Above him, the starlit sky was endless and replete with hidden dangers. With his car parked at the end of the block and concealed behind a Ryder moving truck, the sheriff's deputy wouldn't see him.

Soto's pulse quickened when the deputy approached the house and rang the doorbell. He wished he could eavesdrop on their conversation. After a brief exchange, the deputy reversed course and hopped into his cruiser. The lights flared, and the deputy drove away and turned the corner.

Which meant Robyn was alone now.

A man walked two pugs down the sidewalk. Soto wiggled beneath the steering wheel and tensed when the dogs growled. Though the neighbor hadn't spotted Soto hiding inside the car, the dogs had sniffed him out.

"Easy," the man said as the dogs yipped and pulled their leashes. "Knock it off, or I'll take you home."

Soto released a held breath when the man continued down the sidewalk with the dogs. He emerged with caution, poking his head above the wheel until a pair of headlights swept over the windshield and blinded him. He ducked again. A minivan drove by.

When it was safe to sit upright in his seat, Soto glassed Robyn's house. The curtains blocked his view through the window. He glimpsed her shadow as she crossed the living room. His mind swam with confusion and anger. Six years ago, he'd loved Robyn more than any woman he'd dated, yet she hadn't shared his affection. Then she'd slammed him with the news that she was pregnant. He'd needed to do something. Pleading with Robyn to take his money for the abortion had gotten him nowhere. The news that she'd had the baby almost crippled him. Why hadn't she told him the truth?

The minutes passed like a ticking time bomb. Robyn's neighbors hunkered down inside their homes for the night. Soto stared at the dashboard clock, shocked he'd been watching her house for three hours. It was almost midnight now, and no cruiser had replaced the departed deputy.

The lights switched off inside Robyn's house. How could she sleep when her child was missing? What kind of woman was she? He meant to find out.

Soto checked the empty street before he stepped onto the pavement. He was almost at the curb when Robyn's front door opened and the woman peered through the night, dressed in black.

Soto froze as she stepped into the dark and hurried to the driveway.

28

Robyn Fournette waited inside the shadows while she studied the neighborhood. Every nerve in her body stretched with trepidation. Down the road from her house, a Ford F-150 she didn't recognize lingered curbside. It had stood there since sunset, but it was too dark beneath the sycamore tree to determine if anyone was inside. A moving truck at the opposite end of the block claimed her attention. Someone had parked behind the truck.

No messages had arrived on her phone since this morning, when the kidnapper told her to meet him at the village park at midnight. She sensed a trap. Was the kidnapper in her neighborhood planning to ambush Robyn? The Glock pistol rested against her hip, lending her a small vestige of comfort. An oversize black sweatshirt covered the weapon. With the hood pulled over her head, it was impossible to recognize Robyn in the dark.

She crossed the lawn, the night as chilly as it had been before summer's arrival. Her breath puffed out condensation clouds as she sifted through her keys.

Robyn aimed the fob and unlocked her car doors. Before she climbed inside the car, the silhouette of a man materialized on the sidewalk, stalking toward her. A second later, he disappeared behind a privacy fence.

She reached for the pistol, determined to pull the trigger if the man lunged out of the shadows. But if she killed her stalker before he told her where he'd hidden Dylan, she'd never recover her son. She needed the kidnapper alive.

Pretending she hadn't seen the man, Robyn climbed inside the car and backed into the street. The moonlight made the sleeping neighborhood look like a graveyard. She turned up the road, directing the car toward the village park inside Wolf Lake. As she paused at a stop sign, two headlights flashed behind her.

Robyn monitored the mirrors as she drove. Twice she spotted a vehicle following two blocks behind, too distant for Robyn to recognize the make and model. By the time she passed the village square, she didn't see anyone in the mirror. Robyn hid the car behind an Italian restaurant, the scent of garlic bread seeping through the vents while she crept through an alleyway.

Two rows of rose bushes welcomed visitors to the park. Impenetrable darkness lay ahead. Somewhere in the night, a fountain splashed and gurgled. Robyn crouched below the roses and sneaked down a walkway. After her vision adjusted, the park rendered itself in strange shapes and shadows, the trees like sleeping monsters.

Hiding the pistol beneath her sweatshirt, Robyn edged deeper into the park. Cricket songs filled the night, and a mist thickened between the trees, leaving a damp sheen in its wake. Minutes passed. The cold worked into Robyn's bones.

Where was the kidnapper?

"Hello, Robyn."

The voice made her jump. She spun and found him standing in the center of the walkway, a thick tree limb hanging above his head and obscuring his face.

"Where's my son? You promised to bring Dylan."

"He's here."

"Show me, or I'll walk away."

"Aren't you the brave one? Dylan is close."

"Show me."

"No."

"Then we're through."

Robyn backed away. The kidnapper raised a placating hand.

"Don't rush off," he said. "I waited so long to meet you again."

Though he kept his voice barely above a whisper, she recognized him from somewhere. TJ Soto? She squinted, fighting to pick out the man's facial features, but he hung back.

"Dylan is inside the park."

"I don't believe you."

"I keep my promises. He's right over there."

The kidnapper pointed toward a gazebo bathed in darkness. At first, she didn't see anyone. Then a tiny shape shifted inside the gazebo—a boy with his wrists bound behind his back and a gag yanking his lips into an agonizing rictus.

Dylan. He was so close she could reach him in seconds.

When her gaze returned to the kidnapper, he pointed a gun at her chest.

"Come with us, Robyn."

"You lied to me." Robyn shifted the gun underneath her shirt, aiming it at the kidnapper. "You swore you'd return Dylan if I came to the park."

"I didn't lie. We're all reunited now—mother, son, and father."

Robyn swallowed. "Why are you doing this to us, TJ?"

The man chuckled. He still hadn't spied Robyn's gun. Her finger groped blindly for the trigger. One shot. That's all it would take to end this nightmare and save her child. But could she fire the gun accurately while concealing it?

"No more games. Follow me, Robyn. If you scream, I'll shoot you and take Dylan."

"You wouldn't."

"And why is that?"

"Because it's me you want."

His jaw worked back and forth. The kidnapper's gun pointed at her forehead. If she could distract him somehow and pull out the pistol—

"I told you, no cops."

Robyn blinked as the man tensed. "I didn't bring the police."

"You lie."

She swung around. There was no one in the park except them. He shifted his body, inching toward the gazebo.

"I should kill you for disobeying my orders," he said, taking another step toward Dylan.

"But there's no one here but us."

A bush rustled behind her. The kidnapper lunged off the walkway. Seeing her chance, Robyn pulled the gun from beneath her sweatshirt, aimed, and squeezed the trigger.

The bullet flew over the man's head. Without breaking stride, he whipped around and fired twice. The bullets tore into Robyn's shoulder and drove the wind from her lungs.

She toppled onto the concrete walkway and struck her head. Her arms and legs refused to respond.

As Dylan's muffled cries echoed from the gazebo, Robyn's eyes drifted shut.

29

Hushed voices pulled Thomas toward the center of the park. He'd lost sight of Robyn after she stashed her car behind a restaurant and rushed across the street. But now he'd found her. She wasn't alone.

"I told you, no cops," a man said, just beyond Thomas's vision.

The sheriff groped for his radio and contacted Deputy Lambert, who'd circled the park in case the kidnapper turned and fled. Was TJ Soto speaking?

Thomas knelt behind a rosebush and carefully peeled the thorny stems aside. Two silhouettes stood on the walkway, fifty feet from a tree-cloaked gazebo.

The bushes rustled. Thomas cursed himself, worried he'd caused the commotion before a raccoon scurried through. Then three deafening gun blasts.

Thomas jumped out of hiding and raced toward the walkway. Tree branches whipped at his face. In the distance, a woman screamed as a man's footsteps beat against the concrete path.

Gun raised, Thomas crashed through a hedgerow and

discovered Robyn Fournette lying in a pool of her own blood. The woman's eyes stared into the sky without blinking.

Clearing the scene, the sheriff radioed for an ambulance and checked Fournette's pulse. Weak and fading. He needed to stop the bleeding. Off to his right, the kidnapper pushed through the bushes.

"Hostile fleeing through the east end of the park," Thomas said into his radio.

"I'll cut him off," said Lambert, breathless, as he sprinted toward the suspect.

Before Thomas checked on Fournette, the brush parted behind him. He swiveled and raised his service weapon.

"Don't shoot!" TJ Soto stood before Thomas, his eyes darting from the sheriff's gun to the prone woman. "Is that . . . oh, no. Not Robyn."

"Keep your hands where I can see them."

Soto stared at his palms, as though his hands belonged to someone else. "You don't think I did this, do you?"

Thomas frisked Soto. The man didn't carry a gun, but that didn't prove he wasn't the shooter. Soto might have ditched his weapon and circled back to Fournette, hoping to convince the sheriff he was innocent.

"I didn't do this, I swear." Soto's throat bobbed when he swallowed. "All I wanted to do was protect Robyn. Tell me she isn't dead."

Soto's sudden arrival wasn't coincidental. Thomas took nothing for granted. He needed additional backup. With Lambert on the east end of the park, Thomas divided his attention between the unarmed suspect and the victim, who bled out on the walkway. He removed a clean handkerchief from his pocket and pressed it against the bubbling wound.

Tires screeched. Thomas's head swung as an SUV sped away, traveling toward the lake road at highway speeds.

"I lost him," Lambert said over the radio. "Running back to my cruiser. Will pursue the suspect."

Thomas cursed and grabbed his radio. "Suspect fleeing in a dark-colored SUV and heading toward the lake on Third Street. Repeat, suspect is driving toward the lake on Third Street in a dark-colored SUV."

"Now do you believe me?" Soto asked, lowering his hands.

"Hold this," Thomas said, nodding at the bloody handkerchief. "Keep pressure on the wound. I need to call for backup."

"What if I can't stop the bleeding?"

"Talk to her. Tell her she's doing fine."

While Soto knelt over Fournette, his voice jittery as he stroked the hair off the woman's face, Thomas contacted the state police. With the aid of the state police, law enforcement could cast a net ahead of the kidnapper before he made it to the highway. Sirens blared in the distance, cutting the silence like a knife.

Thomas checked Fournette's vital signs. She was still breathing, but each inhalation sounded more ragged than the last. What was Fournette thinking? She'd agreed to meet a kidnapper alone in the park at midnight and never informed the authorities. If Thomas lost someone he loved, would he do the same? He pictured Chelsey, Scout, his mother, or any of his friends held hostage by a madman. Would he make clear-headed choices? He'd stop at nothing to save the people he cared about.

Whirling lights approached the park as the ambulance arrived. He hoped the medical team could save Robyn Fournette.

30

The shooter escaped Lambert and the team of state police officers tasked with capturing him. Thomas lingered in the hospital corridor, waiting for an update from the doctor. The bullet had cut through Robyn Fournette's shoulder. She'd lost too much blood. The medical team worked desperately to stabilize the victim.

While he awaited word from the doctor, Thomas checked the lounge at the end of the hall. TJ Soto slumped in a chair, his hands buried in his pockets, the man's chin touching his chest as he waded in and out of sleep. The last time Thomas had questioned Soto, the suspect had fallen silent, except for a promise to call his lawyer. Fournette's old boyfriend knew something about the case. Even if Soto wasn't the shooter, Thomas sensed his involvement.

Soto blinked the haze out of his eyes and raised his head.

"I told you before, Sheriff. I didn't kidnap Robyn's son. Until my lawyer arrives, I have nothing to say."

"You're not under arrest, Mr. Soto. Why were you in the park at midnight? Did you see who shot Robyn Fournette?"

"No, I didn't. I arrived too late."

"Were you following Robyn?"

Soto opened his mouth to answer and shook his head. "All questions go through my lawyer from this point forward."

"I can hold you on suspicion. You understand that, correct?"

The confidence fled Soto's face. "But I didn't shoot her. It's not my fault the kidnapper got away."

"You aren't telling me everything. Ever since the interview at the station, you've held back. Why? If you're involved with the kidnapping—"

"I would never endanger a child, Sheriff." Soto stared at the floor. "What did the doctor say? Will she make it?"

"You're quite concerned for someone who hasn't spoken to Robyn since college, and you swear Dylan isn't your son."

"I'm human. There's no reason to suspect me just because I'm concerned."

Thomas leaned in the doorway, uncertain how much he should tell Soto. "The doctor hasn't returned from surgery. For now, no news is good news."

Soto nodded and lowered his head again.

Thomas left Soto and returned to the corridor. At the end of the hall, a deep blue coloration mingled with the starlit sky, portending dawn, which was still an hour away. He stared at the clock, shocked the time had ticked past five in the morning. He'd been awake for over twenty-four hours. Malcolm Chaney's vandalism seemed as though it had happened a decade ago.

Deputy Lambert squeezed between two orderlies and strode toward Thomas. Lambert carried two Styrofoam cups of coffee. He handed one to Thomas.

"The state police swept eight square miles between the lake road and the highway. No sign of the SUV."

"Wonderful," Thomas said, taking a long sip, not caring when the heat singed his lips.

"Can you think of any defining feature that can help us narrow down the make?"

"At night, it could have been any of a hundred different SUV models."

"You didn't catch the license plate?" When Thomas gave Lambert a *you-must-be-joking* stare, Lambert smirked. "I know. Dumb question."

"How long have you been on shift, Lambert? It must be going on twenty hours."

"I could ask you the same question. How's Fournette?"

Thomas glanced at the double doors leading to the surgery area. At any second, he expected the doctor to return with an answer. "They're trying to stabilize her. Let's hope she wakes up and remembers what happened. With any luck, she'll identify our perp."

Lambert hung his head. "I let him get away, Thomas."

"He had a head start. There's no way I would have caught him if I'd had my cruiser. Whoever this guy is, he's good. He evaded the state police vehicles."

"If I'd captured him, we'd know where Dylan Fournette is."

"Don't do that to yourself. This battle isn't over. We'll save that kid, but first we need Robyn Fournette to wake up and tell us who shot her."

As a doctor hurried past with a clipboard, Lambert gestured at the waiting room. "I noticed TJ Soto inside. Do we have anything on him?"

"Only that he was in the park when the kidnapper shot Fournette."

"Soto tell you why he was there?"

"He wants a lawyer before he opens his mouth."

"If he's innocent, he should spill the beans. Every second he clams up makes me think he's working with the kidnapper."

"Soto knows more than he's letting on," Thomas said,

gulping more coffee. "He followed Fournette from the house to the park. That much I'm sure of."

"Did you spot him in the neighborhood?"

"No. Wherever he was, he hid himself well."

"Why would Soto scope out his old girlfriend's house and follow her to the park if he wasn't involved?" Lambert chugged the last of his coffee and tossed the cup into the garbage. "I'm going in there."

Thomas grabbed Lambert's arm. "Don't push him. We'll get Soto to talk. Give him time."

"Do you intend to stay until the doctor returns?"

"Yes."

"Don't take this the wrong way, Thomas, but you look like hell."

"Then I must be looking into a mirror." Thomas removed the phone from his pocket. "I hate to do this, but I'm calling Aguilar in."

"Will you go home after she arrives?"

"Not before you."

Ignoring Lambert's flustered sigh, Thomas found a quiet corner and dialed Aguilar's number. His lead deputy left her ringer on at all times, in case of an emergency.

Strange. The call bounced into Aguilar's voicemail.

Thomas redialed, assuming the first call had awakened Aguilar. Again, she didn't answer. Shaking his head, Thomas returned to Lambert.

"She's not coming in?" Lambert asked, throwing up his hands.

"Aguilar didn't answer."

"That's not like her."

"Today was supposed to be her day off. Maybe she turned off the ringer."

Thomas doubted that was the case. For Aguilar, the job was her priority.

So why wasn't she answering the phone?

31

After sunrise, Chelsey called every member of Wolf Lake Consulting into the office, including volunteer Darren Holt, who'd slipped away from the state park to help the investigators catch the fugitive kidnapper.

At ten o'clock, Darren worked beside Raven on one computer, while LeVar and Scout teamed up at LeVar's workstation. As Chelsey coordinated the search effort, she couldn't pull her eyes away from LeVar and Scout. The friends worked side-by-side, their knees brushing together as LeVar loaded a map and Scout gestured at the screen. From Chelsey's vantage point, LeVar and Scout were more than friends. The age difference worried Chelsey. She trusted LeVar, but young people made poor choices when hormones drove their decisions. Darren and Raven had promised to have a heart-to-heart talk with LeVar and Scout. To this point, they hadn't followed through.

"What's the latest from the hospital?" Scout asked, looking up from LeVar's monitor.

"Robyn Fournette made it out of surgery," said Chelsey. "But she's still asleep, and the doctors won't allow Thomas to question Fournette until she's strong enough."

LeVar groaned. "Which means we don't know who the shooter is."

"Keep working. Fournette might not wake up for hours. Find something that leads us to our shooter."

"I still say it's an inside job," Darren said, leaning back in his chair with his hands clasped over his stomach.

"Thomas questioned two suspects at Empire Coasters. Neither Malcolm Chaney nor Marlee Greenwood kidnapped Dylan Fournette."

"Then it's someone else. Someone who understood how to traverse the tunnels, a person Dylan trusted."

"Darren is right," Scout said, drawing everyone's attention. "If a stranger grabbed Dylan at the park, the boy would have screamed and fought back. That would draw attention, but nobody witnessed a man abducting a child. That tells me Dylan trusted the unsub. Secondly," Scout said, ticking the points off with her fingers, "the kidnapper escorted Dylan out of the park before the gates closed. That's too far to walk through a crowd. He used the tunnels. Our unsub works for Empire Coasters, possibly a character or a security team member."

"The head of security, Ron Faustin, gave Thomas trouble. What if he's the kidnapper?"

The phone rang, interrupting Darren. Chelsey held up her forefinger and answered.

"Chelsey. Good, I'm glad I caught up to you."

Chelsey lowered the phone against her chest and whispered to the others, "It's Thomas."

She walked the phone into the kitchen while the others continued working in the office. "Please tell me you're calling from home."

"I caught an hour of sleep in my truck. Back at the office now. No way I can head home before Fournette wakes up."

"What about Lambert?"

"I sent him home three hours ago. Trooper Fitzgerald is staying at the hospital, in case the kidnapper shows up to finish the job."

"This isn't optimal, Thomas. Your body will shut down unless you rest. What about Aguilar? Can't she relieve you?"

"That's why I called. I've been trying to contact Aguilar since early this morning. No luck. I'm tied up with another case right now. How hard would I need to twist your arm for you to swing past Aguilar's house?"

"I'm busy at the office, but I can spring an investigator or two. I'll send Darren and Raven. What do you want them to tell Aguilar?"

"That I need her at the office. Even if she only comes in for three or four hours while Lambert rests."

"You mean while *you* rest."

"If you insist."

"Consider it done. Besides, I don't want to leave LeVar and Scout alone in the office."

"You're still convinced something is going on between them?"

"I'm convinced I need to intervene if they're together. Scout is too young."

"If either gives you grief, I'll talk to them."

"Thanks, Thomas. By the way, Scout and Darren suspect our kidnapper works for Empire Coasters."

Thomas fell silent for a moment. "The possibility occurred to me. That's why I questioned Marlee Greenwood and Malcolm Chaney."

"Start with the security team. Find out who worked that night."

"All the more reason I need Aguilar to help me research suspects."

Chelsey returned to the office and sat on the edge of Raven's desk. Darren's head popped up.

"Thomas needs a favor," Chelsey said. "The sheriff's department wants Deputy Aguilar to fill in today, but she isn't answering her phone. Will you drive over and bang on her door?"

"You got it, boss," Raven said, tossing the bag strap over her shoulder.

"Thomas thanks you in advance. They're understaffed at the office and desperate for help."

ON THEIR WAY to Aguilar's home on the west side of the village, Darren and Raven stopped at The Broken Yolk and purchased bagels for the office. Both expected a long day at Wolf Lake Consulting. Snacks would keep morale high.

Sliding into Raven's black Nissan Rogue, Darren swept a nervous hand across his forehead.

"After we run this errand, I should stop at the park. I don't feel right leaving it unattended."

"What about your summer help?" Raven asked. "They'll contact you if there's a problem."

"Yeah, but they're high school and college kids."

"While the cat is away, the mice will play."

"Something like that." Darren lowered his window, inviting the August sun into the vehicle. "There's Aguilar's place. Park beside the tree."

Raven checked her messages as Darren rang the doorbell. Nobody answered. Darren cocked his head around the wall and spotted two vehicles in the driveway—Aguilar's red Rav4 and a white hatchback blocking it in.

"Their vehicles are here," said Darren.

"Maybe they went for a walk."

Darren pressed the bell again. Inside the house, a chime rang. Several heartbeats later, soft footsteps approached the door. A woman with brunette bangs peeked through the window and gave them a skeptical look. This had to be Simone Axtell.

"We're looking for Deputy Aguilar," Raven said, raising her voice at the closed door. "Can we speak to her?"

Simone rolled her eyes and pressed a finger against her lips. Quietly, she pulled the door open and squeezed into the opening.

"Will you keep your voices down? Who are you?"

"Darren Holt and Raven Hopkins," Darren said. When the woman gave them an expectant stare, Darren elaborated. "We're investigators with Wolf Lake Consulting. The sheriff is trying to contact Deputy Aguilar, but she isn't answering her phone."

Simone harrumphed. "Doesn't anyone have the common courtesy to let people rest on their days off?"

"Will you get Aguilar?" asked Raven. "It's important."

"No."

"No?"

Simone stepped outside and blocked the entrance. "Veronica needs her sleep."

"It's almost eleven."

"She caught the flu, probably because you people made her work like a slave."

"But why didn't she answer her phone? If she gives the sheriff's department her availability, they can plan around her."

"Because I turned her ringer off. I don't want that damn phone waking her up when she's sick. Now, if you'll excuse me, I need to check on my friend."

"I'd like to see her," Darren said, suddenly squeamish. This woman struck him as untrustworthy.

"Absolutely not. You show up unannounced and claim you're private investigators, but I've never met you. I'm not letting strangers inside Veronica's house while she's asleep."

"If you tell her we're here, she'll—"

Simone closed the door in their faces. Darren shared a glance with Raven.

"What was that about?" asked Raven.

Darren made a swirling motion beside his head with his finger. "Nuttier than a fruitcake, that one."

"We can't leave without speaking to Aguilar."

"You heard the woman. We're strangers, and we aren't entering the house."

Raven rubbed her chin. "The only stranger in this picture is Simone Axtell. What hole did she crawl out of?"

"Chelsey says Aguilar and Simone were college roommates."

"And she's in town because . . ."

"Because Wolf Lake needs drama." Darren glanced at the window as Simone pulled the curtains together. "On second thought, let's skip the state park and head back to the office. It's time someone looked into Simone Axtell."

32

Peeking between the curtains, Simone Axtell ground her teeth until the two private investigators crawled into a Nissan Rogue and drove off. After the vehicle rounded the corner, she tugged the curtains open and illuminated the living room with sunlight.

Her shoulders clenched with tension. It seemed every time Simone and Veronica had time alone, someone pounded on the door or called on the phone, intent on driving a wedge between them.

Jealousy.

That's what drove the sheriff's department and private investigators to interfere. They couldn't compete with the friendship Simone and Aguilar shared. Since college, Aguilar had been the only person who understood Simone, the only trustworthy friend in her life. And despite what Aguilar believed, they'd shared a beautiful night together two decades ago, an unexpected romance Simone would never forget. Aguilar suppressed the memory because her fake friends clouded her mind.

Fury rippled through Simone's body. She hated that name—

Aguilar. The woman's name was Veronica. Her friends had brainwashed the poor woman.

Aguilar and Simone were inseparable. After today, they'd always be together. And Aguilar's meddling friends would never interfere again.

Simone slipped the pill from her purse.

Down the hallway, the door to the master bedroom squealed open. Simone muttered a curse and hid the pill inside her pocket. She swung around just as her best friend staggered into the living room, holding her head.

"That's why I never nap during the day unless I'm working overnight shifts." Aguilar moaned. "If it wasn't for the clock, I wouldn't have any idea what time of day it is."

"That's your body sending a message. You work too much, Veronica. If the department gave you a chance, you could catch up on sleep and regain your energy. Word to the wise: studies link sleep deprivation to disease and premature aging."

"Aren't you the morbid one this morning?" Aguilar slumped onto the couch and rubbed her eyes. "I heard the bell. Who was at the door?"

Simone's mouth twitched. "UPS. I suspected the dullard woke you up. I should file a complaint."

"The UPS deliveryman? What did he want?"

Simone waved Aguilar's concern away. "The idiot rang the wrong doorbell. He tried to deliver your neighbor's package."

Aguilar grinned. "Last week, the mailman gave me a catalog for a woman who lives a block away. I didn't realize they still made catalogs."

"Anyway, I sent the man away and chastised him for disturbing your sleep."

"That was unnecessary."

"If you allow these imbeciles to mess up, they'll do it again."

As Simone shifted her feet, the pill feeling like a jagged

boulder inside her pocket, Aguilar searched the room with her eyes.

"Have you seen my phone?"

"Um, no." Simone's gaze automatically flicked to her purse, where she'd hidden the phone. She found no joy in deceiving her friend, but she had no choice. Until she got Aguilar alone, someone would always ruin their relationship and drag them apart. "Did you leave it in the bedroom?"

"I checked the bedroom first." Aguilar ruffled her hair. "I'm positive I put my phone on the nightstand. That's where I always leave it so I know when the office calls."

"You were so tired when you came home last night. Don't blame yourself for misplacing your phone."

"Let me borrow yours. I should contact the office and get an update on the kidnapping case. Before my shift ended, the sheriff drove to Robyn Fournette's house. I wonder what ended up happening."

"Eat something first. Your health should be your priority."

"I suppose."

Aguilar shuffled into the kitchen, with Simone trailing a few steps behind. Simone cast a glance out the window, ensuring the snooping investigators hadn't returned.

"What's with all the melon rinds in the sink?" Aguilar asked.

"Oh, that. I made a scrumptious fruit salad with melon and fresh berries."

"You're a guest, Simone. Stop cooking meals and making snacks. Though I admit fruit salad sounds terrific."

"It's not for you, silly. I dropped it off at your office."

"The sheriff's department? Whatever for?"

"Because I caused so much trouble for your friends. It was the least I could do."

"That's a gracious gesture, but I asked you to stay away from the office."

"No worries. It's a shame I didn't run into your sheriff friend or that hunk deputy."

"Lambert?"

Simone batted her eyelashes and placed a hand over her heart, swallowing the bile surging into her throat. The oaf deputy disgusted her. As if a Neanderthal like Deputy Lambert would ever interest Simone. "Sadly, he wasn't at the office. I spoke to . . ." Simone snapped her fingers a few times to make it seem as if she was jogging her memory. "Maggie, the administrative assistant."

Aguilar relaxed. "So, you only talked with Maggie."

"Yes, I handed over the fruit salad and told her to share it with the office. She was quite thankful."

"Thank you, Simone. That was very kind. Please, though. In the future, if you want to make amends with anyone at the sheriff's department, come to me first."

"Of course. I have a special surprise."

"You're full of surprises this morning."

"I packed my bags. By five o'clock, I'll be out of your hair."

"What are you talking about? You're welcome to stay."

Simone scratched her nose. "This vacation refreshed me in ways I can never explain. I'm finally ready to face my father, return to therapy, and put the past behind me."

"Happy to hear it."

"Don't be concerned about the way I flew off the handle over my father. It was therapeutic to get that out of my system. I'm not planning to drive to my parents' house in the middle of the night and cause a scene. Instead, I pulled some strings and discovered the perfect bed-and-breakfast on Coral Lake. And guess what? They had one vacancy."

"Meaning what?"

"Meaning you have your house to yourself again, and I'm

booked for a healthy dose of rest and relaxation. Now, if you'll help me load my trunk, we can grab lunch and celebrate."

"This all seems rather sudden. No offense, Simone, but you weren't in any shape to drive the last time we discussed your father. Are you sure you're okay? I mean, really sure?"

"As sure as I've ever been in my life."

"Then I won't stand in your way. Are your belongings in your room?"

"They are. And if you'll be a dear and carry a few things out to the car, I need to use the little girl's room."

"I'll get right to it."

"Yay! I'll meet you outside."

Simone waited inside the bathroom. After Aguilar passed by with two bags hoisted over her shoulders, Simone checked the hallway. Outside, Aguilar's sneakers scuffed in the driveway. Simone needed to hurry. She played a dangerous game, drugging a law enforcement officer. This was the only way to force Aguilar into the car. Simone wasn't strong enough to overpower the sheriff's deputy, and Aguilar continued to lie to herself, denying their bond.

Hurrying into the kitchen, Simone poured champagne into two flutes she'd discovered tucked in the cupboard behind discount store glassware and a mixing bowl. Her hands trembled, and she almost dropped the pill before it landed in the champagne. A quick stir with her finger, and Simone set the flutes on the kitchen table.

She jumped when Aguilar appeared in the entryway.

"Thought you needed to use the bathroom," Aguilar said, narrowing her eyes.

Simone giggled. "I fibbed."

Aguilar gestured at the champagne. "What's this?"

"A surprise. I knew you wouldn't agree unless I poured you a little bubbly."

"I told you I don't drink."

"But this is a special occasion. We're celebrating."

Aguilar lifted the flute and focused on the bubbles congregating along the rim. The way she studied the drink made Simone squirm. Did Aguilar suspect Simone had dropped something in her glass?

"I'm not sure about this," Aguilar said.

"Don't be a spoilsport. Look, I'll drive if it makes you feel better."

Aguilar tapped a finger against her chin, still examining the glass.

Simone stomped a foot and said, "Just one toast together. Will you do that for me? This is my life we're talking about."

"What are we celebrating?"

Simone lifted her flute and held it out. "To new beginnings."

"To new beginnings," Aguilar echoed, and clinked her glass against Simone's.

Simone watched Aguilar over the rim. For a terrifying moment, she panicked, worrying she'd grabbed the wrong drink. Then Aguilar smacked her lips and smiled with satisfaction.

"I haven't sampled champagne since my cousin's wedding," Aguilar said. "Not bad."

"Only the best for you."

Simone tipped back the flute and swallowed the last of her champagne, encouraging Aguilar to follow suit. The deputy wore the mischievous grin of a teenager who'd broken into her parents' liquor cabinet. It was enough to tug Simone's heartstrings and wish it didn't have to be this way.

"I'll grab the rest of my bags," Simone said. "Wait in my car. We'll have the most wonderful day. Just the two of us."

"You're setting the bar high." As Aguilar finished speaking, she tottered and grabbed the chair. "Whoa. It's a good thing you agreed to drive. Guess I can't handle alcohol so well."

"Same old goody-two-shoes Veronica."

Simone kissed her friend on the cheek. In a matter of minutes, the deputy would be at her mercy.

33

After the lunch hour traffic cleared in Wolf Lake, Thomas drove his cruiser to the hospital. Last night's shooting replayed in his mind. It was his fault the kidnapper had shot Robyn Fournette and escaped with Dylan. If Thomas hadn't lost the woman after she hid her car behind the restaurant, he would have arrived in time to help. By now, the kidnapper should be behind bars, with Dylan safe in his mother's arms.

He crossed the hospital lobby and punched the elevator button. The doctor had moved Fournette to a recovery room on the third floor, where Thomas found Trooper Fitzgerald seated in an uncomfortable chair outside Fournette's door, with a baseball magazine open. In the midst of Deputy Aguilar's darkest moments, after she shot and killed a corrupt police officer and blamed herself, Trooper Fitzgerald had been a guiding light to Aguilar, confessing his own fears as he helped the deputy face her demons. The two law enforcement officers had formed a bond since.

Fitzgerald rose when Thomas approached.

"How's she doing?" Thomas asked.

Fitzgerald rolled the magazine and stuffed it into his pocket. "Fournette is in and out of sleep. She might be delusional, too."

"Why do you say that?"

"She took one look at me and became hysterical, telling the medical staff I'd get her son killed."

"It's not you, it's us."

"Come again?"

"The kidnapper threatened to murder her kid if Fournette contacted the police. All the more reason that I need you here, guarding her room."

Thomas peeked through the doorway. Half-awake, Fournette stared at the window.

"I'll convince her to talk," Thomas said, slipping inside the room. "If you see anyone who looks out of place—"

"No worries. Nobody is getting past me."

Thomas closed the door.

Robyn Fournette's face seemed a shade paler than when he'd last encountered her deep in the bowels of Empire Coasters. Probes stretched from her body to monitoring equipment beside the bed. A thick slice of gauze covered the woman's shoulder, where the bullet had blown through her flesh and exited.

"Ms. Fournette, do you remember me from the night your son disappeared?"

The woman's eyes trailed from the window to Thomas, then back to the window. "I remember you."

"How are you feeling this afternoon?"

Fournette choked on a sob. "I failed my son."

"I'll find your boy. But I need you to tell me who did this." When the woman didn't reply, Thomas pulled a chair beside the bed and sat. "Please, Ms. Fournette. Who shot you?"

"You shouldn't be here."

"Why? Because the kidnapper told you not to involve the police?"

Her gaze swung to his. "How did you know that?"

"Your cell phone records. We intercepted his texts, and I overheard what he told you in the park."

"If he finds out I talked to you, he'll kill my son."

"He won't find out."

"Yes, he will. He sees everything."

"Ms. Fournette?"

"Just go. I can't tell you who shot me last night. It was too dark to recognize a face."

"What about his voice? Did you recognize his voice?"

She pulled the blanket toward her chin and clasped her hands together. "You can't be here. He's watching."

Thomas moved to the window. Standing with his palms braced against the sill, he peered at the street below. An orderly wheeled a man from the exit to a waiting car. On the opposite side of the street, a woman carried a bag of takeout. Nothing suspicious stood out amid the sea of vehicles clogging the parking lot.

"He's not out there. If he approaches the hospital, I'll catch him."

"You don't understand. The police never caught him."

Her words trailed off. Thomas motioned for Fournette to continue, but all she did was swipe a tear off her eye.

"How long has this man harassed you?"

No answer.

"If you don't tell me the truth, I can't find Dylan."

"I want to go home. At least I'd have my gun and be able to defend myself."

"You need to heal, and your gun is in safe keeping."

The woman turned away and became an impenetrable stone wall.

"I need to check with my office," Thomas said. "In the meantime, the state trooper outside your door will ensure you're safe."

"You're signing my son's death warrant."

Thomas exited and closed the door behind him.

"No luck?" Fitzgerald asked.

"She's convinced the shooter is watching. There's something she isn't telling me. I suspect Fournette went to the police before, and they didn't help her."

"What do you think she's hiding?"

"Robyn Fournette moved from Illinois with a newborn, leaving her family and friends behind. She claims she came to New York for work, but I'm not so sure. If this guy stalked her for six years, I need her to talk."

"I tried. She wouldn't open up to me."

"I know someone who can help."

Thomas left Fitzgerald beside the recovery room and dialed Chelsey's number. The investigators were busy at the office, but Chelsey agreed to drive to the hospital. Chelsey had dealt with her own stalker, a deranged man named Ken Wendle who'd been obsessed with Chelsey since they were young.

Twenty minutes after Thomas called, Chelsey emerged from the elevator.

"Where is she?" Chelsey asked.

Thomas nodded toward Fitzgerald. "Behind that door. Don't acknowledge that you're a private investigator unless Fournette asks. She refuses to speak with law enforcement. I don't know how she'll react to a PI."

"I know what to say."

Thomas sat beside Fitzgerald, who slapped the baseball magazine on the sheriff's lap.

"Reading material to help you pass the time," the state trooper said. "Do you think Chelsey will get through to Fournette?"

"If anyone can, it's Chelsey."

Before Thomas opened the magazine, movement in the corridor caught his attention. A man hiding behind sunglasses carried a bouquet.

Thomas nudged Fitzgerald. "See the guy with the flowers?"

Fitzgerald tensed. "Straight ahead by the elevators."

When the man spotted Thomas and Fitzgerald, he swerved and headed in the opposite direction.

Thomas stood from his chair. "Radio security. Stay with Fournette."

The man veered down another hallway and quickened his pace. Thomas rushed to catch up. Another corridor opened to the right, and the man swung around the corner and hurried away.

"Nightshade County Sheriff's Department. Stop where you are."

The man stopped and raised his arms, his back to Thomas, the bouquet clutched in his right hand. He wore a brown leather jacket that seemed too warm for an August afternoon. Thomas worried about a concealed weapon.

When the man twisted his head, Thomas recognized him.

"TJ Soto. Why did you run?"

"You all but threatened to arrest me this morning. I didn't want trouble."

"Keep your hands up," Thomas said, frisking Soto.

The man carried nothing in his pockets besides his wallet and keys.

"I did nothing wrong. This is harassment."

"Why are you here, Mr. Soto?" Thomas lifted his chin at the flowers. "A gift for your old girlfriend?"

"I'm worried about her."

The sheriff's radio squawked as security rounded the corner.

Thomas held up a hand. "False alarm. I have the situation under control."

The guards kept advancing until Thomas shot them a pointed look. Thomas sensed Soto was on the verge of spilling the beans. After the guards left them alone in the hallway, Thomas pressed a finger against Soto's chest and backed him against the wall.

"You're lucky Robyn Fournette survived the shooting. Otherwise, you'd be a murder suspect."

"Why would I shoot Robyn, then bring her flowers?"

"To finish the job. You could have ordered the flowers and paid someone to deliver them. Instead, you're here, and you need to tell me why. Are you certain Dylan isn't your son?"

"Positive."

"How can you be so sure?"

Soto stared at the floor.

"Until you tell me the truth, you're my top suspect."

"I might know who the father is," Soto said, pacing.

"Might?"

The man pressed a hand against his forehead and closed his eyes. "While Robyn and I were dating, something happened at a party."

Conflict masked Soto's face. The sheriff waited for the man to continue.

"Tre was my best friend, but he had eyes for Robyn and had since we started dating. We were all drinking that night, and I lost track of Robyn, who'd gone upstairs to lie down. The party got too loud for her. She must have passed out. After I realized she wasn't downstairs, I asked if anyone had seen her. But when I found her in the bedroom, Tre was coming out of the room and buckling his belt. I looked over his shoulder, and there was Robyn on the bed, unconscious with her shirt off and the covers pulled over her hip."

Thomas couldn't believe what he was hearing. "Your friend raped Robyn while she was asleep?"

Soto swiped a hand across his nose and composed himself. "Tre swore he never touched Robyn, that he'd gotten sick and crashed on the floor until the room stopped spinning."

"And you believed him?"

"How could I prove Tre raped Robyn?"

"What happened next?"

"I told Tre he wasn't welcome around the house, and that if he ever came anywhere near Robyn, I'd make him sorry. Tre dropped out of school. Last I heard, he transferred to finish his degree. We never talked after he left Chicago." Soto knocked the back of his head against the wall, filling the corridor with low thumping noises. "Then Robyn told me she was pregnant. At first, I thought maybe the baby was mine. Robyn and I had slept together a lot that semester, and even though I used protection, I understood the risks. Sometimes, things happen."

"You didn't suspect the baby belonged to Tre?"

"Again, I couldn't prove anything, and Tre swore he never touched Robyn that night."

"So, you didn't tell Robyn or go to the police."

Soto glanced away and shook his head. "After I offered to pay for the abortion, Robyn broke up with me and said she'd take care of everything. Why didn't she tell me the truth?"

"Are you kidding?" Thomas wished he could toss Soto in jail, but he couldn't prove the man had covered up a rape. "You should have told Robyn about your suspicions. I need your friend's full name. Tell me everything about this guy."

"His name is Tre Kelly. He grew up south of Chicago and planned to go into law enforcement. The guy came from money. While the rest of us survived on loans, Tre's parents paid for college out of pocket. After Tre dropped out of school and transferred, I lost track of him."

Tre Kelly. Why did the name sound familiar? Thomas remembered the security guard who'd escorted Thomas and Aguilar into the tunnels. Officer Kelly.

"And now you're worried Tre kidnapped Robyn's son."

"I'm not sure what to believe. All this time, I assumed Robyn had gone through with the abortion. Then you told me about Dylan, and it made me wonder if the boy belonged to Tre."

"Think hard before you answer the next question. And you'd better answer honestly. Did you ever tell Tre about Robyn's pregnancy?"

Soto pressed his lips together and closed his eyes.

"Answer me."

"Before he transferred, I told Tre that I'd offered to pay for Robyn's abortion. I wanted to corner Tre and force him to admit what he'd done. But he refused to tell the truth. We never spoke again."

Thomas grabbed Soto's elbow. "You're coming with me."

"You can't arrest me."

"I'm not arresting you, Mr. Soto. But you're not leaving until I speak with Robyn and get a full statement from you on what happened six years ago."

34

Thomas bristled with nervous energy. Before he entered Robyn Fournette's hospital room, he phoned his department. With Lambert asleep at home and Aguilar nowhere to be found, the sheriff needed an experienced investigator to link Tre Kelly to the kidnapping. Again, he leaned on Wolf Lake Consulting for help.

Inside the recovery room, Fournette opened up to Chelsey after the private investigator shared her stalking experience. It didn't surprise Thomas that Chelsey bonded with the shooting victim. After Fournette calmed down, Thomas told her about TJ Soto.

Sitting up in bed, Fournette glanced from Thomas to Chelsey in disbelief.

"TJ is here?"

"He's down the hall, giving a full statement to the state trooper," Thomas said. "TJ told me something you need to know."

Thomas repeated Soto's story about Tre Kelly. Robyn's lower lip quivered. She pulled the blanket to her shoulder, as if she wanted to crawl beneath the covers and block the ugly truth.

"I remember Tre. He was so creepy. Sometimes, I caught him

staring at me, but I never told TJ because they were close friends. My God, are you saying Tre is Dylan's father?"

"We only have TJ's word to go on, but we'll talk to Tre Kelly. There's a Tre Kelly who works at Empire Coasters with the security team."

"He can't be the same Tre Kelly."

"That's what we're trying to establish."

"But the Tre Kelly I knew wasn't in the security office during the interview."

"No, but Tre was at the park on the night of the kidnapping. He would have avoided you, afraid you'd recognize him and wonder if he'd had anything to do with Dylan's disappearance." Thomas adjusted his hat. "Is there anything the kidnapper told you that proves he's TJ Soto's friend?"

Fournette inhaled. "I just remembered. My phone. There's an audio file of the kidnapper. I recorded him when he called yesterday."

Chelsey met Thomas's eyes. "If it's Tre, you can match his voice to the audio."

"It will take days before the lab analyzes the voice and gives a definitive answer," said Thomas.

"Forward the audio to my team. We'll work on the recording while you pursue Kelly."

LeVar tossed the dreadlocks over his shoulder and placed his hands against his cheeks, his mouth agape as Raven and Darren waited for him to respond. Beside LeVar, Scout's face turned crimson.

"You think I'm dating Scout? Are you out of your minds?" LeVar turned to Scout. "No offense."

"None taken," Scout said, hiding her face in her hands.

"Hundred percent. We aren't dating. I mean, she's fifteen. Be real."

"But you're always together," said Raven, leaning closer and touching her brother's arm.

"Maybe because we're friends? Come on. You're better than that. Scout and I exercise together and work on cases in the guest house."

"Right," Darren said. "With the guest house locked and the shade drawn on the back door. Put yourself in our shoes. If you visited my cabin and found the door locked and the curtains drawn over the windows, what would you assume?"

"Damn, I'm not sleeping with my fifteen-year-old neighbor. Who else believes this nonsense?"

"Nobody is accusing you of anything," Raven said. "We just worry and want you to understand what it looks like from an outsider's perspective."

"If it will make everybody happy," Scout said, "I won't visit the guest house anymore. And I can run alone."

Darren sighed. "That's unnecessary. Truth be told, I didn't buy the relationship thing."

Raven elbowed Darren. "Since when?"

"I realize I was born before the invention of electricity, but I remember being a teen. Everyone suspects the worst when a boy and girl spend a lot of time together. That's how rumors start."

"Sounds like you have experience with unfounded rumors. Bet you were a teenage Casanova."

Darren shrugged. "If LeVar and Scout say they're just friends, who am I to question them?" Darren shifted his chair to face LeVar. "But you need to exercise better judgment. If you want to hang out together, do it in the yard, where people can see you. And when you're in the guest house, don't pull the shade or lock the door. Someday, you'll have kids of your own. Not together, I mean, but . . ."

Raven laid a hand on Darren's shoulder. "What Darren is trying to say is, when you become adults, you'll have a different perspective."

The office phone rang, saving LeVar from the awkward intervention. He held their gazes as he answered.

"Wolf Lake Consulting." Recognizing Chelsey's voice, he held up a hand, signaling everyone to quiet down. As Chelsey spoke, LeVar jotted notes on a blank sheet of paper. "I'll download the file now."

Raven and Darren questioned LeVar with their eyes. Scout appeared as if she wanted to shrink and scurry into a mouse hole.

"That was Chelsey," LeVar said, opening the company email account. "Robyn Fournette recorded a phone conversation with the kidnapper. The file just arrived."

"This is huge," said Raven. "Is it TJ Soto?"

"Soto confessed to Thomas that his friend date-raped Fournette at a party during college. The guy's name is Tre Kelly. Nobody ever told Fournette."

Darren knuckled his forehead. "Tre Kelly might be the father. Are we to assume this guy followed Fournette to New York?"

"Worse. There's a Tre Kelly on the Empire Coasters security team."

"I knew it," Darren said, locking eyes with Scout, who nodded. Scout and Darren shared the theory that the kidnapper worked at the amusement park.

"Now, we have to prove Tre Kelly's voice is on the recording."

The team sprang into action, with Darren and Raven rolling their chairs to Raven's computer, while Scout shifted uncomfortably.

"We can work together," LeVar said, gesturing at Scout to

join him. "Especially now that these fools understand we aren't having a steamy relationship."

LeVar cocked an eyebrow at Darren and Raven, who busied themselves with the recording. Scout reluctantly sat in the chair beside LeVar, her cheeks still pink.

Raven's fingers flew across the keyboard as she ran a background check on Tre Kelly at Empire Coasters.

"It's the same guy," Raven said. "Tre Kelly attended the University of Chicago before he dropped out and transferred the year Robyn Fournette graduated. The records show he took the Empire Coasters job twenty-two months ago."

"He may have been watching Robyn and Dylan Fournette the whole time," Darren said.

LeVar hit the play icon and sat back, a prickle forming along the back of his neck as the kidnapper threatened Robyn Fournette.

"Don't pretend you care about your child's life. If you gave a damn about Dylan, you wouldn't have considered an abortion."

Raven and Darren turned to look when the kidnapper's voice boomed through the speaker.

"You wouldn't have considered an abortion," Raven said, repeating the kidnapper's words. "Only someone who knew Robyn Fournette six years ago would have that information."

As the kidnapper continued to speak, a high-pitched sound played in the background.

Darren pointed at the screen. "What was that sound? Play it back."

LeVar clicked the rewind icon. There it was again. LeVar clamped his eyes shut, trying to home in on the familiar sound. "I can't tell what that is. Can we filter out Kelly's voice?"

"Not entirely," Scout said. "But I can bring out the background. Let me try."

Under LeVar's supervision, Scout adjusted the noise filters

until the volume of the kidnapper's voice dropped, allowing the background to come through with added clarity. Replaying the conversation, Scout's eyes widened when the sound came again.

"That's a dog howling," Scout said.

"Not just any dog," said LeVar, increasing the monitor volume. "That's the sound effect from the haunted house at Empire Coasters. I'd recognize it anywhere."

Darren wheeled his chair over to LeVar's computer. "But Dylan's voice is on the recording. Kelly can't be holding a child captive in the park. That's insane."

"Even when you drive past the park, you hear that dog howling," Raven said. "He must be hiding Dylan in a house close by."

"Where does Kelly live?" asked LeVar.

"Twenty-six Brandywine Lane in Treman Mills. That's ten miles from Empire Coasters. No chance the sound travels that far."

LeVar called up a digital map and located eighteen rural houses outside of Empire Coasters. Dylan Fournette might be in any of them.

"Narrow the search to unoccupied homes," Darren said.

"I found five."

Scout clapped her hands together. "Guys, guys. Which way was the wind blowing when the kidnapper called Robyn Fournette?"

Darren opened his mouth to ask why it mattered. The reason dawned on his face. "Of course. Sound travels farther depending on wind speed and direction."

"Give me the time of the call."

Raven scanned the file Thomas had sent over. "Eleven in the morning."

LeVar moved aside while Scout accessed the wind and weather archives from the local National Weather Service office.

"The wind traveled from the west at twenty-two miles per

hour," Scout said. "We should focus on residences east of the park. Given the strong wind speed, we may need to widen the search area."

Pointing at the map, LeVar said, "There aren't any vacant homes east of the park. Not unless you travel five miles, and you wouldn't hear the haunted house from that far away. Any suggestions?"

Nobody answered. Where was Tre Kelly hiding Dylan Fournette?

35

Sunlight glinted through the trees as Thomas stopped the cruiser outside Aguilar's house. His lead deputy lived between the station and the highway, which would take Thomas to Tre Kelly's residence. When he removed the keys from the ignition, the road tilted, as though he'd stepped off the amusement park's fastest roller coaster. He wiped the blur out of his eyes and staggered across the blacktop, grabbing the truck to steady his balance. Except for an hour of shuteye this morning, he hadn't slept in almost thirty-six hours. The more he zeroed in on Dylan Fournette's kidnapper, the harder it was to stay awake. He wasn't sure he could drive to the amusement park and keep the cruiser on the road, let alone capture a sociopath. Thomas needed Deputy Aguilar.

He stood at the end of the driveway. Aguilar's red RAV4 slumbered in front of the garage. The gusting wind had ripped leaves off a maple tree and littered the windshield and roof of the SUV, suggesting Aguilar hadn't driven her vehicle today. His eyes moved to the front window. A sliver of darkness crept between the parted curtains. It didn't look as if anyone was home.

Thomas climbed the steps and rang the bell, recalling the first time he'd done so after he moved from California. On a dare from Lambert, Thomas had escorted Aguilar to the Magnolia Dance, Wolf Lake's popular springtime festival. Now nobody answered. He rang the bell again.

Crossing the lawn, he stood on tiptoe and peered between the curtains. There was enough light to make out the living room furniture. A flash of reflected sunlight caught his eye. Aguilar's keys lay on an end table.

Where was she?

Thomas pulled out his phone and dialed Aguilar's cell. After several rings, he got her voicemail. He tried again, this time placing his ear close to the window. Either Aguilar had silenced the ringer, or her phone wasn't inside the house. Logic told him Aguilar was out with her friend, Simone. Except that made little sense. Loyal to her job, Aguilar would answer Thomas's calls if she was awake. Worry prickled at Thomas. Maybe it was the lack of sleep playing tricks on him, but the situation didn't feel right.

When Thomas returned to the cruiser, Wolf Lake Consulting called. The sheriff didn't know how his department would survive without Chelsey and her team of private investigators. A short conversation with Chelsey, who'd just arrived at her office, confirmed that the Tre Kelly employed by Empire Coasters was the same Tre Kelly from the University of Chicago. Chelsey's news that her team had identified sound effects from the park on the recording struck Thomas as strange. Where could Kelly hold Dylan inside a crowded amusement park?

"We think he's keeping Dylan east of the park," Chelsey said. "I didn't locate a vacant home in the area, but we're working on alternative locations."

"Perfect. I'm heading to Tre Kelly's house next. It appears I need to call Deputy Lambert back to work."

"Wait, you haven't contacted Deputy Aguilar?"

"Not yet. Have you heard from her?"

The pause on the other end told Thomas that Chelsey was considering how much she should divulge.

"Chelsey, what's wrong?"

"It's Simone Axtell. I don't trust her. Darren and Raven were about to run a background check on Simone before you emailed the recording."

"Seems Simone was busy today. Maggie contacted me from the office. Simone showed up with a fruit salad while I was at the hospital. Says she wanted to make amends for causing a scene."

"I can't decide if that's a kind gesture, or a mega-weird one. You want us to check into this woman?"

"I don't even have her phone number. At the very least, I need to contact Simone to find out where Aguilar is."

Keeping Chelsey on the line, Thomas gunned the engine and pointed the cruiser toward Tre Kelly's house. Despite his exhausted state, he might need to take a kidnapper down without help from his deputies.

AFTER THE CALL with Thomas ended, Chelsey leaned over Raven's shoulder. Nobody on the investigation team needed Chelsey's encouragement to look into Simone Axtell. Like Chelsey, Raven and Darren suspected Deputy Aguilar's friend was hiding a secret. There was a dangerous edge to Simone, though Chelsey couldn't pin down why the woman worried her.

"Weird," Raven said, clacking away on the keyboard.

"What did you find?" Chelsey asked.

"Fifteen calls to resort hotels within a ten-mile radius of Coral Lake, and nobody has a record of Simone Axtell staying in the last month. And I searched her employment records and can't find anything over the last seven years."

"What about self-employment? Didn't Deputy Aguilar tell Thomas that Simone owned a business?"

Another search produced zero results. In the background, LeVar and Scout replayed the kidnapper's voice, searching for any clue they'd missed.

Chelsey bit her lip. The sheriff was fifteen minutes from Tre Kelly's house, intent on encountering the kidnapper, with no one to back him up. Chelsey wished Thomas would stand down until the state police arrived, but she knew the sheriff better than that. With a child's life on the line, Thomas wouldn't rest until he captured the kidnapper. She only hoped the state police would arrive to help.

Darren rubbed his chin. "Seven years without gainful employment, yet Simone spends all summer vacationing, stays in lavish resorts, and lives in the most exciting cities in the world. Does that make sense to you?"

"Nothing about that woman makes sense to me. And where's the proof that she visits resorts?"

"It's possible the parents are wealthy and finance Simone."

"Unlikely. According to Deputy Aguilar, Simone doesn't get along with her parents, though she wouldn't elaborate."

Chelsey worked her jaw from side to side. Deputy Aguilar had asked Chelsey not to reveal Simone's background, not even to Thomas. Instinct warned Chelsey to place all the cards on the table before something terrible happened.

"I know why Simone doesn't speak with her parents," Chelsey said.

They all stared at Chelsey, waiting for an answer. She told them about Simone's father.

Raven broke the stunned silence. "I smell BS. There's one way to find out the truth."

"I see the wheels turning in your head, Raven. What's your plan?"

"Simone's parents are Albert and Maia Axtell. They live outside Buffalo. I'm calling them."

LeVar and Scout strode to Raven's workstation.

"Wait," said LeVar. "You can't call two complete strangers and ask them why Albert Axtell sexually abused his daughter."

"Watch me."

The office fell silent, the only sound the phone ringing through the speaker as Raven hovered over her desk. The tension made Chelsey want to pull the cord out of the phone before anyone answered.

"Hello?"

A woman's voice.

"Is this Maia Axtell?"

"Yes. Who's calling?"

"Mrs. Axtell, my name is Raven Hopkins. I'm calling from a private investigation firm in Wolf Lake."

"What's this about?"

"It's about your daughter, Simone."

A pained croak fled Maia Axtell's throat. "She's dead, isn't she? As much as I prepared myself for this call . . ."

Sobs stifled the woman's words.

"No, your daughter isn't dead," Raven said, softening her voice.

"Then something happened at the facility. Please tell me she didn't hurt anyone."

"Excuse me, what facility?"

More crying. A man's voice called to Maia, asking who was on the phone. The woman must have placed the receiver against her chest, for her answer sounded muffled.

"It's a private investigator asking about Simone," Maia said.

"Why would a private investigator call about our daughter?"

"Sorry, that was my husband," the woman said, returning to the phone.

"Mrs. Axtell, your daughter is visiting a colleague of ours, and now our colleague is missing. Simone might be the only person who knows where she is."

"But that's impossible. Simone can't visit anyone. She's lived in an institution for seven years."

Raven looked at the other investigators. "An institution. Like a mental facility?"

"My goodness. Did they release her?"

"Wouldn't the facility notify you if they released your daughter?"

"No. She's an adult, and she emancipated herself from us years ago."

"Because of the issue between Simone and her father?"

"What? There were no issues between Simone and Albert. Our daughter is a sick woman, and she blames us for her problems. We begged her not to go through with the emancipation papers, but there's no talking Simone out of a decision once she makes up her mind. What on earth did Simone tell you?"

Raven lowered her voice. "That your husband molested Simone when she was young."

Maia Axtell burst into tears. It took her a long time to compose herself. "She lies to get attention. That's the way Simone has always been, ever since she was a child. The lies became worse as she grew older. But this?"

"It's not true?"

"Albert has Parkinson's and has been in a wheelchair since Simone was a baby. He couldn't force himself on anyone. I can't believe Simone claims . . ." Another sob. "She needs help. They never should have let her out of the institution."

Chelsey approached the phone. "Mrs. Axtell, my name is Chelsey Byrd. I'm another investigator at Wolf Lake Consulting.

Will you tell us why your daughter entered an institution? We need to know if our colleague is in danger."

"Seven years ago, Simone worked in New York City and seemed on the verge of turning her life around. But the job was so high paced, and I believe the city wore her down."

"Go on."

"Simone had a mental breakdown and poisoned her coworkers at a holiday party. She slipped something into the dessert. Several people left in an ambulance, and a few ended up in critical condition. Thank goodness they survived. It might have been so much worse."

Chelsey snapped her fingers. Across the room, LeVar contacted the sheriff's department. Chelsey prayed Maggie, Thomas, and the deputies hadn't consumed the fruit salad.

"Do you have any idea where Simone is right now? It's critical we find her."

"I'm sorry, but I can't help you. Simone refused to accept our calls at the facility. We haven't spoken to our daughter since she poisoned her coworkers."

Chelsey thanked Mrs. Axtell.

Now they had two fugitives to capture, their colleagues with the Nightshade County Sheriff's Department might have life-threatening illnesses, and Aguilar's life hung in the balance.

36

Two state police cruisers screeched to a halt outside Tre Kelly's residence when Thomas arrived. He juggled the kidnapping investigation and the madness occurring at his office, where the afternoon radio dispatcher and Maggie Tillery had left the station in ambulances. Both experienced severe stomach pain, and Maggie had vomited an hour ago.

The sheriff wiped the sweat off his forehead, his mind on his coworkers as he greeted Trooper Gaines, a veteran officer from Kentucky. Two female troopers and a rookie male joined them. Thomas wished Fitzgerald was here to lead his team. After Thomas laid out a plan, he climbed the steps with Gaines.

A knock on the door produced no result.

Gaines peeked around the corner and shook his head. "No vehicle in the garage. It doesn't appear he's home."

Thomas raised his hand to knock again, and a thump echoed inside the house.

"Mr. Kelly? This is Sheriff Thomas Shepherd with the Nightshade County Sheriff's Department. Are you injured?"

Nobody responded. When the sound came again, Thomas shared a look with Gaines. Someone was inside the house. A weak cry, muffled by the walls, emanated from inside.

"That sound like a child's voice to you?" Gaines asked.

"We'll go in quietly. Kelly might be in there, and so might Dylan Fournette."

Gaines motioned for his troopers to circle the home and breech the back door. On a silent three count, Thomas shouldered the door open. An alarm shrilled, causing the sheriff to flinch and cover his ears before he regained control.

Thomas braced himself as he turned every corner, picturing Kelly on the other side of the wall, with a gun aimed at the sheriff's forehead. He found nobody in the living room and dining room. The home barely appeared lived in, it was so neat.

"Dylan Fournette, are you in the house? We're the police. Call out, and we'll come to you."

With the security alarm screeching, Thomas couldn't hear the child, even if the boy yelled from the next room.

Thomas and Gaines cleared the downstairs. The other three troopers met them in a spotless kitchen with gleaming floor tiles. Gaines waved his hand and sent his team to investigate the basement, which lay beyond a hallway door between the kitchen and living room. Gaines started up the staircase to check the upper floor, when Thomas paused on the lower step. The trooper wheeled around, wondering why Thomas had stopped. The sheriff held up a hand and pointed at a door cut into the side of the stairway. A padlock barred entry. Thomas pointed at the lock. Gaines nodded with understanding. Though the lock appeared stout, the door was flimsy enough for Thomas to pry it open until the board warped, allowing the sheriff to squeeze through the opening.

He caught his breath. Toys and comic books littered the tiny space beneath the stairs. Covered by a pale-blue blanket and pillow, a mattress lay in the corner. A young boy curled on the floor, clutching his shoulder. Dylan Fournette.

Thomas knelt beside the child and brushed the hair off his brow. The boy's eyelids fluttered, the eyes rolling back in his head. Dylan didn't respond to Thomas's consoling words. The sheriff turned to Gaines, who struggled to force his way into the storage space beneath the stairway.

"He's losing consciousness. Call an ambulance."

Gaines retreated and made the call, as one of the female troopers spoke to the security company and convinced them to shut off the alarm. The other troopers cleared the upstairs. Cradling the boy in his arms, Thomas kicked the door off its hinges, sending the padlock skidding across the hardwood floor.

"Careful with the arm," Thomas said, setting the boy on the living room rug. "He dislocated his shoulder, attempting to break out of the room."

"Ambulance is en route," Gaines said, returning to Thomas. "Where's Kelly?"

"Not here. He might be working at the amusement park. No doubt the security system alerted him by now, so he knows we found Dylan."

"We'll stop him if he runs. No way he's leaving the county."

"I doubt Kelly is going anywhere," said Thomas, leaning down to check on Dylan. The boy's breathing was too rapid, his lips parched and scabbing, signs that he was dehydrated. "Kelly followed Robyn Fournette from Illinois to New York. He won't stop until he catches her."

"He won't get past Fitzgerald at the hospital."

Thomas wanted to agree with Gaines. He couldn't. Robyn Fournette wouldn't be safe until they captured Kelly.

"What now?" asked Gaines.

"We visit Empire Coasters. This time, we don't tell anyone we're coming until we reach the security tunnels. No reason to tip off Kelly."

"I'll back you up. My troopers can stay with the boy until the ambulance arrives."

37

B y the time the sheriff and Trooper Gaines drove their cruisers into the Empire Coasters parking lot, word had come over the radio that the paramedics had stabilized Dylan Fournette. The ambulance would transport the child to the same hospital as his mother. But now the sheriff needed to find Simone Axtell, who Thomas suspected had poisoned Maggie and his afternoon dispatcher, based on the shocking history Chelsey and her staff had uncovered, and the two coworkers who'd left the station in ambulances. A BOLO existed for Simone Axtell's vehicle. This new emergency divided the already beleaguered law enforcement staff.

One piece of good news—Deputy Lambert, half-awake after grabbing a few hours of sleep, was back at work and leading the search for Axtell and Aguilar. Lambert cared for Aguilar as much as Thomas did. The deputies had worked side by side since before Thomas Shepherd returned to Wolf Lake and later replaced Sheriff Gray. Thomas needed to catch Tre Kelly before he hurt anyone else. The sooner the sheriff captured the fugitive, the quicker he could join the search for Deputy Aguilar and her disturbed friend.

Thomas flashed his badge at the front gate of Empire Coasters. The overweight, mustached guard working at the gate refused to let Thomas and Trooper Gaines pass without Ron Faustin's approval. Gaines blasted the guard for obstructing a kidnapping investigation until the guard allowed them to enter.

"Everyone needs a fiefdom," Gaines muttered while they squeezed through the crowd, angling toward the tunnels. "Give these idiots power, and they think they're kings."

"Something is bugging me," Thomas said.

"What's that?"

"Kelly hid Dylan Fournette inside his house, yet in the phone recording, we heard the haunted house sound effect."

"That tells me Kelly kept Dylan nearby."

"But why?"

"Kelly still needs to work. He keeps Dylan close so he never loses track of the boy."

"But the private investigation firm we're working with checked. There aren't any vacant homes downwind of the park."

The guard at the front gate must have alerted Faustin, as the head of security met them at the entry doors to the tunnels. Usually brash, Faustin drew in a breath when he spied Thomas and Gaines. Faustin glanced behind him, more of a cornered mouse than a king ruling over his fiefdom. After a moment of indecision, Faustin firmed his shoulders and drew himself up.

"Officer Kelly isn't on shift until this evening. He's not here."

"We'd like to search the tunnels, all the same," Thomas said. "I assume Kelly has a locker? Somewhere to store his belongings?"

"I'm under no obligation to admit you into the tunnels. This is private property."

"If you prefer, we'll return with a warrant. Should anything happen to Robyn Fournette or her son, I'll tell the judge that you refused to help us in our investigation."

"Think of the publicity," Gaines said, setting his hands on his hips.

"Fine," Faustin said. "But stay with me. No wandering around on your own."

Faustin led Thomas and Gaines past the glass doorway of the security office toward a gloomy room tucked at the end of the corridor. The head of security swiped his ID card through the reader and pulled the door open.

"That's Kelly's locker," Faustin said, gesturing at a green rectangular locker in the middle of the row.

A long wooden bench stretched the length of the room, dividing one wall of lockers from the other. The room smelled of cologne and Lysol. Faustin lingered beside the door, checking his phone as if expecting a call.

Gaines eyed Faustin while Thomas tugged on the locker.

"It's locked," Thomas said. "Open it for me."

Faustin muttered under his breath and produced a key, which he slipped into the locker door. "There. I've done everything I can to help you. Just find what you're looking for and get out of my hair. No need to turn this into a public relations nightmare."

Thomas opened the door. Two clean security uniforms hung from hooks. A change of clothes, including a gray sweatshirt, lay along the bottom of the locker. Two lockers down from Kelly's, an open door beckoned. Faustin's name was affixed to the open door. A lunch box and a pair of shoes sat at the bottom of the locker. As Faustin stuffed his hands inside his pockets, his gaze moved from his locker to Kelly's.

"Does Officer Kelly own a second property near the park?" Thomas asked.

"No, why?"

"He concealed Dylan Fournette nearby while he worked at the amusement park. He may have even slipped away to check on the boy while he was on shift. Have you noticed Officer Kelly acting strangely or disappearing for an hour at a time?"

"Nothing of the sort. Kelly is a model employee. If he owns a second house, I'm not aware, and it's not my business."

As Thomas searched the locker, he caught Trooper Gaines shifting his body closer to Faustin. The sheriff didn't like the head of security, but he'd had no reason to distrust the man before today. Gaines had picked up on the same mannerisms Thomas noticed—Faustin's edginess ramped up as the sheriff sifted through Kelly's belongings. Was Faustin hiding something?

Moving Kelly's sweatshirt aside, Thomas's hand closed over a black prepaid phone on the bottom of the locker. A second phone—same brand and model—lay beside the first. Kelly used prepaid phones and cloaking technology to mask his number and conceal his identity. Thomas wondered if he'd find calls to Robyn Fournette on either phone.

"These phones are burners. Kelly ever use either phone in your presence?" Thomas asked over his shoulder.

Faustin cleared his throat and backtracked a fraction of an inch. "I don't recognize them."

"In a hurry to leave?" Trooper Gaines asked, eyeing the head of security.

"I just wish you'd get to the point and complete this half-ass search. I have a park to run."

When Thomas stood, his leg clipped Faustin's open locker. The shoes toppled out and landed on the changing room floor.

"Sorry," Thomas said, reaching to retrieve the shoes.

"No, don't! I'll take care of—"

Faustin's voice cut off when Thomas eyed the identical prepaid phone inside the head of security's locker. The sheriff had no warning before the gunshot blasted over his head and blew a hole in the locker. He ducked and rolled out of the way as Faustin aimed to fire again.

Gaines struck Faustin from the side and drove the shooter against the jamb. As Thomas jumped to his feet, the state trooper snagged Faustin's wrist and fought to wrestle the weapon free. The gun fired, the bullet exploding through Gaines's thigh and driving the trooper backward.

Thomas tackled Faustin. The gun skittered across the floor. Thomas struggled with Faustin and gained the top position, the shooter lying face-down. Gaines sprawled ten feet away, his hands clutching his thigh, blood welling between twitching fingers. Guards raced down the hall to respond to the commotion. Still fighting to control Faustin, Thomas wondered where their loyalties lay, and if they'd attack Thomas for assaulting their boss.

Sitting atop the thrashing shooter, Thomas wrenched Faustin's wrists behind his back and snapped the handcuffs. The guards watched in shock while Thomas read Faustin his rights.

"Call an ambulance, dammit!" Thomas barked at Officer Wheeler, the tallest of the guards.

Wheeler made as if to protest, then lifted his phone and dialed 911. Holding Faustin's wrists with one hand, Thomas radioed for backup he knew wasn't coming. The two investigations had tied up every officer within driving distance.

"Officer down. I repeat, officer down." Thomas swung his head to Gaines. "Help is on the way."

Gaines gritted his teeth and nodded.

"You live nearby, Faustin?" Thomas asked, wrenching the cuffed wrists up the man's back until he winced. "A mile east of the park, perhaps? Now we know where Kelly hid Dylan while he worked at the park. But what's in it for you? How much did Kelly pay you to help him kidnap a child?"

"Ouch!" Faustin writhed beneath Thomas, unable to unseat

the sheriff. "I'm not saying anything without a lawyer. I know my rights."

"Even with Kelly's knowledge of the security cameras, there's no way he moved Dylan through the tunnels without appearing on camera. Someone erased the footage. That had to be you."

"Like I said, I'm not talking until—ow!"

Thomas yanked harder on Faustin's wrists. Fury rippled through his exhausted body. Two men charged with ensuring the safety of park visitors had collaborated to abduct Dylan Fournette. Obsessed with the kidnapped boy's mother, Tre Kelly wanted to capture his son and terrorize Robyn Fournette. Thomas could only guess Faustin's reason for aiding Kelly, but he figured money was involved. It usually was when unlikely partners worked together.

A second guard, a fair-haired man with a boyish face, knelt beside the sheriff and tilted his head at Faustin. "Sheriff, help the state trooper. I'll cover Faustin."

Thomas wasn't sure if he trusted the guard, but the predicament left him with little choice. If Faustin's armed staff turned on Thomas, there was little he could do to defend himself. The sheriff hurried to the fallen trooper's side.

"I need a clean towel to stop the bleeding," Thomas called to the guards. "This is the most popular theme park in the region. You have an infirmary. Someone must keep a first-aid kit on hand, for goodness' sake."

Gaines grabbed Thomas's arm. "I'm all right. Deal with Faustin."

Officer Wheeler tossed a towel to Thomas. The sheriff pressed the cloth against Gaines's bleeding leg and held it firm.

"No chance, Gaines. I'm not leaving your side until the paramedics arrive. The towel will slow the bleeding. Hang in there. You'll be fine."

Gaines dropped his head against the floor and squinted his

eyes, groaning. The bullet that struck the trooper's leg had blown a hole in the floor. Good news. At least the bullet hadn't lodged in the state trooper's leg. Provided Thomas controlled the bleeding, Gaines would survive.

But as Thomas held the bloody towel against the fallen trooper's leg, icy fear encased him from the neck down.

Where was Tre Kelly?

38

Trooper Fitzgerald massaged his neck and rose to stretch his back. He'd sat in the same plastic chair outside Robyn Fournette's recovery room all morning and afternoon while reading his baseball magazine from cover to cover. Now he paced the corridor, never straying more than a few dozen paces from Fournette's room, as he worked the blood into his legs. The hospital had cleared out over the last hour. With the sun drifting lower in the sky, the day shift had departed, leaving a skeleton crew of evening and overnight workers to run the show. It was the same in law enforcement, Fitzgerald mused. The evening and overnight shifts were always thin.

He touched his hat when a twenty-something nurse with shoulder-length auburn curls passed. At the end of the hall, movement caught Fitzgerald's eye, but it was just a doctor making the rounds and checking patients.

Fitzgerald stopped at a floor-to-ceiling window and peered down at the parking lot. Already the lot appeared deserted, with just a trickle of vehicles driving down the road. The sun dropped behind a gray cloud on the horizon, making the day seem later than it was.

He clenched and unclenched his fists, anxious for news on Deputy Aguilar. According to the latest news, Aguilar had been missing since this morning, and the deputy's house guest was under suspicion for poisoning two members of the Nightshade County Sheriff's Department. A genuine friend, Aguilar was the hardest working deputy Fitzgerald had ever met. It killed him to stay at the hospital while Aguilar's life was in danger, but he wouldn't abandon his post. He'd patrol the hallway until relief arrived or his legs gave out.

As he passed an unoccupied recovery room, a metallic rattle that sounded as though someone had bumped against a tray of medical instruments caught his attention. He stopped and stared, the door open and spilling a shaft of muddy light into the corridor. With one hand resting on his gun, he moved toward the doorway. A made bed stood against the wall, a hazardous waste bin beside the sink. On the counter, a metal tray held various instruments.

After a quick glance down the hallway toward Fournette's room, Fitzgerald approached the closed bathroom door, his body thrumming. On his hip, his radio squawked. Something about a shooting at the Empire Coasters amusement park.

Fitzgerald removed the gun from his holster and stood beside the closed door. He grasped the handle and pulled down. Holding his breath, the state trooper pushed the door open and swung inside the bathroom.

Empty.

Paranoia stalked him like the lengthening shadows outside the window.

Back in the corridor, Fitzgerald studied the hallway. No doctors, no orderlies, just the lone nurse with the curly hair seated at her station. She widened her eyes upon spying the state trooper's gun. He slipped the weapon into the holster and raised a calming hand.

When the nurse returned to her work, Fitzgerald hustled to Robyn Fournette's recovery room and opened the door. The woman slept, her head supported by two pillows. Fitzgerald eased the door shut and picked up his radio to contact hospital security.

"Anything suspicious?"

"Negative," the security guard said. "It's as quiet as a tomb."

The gallows humor struck Fitzgerald as strange, seeing as some patients fought for their lives in the hospital.

"I thought someone was inside an empty room. Keep your eyes open."

"Probably a nurse poking around, or the maintenance staff cleaning."

Fitzgerald grunted, unconvinced. He slid down the hall and arrived at a second corridor. A glance revealed a doctor exiting a room several doors down. Maybe that's who Fitzgerald had heard.

But when he turned around, he didn't see anyone at the nurses' station. It seemed this wing of the hospital had been abandoned.

"Hello?"

Nobody answered.

With renewed suspicion, Fitzgerald hurried along the wall, wary of the open doors. Robyn Fournette's room stood directly ahead, the door closed. The trooper's skin crawled. He didn't trust the deepening shadows spilling out of the unoccupied rooms.

Fitzgerald was about to poke his head inside Fournette's room, just to be sure the woman was still safe, when shattering glass brought him around. He moved his gaze across the hall-way, searching for the source of the noise. His eyes landed on the closed door of a storage room. It bothered him that nobody cursed. Usually, when someone dropped a fragile item and it shattered, a colorful expletive followed. Not this time. Dead silence trailed down the corridor.

He approached the storage room and turned the handle on the door. It was dark inside. There should have been a ceiling full of LED lights casting bright illumination upon the room. Someone had turned the lights off. His shoes crunched down on glass shards. Fitzgerald reached for the wall switch.

As he flicked the lights on, a heavy object struck him from behind and pitched him forward. The breath flew from his lungs as he landed on the storage room floor. Then a hand pressed a cloth over his nose and mouth, the sickly sweet scent of chloroform sapping his strength as he flailed beneath his assailant.

After a long struggle, Fitzgerald fell still.

39

Thomas walked alongside Trooper Gaines as the paramedics wheeled the injured officer on a gurney through the exit gates of Empire Coasters. Inside the tunnels, the medical team had treated Gaines and further slowed the bleeding. The sheriff spoke comforting words to ground the fallen trooper, assuring Gaines he'd find Tre Kelly and stop the psychopath before the man caught Robyn Fournette.

The scene pulled the attention of park-goers, many pushing closer for a better look, snapping photographs with their phones, rubbernecking as the paramedics loaded the injured officer into the ambulance. Others edged back, worried the person who'd attacked Gaines was still loose in the park. Already, rumors of the shooting circulated. Thomas overheard *terrorist* and *crazy man with a gun*. Some argued there hadn't been a shooting, that Gaines had hurt himself fighting an unruly guest.

Gaines reached out and clasped Thomas's hand before the paramedics kicked the sheriff out of the ambulance.

"What happened to Faustin?" asked Gaines, his voice

strained and his forehead beaded with sweat. The officer had lost consciousness for several minutes after Thomas detained Faustin.

"Two of your team members arrived and took Faustin away. He still hasn't admitted he aided Kelly. We confiscated the phones. Now it's a matter of piecing the evidence together."

"You don't have time to build a case." Gaines hissed and reached for his leg when the gurney shifted. "Kelly is on the run. Someone needs to warn Fitzgerald."

"Trooper Fitzgerald knows what happened here. He's ready if Kelly sneaks into the hospital. Take care of yourself. I'll check on you as soon as I'm able."

"The doctors have it covered, Sheriff. Catch Kelly. That's all I want."

Thomas hopped down from the ambulance. Only adrenaline kept him upright, and Thomas figured Lambert couldn't be much better off. The doors swung shut, and the siren whooped, clearing away the onlookers. After the ambulance motored away, Thomas blinked upon seeing Chelsey and LeVar in the parking lot. For a second, he wasn't convinced they were there. Perhaps his exhausted eyes played games with him. Chelsey lifted a hand.

Thomas strode across the parking lot, dodging the drivers intent on fleeing the amusement park. "What are you doing here?"

"We learned about the shooting over the radio," Chelsey said, her eyes red from crying. She threw her arms around Thomas. "I needed to know you were okay."

"It wasn't me. A state trooper got shot."

"Was Tre Kelly the shooter?"

"No. Ron Faustin, the head of security."

LeVar's mouth fell open. "You're kidding."

"I wish I was. Seems Faustin and Kelly are working together.

I confirmed Faustin owns property east of the park. Kelly used Faustin's house to hide Dylan Fournette."

"That explains why the haunted house sound effects showed up in the recording."

Thomas turned to Chelsey. "Any news on Aguilar and Simone Axtell? I've kept my radio on, but the last hour has been too hectic for me to pay close attention."

"Nothing yet," Chelsey said. "I'm starting to worry, Thomas."

"Axtell won't escape the county without the state police catching her."

"Are you sure about that? They're spread thin, and so is your department. Let my team help. Darren and Raven are at the office and ready to hit the ground running. Scout can field calls and coordinate the search effort."

"I won't let you pursue Axtell. She already poisoned my staff and might have abducted Aguilar. This is a job for the sheriff's department and state police."

"We have to help somehow," LeVar said, straightening his shoulders, suggesting he wouldn't take no for an answer. "Come on, Shep Dawg. You've seen our work. Who caught Mark Benson after he attacked Raven?" LeVar poked a thumb against his chest. "That was us."

"Yes, with my deputies' aid. Which reminds me, Deputy Lambert is on duty and patrolling the county with the state police."

"You still need more bodies."

An argument formed on Thomas's lips. Yes, he needed help from the private investigation team. With a little creativity, he could make this work.

"I have an idea," Thomas said.

"Anything you need. Say the word."

Thomas blew out a breath. "Chelsey, go back to the office

and coordinate the search effort with your team. LeVar, I want you to link up with Deputy Lambert and ride with him."

"What are you saying?"

"I have the power to deputize civilians. Understand, I can't authorize an untrained civilian to carry a gun."

"Shep, I know how to use a gun. Back when I ran with the Kings—"

Thomas held up a hand. "It's better if you don't tell me. Look, I've wanted you on my team for months, and I never would have pulled the deputy offer if I wasn't worried about your education. But I can't think of anyone I trust more to handle the job."

"One night only?"

"Strictly temporary."

Chelsey smirked. "This reminds me of when Santa asked Rudolph to pull his sleigh."

"What do you say, LeVar? I need you and Lambert to bring Aguilar home. Can I count on you?"

"You know you can," LeVar said, giving Thomas's shoulder a playful jab. "Nightshade County Sheriff's Department deputy." Grinning, he let the idea roll around in his head. The smile fell from LeVar's face as the gravity of the situation struck. "Hook me up with Lambert. I won't let you down."

R obyn Fournette bolted awake in her hospital bed, as though a bucket of ice water splashed over her body. Her breaths came too quickly, and a black, hazy curtain unfurled over her eyes as she hyperventilated.

Something had yanked her out of sleep. A noise.

Night perched at the window. On the street below, the headlights of a lone car crawled through the darkness.

"Is anyone there?"

The corridor seemed too quiet, the hospital wing guarding a secret. When nobody answered, she reached for the call button and jammed her thumb down. After thirty seconds, she pressed the button again. The nurse didn't respond.

Outside the closed door, footsteps scuffed down the corridor. Probably the state trooper patrolling. Except the person outside her door moved to avoid detection, hiding his presence. Why would the trooper sneak through the hallway?

Heart racing, Robyn sat up and lowered her socked feet to the floor. The IV tugged her arm, and she yanked the catheter out and pressed the bandage to stop the bleeding. The scuffing footsteps came again. Her spine drew erect. Robyn stood and gripped the counter until her legs stopped trembling. She crept to the door and pressed her ear against the wood, afraid to call out again until she was certain the state trooper still guarded the corridor.

Patients recovered in rooms down the hallway. Robyn should have heard the medical staff moving about the corridor, voices as nurses checked on patients. Only silence and the scraping of shoes against the floor spilled beneath the doorway.

Robyn worked up the courage to open the door. She pictured the stalker waiting outside, an insane grin stretching his lips. Had the sheriff been right about Tre Kelly? My God, was he Dylan's father? The idea of Kelly stalking Robyn for six years stretched her nerves to the point of ripping. The police couldn't help Robyn, and she wasn't safe in the hospital. She had only one choice.

Escape and rescue Dylan.

Holding her breath, Robyn edged the door open and peered through the crack. Nobody in the hallway.

Halfway down the corridor, the nurses' station appeared unmanned. The sudden shriek of a ringing phone made Robyn leap out of her skin. Her eyes landed on a blinking light at the nurses' station as the phone continued to ring, but no nurse responded to her call for help.

She walked toward the station, her gaze darting from room to room—some occupied with sleeping patients, others vacant and dark. The echoes of footsteps followed her. She prayed it was her own footsteps.

Robyn stopped before she passed the station. A white stockinged leg jutted out from behind the desk. Her heart thundering in her ears, Robyn slipped around the desk and discovered the auburn-haired nurse sprawled on the floor, her lifeless eyes staring up at the ceiling, a trail of blood trickling from her gashed scalp toward the wall.

With a scream, Robyn whirled around to run. She pulled up short and read the message scrawled across the wall in red marker.

I FOUND YOU.

41

Inside the crowded office of Wolf Lake Consulting, Chelsey repeated the mantra inside her head—her friends would survive the night. Convincing herself that all would be well was the only path to sanity. But with Deputy Aguilar missing and in the hands of a deranged woman, Chelsey fought to compartmentalize her emotions. She had a duty to help the authorities track Simone Axtell. But that wasn't easy, especially after Thomas deputized LeVar. She fretted over her student intern, worried he was unprepared to chase a hostile fugitive. Chelsey told herself LeVar had crossed far more dangerous bridges, but it didn't calm her nerves. And now she worried about Thomas, the sheriff working on an hour of sleep over the last two days as he pursued a kidnapper.

Two police band radios positioned on opposite sides of the office kept Chelsey informed of the investigation's progress, no matter where she was in the room. Raven and Darren worked at one computer, with Scout at LeVar's workstation. Chelsey sifted through public sightings of Simone Axtell and her vehicle. Most, if not all, would be false leads. Still, she owed it to Deputy

Aguilar and LeVar to scrutinize each report and determine if the lead might be valid.

Across the office, Chelsey locked eyes with Raven. It was obvious Raven was a bundle of nerves. This was her brother. Though they all expected LeVar would join law enforcement after graduation, the reality that it was happening tonight overwhelmed the investigators and made them act like parents waiting for their child to return home after a midnight party.

"LeVar knows what he's doing," Darren said, offering comforting words. "And he's riding with Deputy Lambert. Stop worrying."

"Scout, any new reports come in?" Chelsey asked, staying busy.

"One. A man in Syracuse claims he spotted Axtell's car outside a gas station on the west side of the city."

"Do you buy the report?"

"Not really. According to the report, the man didn't see anyone in the passenger seat and wasn't sure if the driver had blond or dark hair. Plus, he first reported the vehicle had Pennsylvania plates, before he changed his story and said they were from New York."

"Mark it down on the map, just in case."

Scout pressed a pin into a wall map of potential sightings. As Chelsey studied the map, paranoid she'd overlooked a vital clue, the radio squawked with activity.

Darren rose from his chair. "Did you catch that? Kane Grove PD found Axtell's car in a mall parking lot in the center of the city."

Chelsey leaped out of her seat, as though she wanted to drive to the mall and rescue Aguilar herself. "That doesn't sound right. Simone Axtell is trying to escape the county with Deputy Aguilar. Why would she stop at the mall?"

"Right," Raven said. "She's crazy, but not an idiot. If Axtell poisoned Aguilar like she did Maggie and the dispatcher, Aguilar wouldn't be in any condition to shop."

"It's a trick." They all stared at Chelsey. "You remember the old saying about hiding in a crowd? Axtell ditched her car in the mall parking lot because it's difficult to spot in a mass of similar vehicles. Only this time, the plan backfired. I guarantee she stole a vehicle to throw the police off her trail."

"And if the stolen vehicle belongs to a family spending the evening shopping," added Darren, "they might not report it stolen for hours."

Chelsey called Kane Grove PD. She spoke to Detective Presley, whom Chelsey knew from past investigations, and confirmed the license plate and model of Simone Axtell's car. Kane Grove PD was canvassing the mall, searching for Deputy Aguilar and her unhinged house guest.

"Axtell switched vehicles," Chelsey said. "Any reports of vehicles stolen from the mall parking lot?"

"Hold on," Presley said. The detective set the phone down and dialed her contact at the mall. After a brief conversation, Presley returned. "You won't believe this, but a woman just reported her SUV stolen. The parking lot is packed this evening, and she assumed she was searching in the wrong area."

"Make and model?"

"It's a 2017 Kia Sorento LX, dark blue. Hold on, I'll get you the license plate number."

Presley added the Sorento to the BOLO. Chelsey radioed LeVar and Deputy Lambert with the updated information, hoping they could rein Axtell in before she escaped in the stolen vehicle.

∽

HE SHOULDN'T HAVE FELT this uneasy.

LeVar stuffed his hands inside his pockets, so Lambert wouldn't see them shaking. He squinted at the darkness flying at the windshield as Lambert's cruiser raced down a country road between Treman Mills and Wolf Lake. Lambert argued this was prime area for hiding from law enforcement. The countryside fell under county jurisdiction, and the sheriff's department rarely patrolled the region, which featured numerous turnoffs and scenic lookouts—perfect places to conceal a vehicle and wait until the coast cleared.

"And the ramp to the interstate is four miles north of here," said Lambert, driving with one hand as his gaze darted toward the driveways of scattered properties. "Once you hit the interstate, you have a free shot into Buffalo or Albany."

LeVar nodded without responding. His right hand sneaked out of his pocket and grasped the door handle. How could Deputy Lambert drive at the speed limit on an unfamiliar road and carry on a conversation at the same time? Maybe LeVar wasn't cut out for law enforcement. He couldn't shake the sensation that the cruiser would spin off the macadam at any second, or they'd drive past the stolen Kia Sorento with neither noticing the vehicle.

"In through your nose, out through your mouth," Lambert said.

"What are you talking about?"

"Your breathing—it's too fast. Breathe deeply through your nose, relax your shoulders, then exhale through your mouth."

As Lambert demonstrated, LeVar wiped a hand across his lips. He never pictured the deputy as the relaxed, yoga-loving type.

"It's your first gig," said Lambert, slapping LeVar on the shoulder with his free hand. "Totally normal to feel nervous. I've seen you perform in the field. You got this."

"It's just that . . . man, I can't believe this is real. Thomas deputized me."

"Because you can do the job. Now, perform your breathing exercises. We have a fugitive to catch and a friend to rescue."

"*Aight*. I'm breathing, bro."

LeVar drew in a breath as instructed, let his shoulders slacken, and exhaled. It wasn't working. He rubbed his eyes and grasped the handle again, wishing he'd never expressed interest in joining the Nightshade County Sheriff's Department. It wasn't too late to change majors. If he shifted his course load, he could transition into a business or public relations degree. Perhaps forecast the weather. Or teach. Anything but chase criminals with guns.

After another ten minutes of crisscrossing rural terrain, LeVar stopped trembling. What was he worried about? The odds that they'd come across Simone Axtell were slim to none. Nightshade County covered almost 900 square miles, and there was no guarantee the fugitive was still in the county. As much as he wanted to save Aguilar and ensure her safety, it was smarter to leave his friend's rescue to the professionals—experienced officers who knew what they were doing and wouldn't freeze. In fact, LeVar wouldn't be surprised if the state police caught Axtell outside of—

The radio burst with a sighting, cutting off LeVar's thoughts. A trooper had glimpsed a Kia Sorrento matching the stolen vehicle's description, rocketing out of Kane Grove and driving toward the highway.

"That's our target," Lambert said, flipping on the siren and whirling lights. "If we hustle, we'll cut her off before she hits the interstate."

LeVar uttered a silent prayer. But this time, he didn't pray for his nerves to calm. He wanted to save Deputy Aguilar while there was still time.

42

The sheriff's cruiser screeched to a stop outside the hospital. Thomas bounded toward the entryway, where a woman from the hospital security team waited. For the last fifteen minutes, Trooper Fitzgerald hadn't responded to the sheriff's radio calls.

"We locked down the hospital," the security guard said, leading Thomas across the lobby toward the stairwell. An alarm shrilled every two seconds. Each blast of sound frayed the sheriff's nerves. "Trooper Fitzgerald isn't at his post, and Robyn Fournette's room is empty. We're evacuating the hospital, but it will take time to get the patients out, and some can't be moved."

Thomas followed the woman up the concrete stairs, the stairwell gloomy compared to the lobby, their footfalls ringing off the walls.

"Didn't anyone at the nurses' station see Fitzgerald leave his post?"

"There was one nurse manning the desk after visiting hours. We found her dead. Someone dragged her behind the desk. Our security team is sweeping every floor for Robyn Fournette and the state trooper."

"What about the medical staff? Tell me someone saw what happened to Fournette and the state trooper."

"There were two doctors on Fournette's floor. We only staff two nurses on each floor and a handful of orderlies after seven o'clock. This is a small hospital."

Thomas took the stairs two at a time, desperation pulling him forward. He'd promised to keep Robyn Fournette safe, and Trooper Fitzgerald was a friend.

With the elevators shut down and only accessible with a key, the stairs represented the only paths to the exits. Cameras watched every corridor, but so far Tre Kelly had eluded the security monitors.

When they reached Robyn Fournette's floor, Thomas pushed the stairwell door open and rushed into the corridor. He waved the guard down a second hallway, halting when he spied the message scrawled across the wall.

I FOUND YOU.

Gun in hand, he peeked inside recovery rooms, searching for Kelly, Fournette, and Trooper Fitzgerald. Behind him stood the nurses' station and the dead woman stuffed between the desk and wall.

His eyes swept the corridor, seeking a clue that would lead him to either Fournette or the state trooper. Dark splotches interrupted the polished floor every few steps and left a trail down the hallway like a psychopath's breadcrumbs. Thomas knelt and examined the splotches.

Blood.

He followed the trail, which ended outside a closet used by the cleaning staff. Chemical cleaner hung thick in the air outside the door. He jiggled the handle and found it locked. It took three bone-jarring kicks to bust the lock and open the door. He searched the darkened closet for a wall switch or pull string.

Unable to find either amid the pitch black, he aimed a flashlight inside.

Two shelves of cleaning products. A mop in a bucket.

And a man's leg jutting out from under a drop cloth.

With an intake of breath, Thomas ripped the sheet away. Trooper Fitzgerald lay face down. A streak of red colored the floor.

"Officer down. Third floor storage closet."

Thomas set the radio down and touched Fitzgerald's neck. He had a pulse. The state trooper groaned and mumbled something indecipherable.

Footsteps pounded behind Thomas. The sheriff turned and raised his gun. He dropped the weapon upon recognizing the guard who'd led him inside.

"He's alive," Thomas said. "It appears he has a head injury. Have you seen or heard anything?"

Before the woman responded, a crash on the opposite end of the hospital wing shattered the dark.

FINDING the dead nurse and the stalker's message written across the wall sent Robyn into a free-fall panic. Every few seconds, the security alarm burst and caused Robyn to cover her ears. She ran down the gloomy corridor, unaware of where she was or where she was running to. Saving Dylan was her priority, but she had to elude Tre Kelly first.

After yelling for help, Robyn heard footfalls racing down the hallway. It had to be Tre, following her voice.

She ducked into the first room she found. Archived records, pills, medical supplies, and linens lined the shelves of a long room divided into rows. Storage bins rested on shelves, the center row on wheels. With a trembling hand, Robyn reached for the switch and turned the lights off, plunging the interior into absolute darkness. Black dots encased her vision. Slowly, her eyesight adjusted, and she made out the dim shapes of the bins, as she huddled with her arms wrapped around her knees, the hospital gown tearing down the back from all that running. Goosebumps bubbled along her skin.

Someone ran past the room. Robyn held her breath until her pursuer continued down the hallway. She exhaled, believing she'd lost him.

Taking nothing for granted, she strained her eyes, trying to recall where the medical instruments had been. She should have grabbed a weapon before she turned off the lights. Her ankles buckled as she climbed to her feet. Meant to keep her calm and restful, sedatives swam through her bloodstream, impairing her mind and making it difficult to steady herself. One hand grasping the shelves, she groped through the dark.

The door creaked open.

A shaft of light poured through the opening and missed her by inches. Robyn backed away, hoping the person in the doorway was a security guard or a physician. She knew better. Tre Kelly had followed Robyn for six years, hiding in the dark and watching her every move. There was no escaping the lunatic.

Tre isn't Dylan's father. He can't be.

"Come out, Robyn. I know you're in here."

His voice made her skin feel too tight. A sudden glint caught her attention as the light shaft landed on an opaque storage bin. She focused on the scalpel inside the bin. It wasn't a knife or a gun, but it would serve if Tre discovered Robyn hiding between the rows.

"How could you deny Dylan his father? What mother raises a boy without a strong man in the house?"

Robyn reached for the bin. Unclasping the hinge would

make a loud, popping sound and draw Kelly to her. She'd need to move quickly.

"You were wonderful that night, Robyn. Don't pretend you were asleep. That trick didn't fool me then, and it doesn't fool me now. You loved every second. Admit it."

He pushed the door inward another few inches, widening the light shaft, which fell across the tops of her feet like burning sunlight. She lowered her head and crouched with her back to the middle row, fighting to control her breathing as her fingers fumbled with the latch.

"Stop running and tell me where you are. I'm blocking the exit. You can't escape this time."

Kelly's hand crawled across the wall toward the light switch. In a second, he'd cast illumination into the storage room.

Robyn unclasped the top of the bin. The noise was deafening despite the shrieking alarm.

With a growl, Kelly flared the lights. Robyn yanked the top off the bin and hurled it at the stalker, who bounded into the room with a madman's scream. He was almost on top of her when she grasped the scalpel and thrust it at him.

The medical instrument dug into Tre's chest and knocked him backward. Blood welled beneath his shirt. He glanced down at the injury, then raised his eyes to Robyn, fury twisting his face. When he lunged at her, she tore the scalpel across his face and dug a crevice through his cheek, missing his eye by a fraction of an inch. Tre's fist struck Robyn's face and knocked her against the shelves, wrenching her back. He dove at her. She kicked out and drove him away.

Tre stumbled and fell. Before he recovered, she gripped the scalpel and ripped it across his arm, drawing more blood.

"Tell me where Dylan is! Give me my son, or I'll kill you."

The stalker issued a deranged chuckle, even as he shielded himself with a raised forearm.

Seeing her chance to escape, Robyn backed away, the weapon still in her hand. He seemed impervious to pain as he clutched the shelving and dragged himself up. Her legs felt as though they were filled with gelatin, the medication blurring her thoughts.

As she rounded the corner, Tre staggered along the center row, gaining on her. With a heave, she threw her body against the shelves, which rolled toward the stalker, constricting his pathway. Tre recognized Robyn's intentions and pushed back, fighting to drive her against the wall and pin her. Bracing her legs against the shelving behind her, Robyn burst forward with all her strength. The wheels caught on the floor, tipping the middle shelves. Bins of medical equipment and pills tumbled over and crashed down upon Tre, burying him.

With a scream, Robyn stumbled into the hallway and fell against the wall. She struggled to regain her balance as the stalker tossed the bins aside and bellowed inside the storage room. He was coming for her again.

Robyn turned toward the stairwell. Tre darted into the hallway and clutched her neck. She gasped, choking as he strangled the life out of her.

"Ungrateful whore. If I can't have you, no one can."

Robyn's eyelids fluttered before another shape materialized out of the haze and knocked Tre sideways. She saw a tangle of limbs as the two men struggled across the floor. The uniformed sheriff fought his way atop Tre and struck the stalker across the face. Tre's eyes rolled back in his head before the sheriff twisted the madman onto his stomach and cuffed the man's wrists.

Shouts for help mingled with the blaring alarm. Two guards turned the corner and rushed to the sheriff's side as Robyn crawled up to her knees.

Robyn met the sheriff with pleading eyes.

"Where's my son?"

43

Only the seatbelt prevented LeVar from shooting out of the passenger seat on pure adrenaline. For months, he'd dreamed of joining law enforcement and making a positive difference. The moment had arrived, and a close friend needed saving. Beside LeVar, Lambert drove with both hands clutched around the steering wheel, the deputy's eagle eyes picking out every unseen curve in the road before the headlights revealed the turns.

"Follow my lead, LeVar," Lambert said through gritted teeth. "Don't engage the suspect and don't be a hero."

"I got it."

The state trooper who'd spotted Simone Axtell's stolen vehicle had closed the distance on their target, tracking the fugitive down County Route 23 toward Deputy Lambert and LeVar. Except for the occasional driveway, no more turnoffs existed. Axtell was coming this way at highway speed, and she had Aguilar in the front seat of the SUV.

"What's the plan?" LeVar asked over the growl of the motor.

"Prevent her from passing. When she gets close, we'll block the road."

In his mind, LeVar pictured every action movie chase scene, which climaxed with the police barricading a road. Sometimes, those plans backfired. What if Axtell didn't stop? Lambert couldn't predict how the unhinged woman would react when she spotted the sheriff's cruiser blocking County Route 23.

Nothing but infinite blackness lay ahead as the cruiser navigated the twists and turns of the rural route. Along the road, trees sprang out of the night at the very last second, causing LeVar's heart to leap into his throat.

Then two microscopic lights appeared in the distance. They grew larger every time LeVar breathed. This was it. The stolen Kia Sorento rushed at them like a shooting star. Behind the SUV, the whirling lights of the state trooper's vehicle ignited the roadway.

"Hold on tight," Lambert said, a split-second before he braked and swerved the cruiser so it formed a barricade.

LeVar's pulse pounded in his head as he stared out the passenger window. He was in the direct path of the onrushing SUV.

"Out of the vehicle, LeVar," Lambert said, breaking LeVar's trance.

Time stood still as LeVar crawled behind the cruiser with Lambert. The deputy produced a bullhorn and aimed his gun over the cruiser's roof.

And still Simone Axtell's vehicle rushed forth, the headlamps morphing into rising suns as the SUV eclipsed the ridge and started down the other side.

If the SUV struck the cruiser at full speed, LeVar and Deputy Lambert wouldn't survive. LeVar glanced at the deputy in question, but Lambert held steady with the gun fixed on the SUV's windshield.

A thousand yards and closing fast.

Five hundred.

Two hundred.

LeVar refused to leave the deputy alone. He'd stay beside Lambert until the deputy ordered him to flee.

When the SUV was less than a hundred yards away, the tires shrieked. For a frozen moment, LeVar worried the SUV would roll over and crush Aguilar in the passenger seat. He covered his mouth when the Kia Sorento rocked to a stop. A second later, the state troopers stopped behind Axtell. Two shadowed figures interrupted the headlights and crouched behind their cruiser, weapons raised.

"Simone Axtell," Lambert called through the bullhorn, "step out of the vehicle with your hands raised."

LeVar rubbed the imprints of the headlights off his eyes. He spied Axtell behind the wheel and a slumped figure in the passenger seat.

Aguilar.

"Stay here," Lambert said, lowering the bullhorn.

"Where are you going?"

"I'm approaching the vehicle."

"What do you want me to do?"

"Nothing. Stay out of the line of fire. She might have a gun." Before Lambert crept around the sheriff's cruiser, he swung his head to LeVar. "If by freak chance she makes it past me, don't let her get away. Unless she has a gun. Then don't do a damn thing."

"But—"

Deputy Lambert left him alone and strode toward the stolen vehicle. With his head peeking above the hood, LeVar chewed the inside of his cheek, wishing he could help. Aguilar didn't move inside the SUV.

She has to be alive.

The driver's side door opened. Simone Axtell stepped onto the blacktop, dragging Deputy Aguilar with her. There was something wrong with Aguilar, who rested limp in Axtell's arms.

"Freeze!" Lambert yelled. "Show me your hands!"

The tension pulled the night into a taut cord. Behind Axtell, the state troopers crept out from behind their vehicle.

Lambert stopped. His flashlight beam reflected off the knife blade held against Aguilar's throat.

"Let us pass," Axtell said, flashing glares at Lambert and the troopers closing in on her. "If you don't, I'll kill Veronica. I swear, I'll do it."

"Put the knife down!"

LeVar edged out from behind the cruiser as Lambert trained his gun on Axtell. At this distance, the deputy could shoot the woman and force her to drop the weapon. A tiny accuracy error, and Lambert might hit Aguilar. And would the shot prevent Axtell from sweeping the blade across Aguilar's throat before she died?

"We love each other," Axtell yelled over the wind. "Veronica and I are meant to be together."

"This isn't the way, Simone," said Lambert, taking two steps forward. "If you care about Aguilar, you'll let her go and drop the weapon."

"I can't do that. The second I step away from Veronica, you'll shoot me."

"Not unless you threaten her life. Drop the knife, and we'll talk this over."

A strained laugh escaped Axtell's lips. "There's nothing to discuss. You don't know what I've been through, what it's like, or the pain I feel every day. This," Axtell said, tilting her head at the slumped form of Deputy Aguilar, "is the only woman who understands me. We'll be together forever. I won't let anyone tear us apart."

LeVar rose out of his crouch. A sharp moment of tension froze everyone as Axtell's gaze landed on LeVar.

"Who are you?" she asked, eyeing LeVar. She checked over her shoulder for the advancing state troopers. "Back off! I'll kill her if you come any closer."

The troopers didn't back away, but they stopped.

"You're not a cop," said Axtell, turning her attention back to LeVar. "Why are you here?"

Lambert raised an eyebrow, warning LeVar to get behind the cruiser. LeVar stepped into the starlight, each sneaker straddling the centerline.

"I'm a friend of Ag—Veronica's," LeVar said, raising his hands.

"Oh yeah? What's your name?"

"LeVar. LeVar Hopkins."

"How come Veronica never mentioned you?"

LeVar moved beside Lambert, the deputy's gun still aimed at the woman with the knife. "I can't answer that. But I swear I'm a close friend. I can't say I've known her for as long as you have, or that our friendship is as close as yours. But I care for her." As LeVar spoke, the corner of Simone's mouth twitched. "And I care about anyone who Veronica calls a friend."

"Liar. You don't care about me."

Axtell's grip tightened on the knife, and Deputy Lambert reached a hand out to prevent LeVar from advancing.

"Get the hell behind the cruiser," Lambert muttered.

"Give me a chance to talk her down," LeVar whispered.

"You aren't qualified to . . . dammit, LeVar. Do as I say."

"You got a clean shot at Axtell, dawg. She's not going anywhere."

"Axtell has a knife, LeVar."

"She won't hurt Aguilar." As Lambert shot him an incredulous look, LeVar raised his voice. "I don't know what you've been through, but I understand the pain you feel. No matter how hard your life has been, you can turn it around."

Axtell scowled. "What do you know about overcoming pain? Bet you were raised in a perfect home and had everything given to you."

"Nah, it was never like that." Another small step toward Axtell and Aguilar. "I grew up in Harmon. My father walked out on us when I was too young to remember his face. Mom worked two jobs and still couldn't pay the bills. Then the pressure got to be too much, and she turned to drugs. Heroin. I made the same mistake, but for me, it was the Harmon Kings gang instead of heroin. That was my life from the day I became a teenager until a little over a year ago."

"What happened a year ago?"

"Mom got help. She's a recovered addict now, owns her own house down the road from me, and finds strength in her friends."

"And you?"

"There isn't a day that I don't wake up and experience impostor syndrome. You understand what that is? It's believing I don't belong, that I don't deserve the good things in my life, that every inch I've gained is an illusion, and it's a matter of time before someone comes along and snatches it from me."

The knife slid a fraction of an inch away from Aguilar's throat. Axtell bobbed her head, as if LeVar had struck a chord.

"I wouldn't survive without the people I surround myself with," said LeVar, keeping his palms raised. "And Deputy Aguilar . . . Veronica . . . is someone who has my back. So I beg you to think about what you're doing and who you'll injure if you make the wrong decision. Please, drop the knife. Nobody will hurt you. I won't let them."

A tear ran down Axtell's cheek. Her arm fell slack, the knife hanging at her hip as she cradled Deputy Aguilar's head with her free arm. The state trooper moved so silently that LeVar never noticed him before he struck Axtell from behind. A cry, then the knife flew from the woman's hand and clanged against the blacktop.

As the first state trooper subdued the struggling, cursing woman, the second supported Deputy Aguilar. Lambert ran to his partner, LeVar trailing behind.

Lambert took Aguilar in his arms.

"She's breathing," Lambert said, closing his eyes and lifting his face to the night sky. When the deputy's eyes opened, they fixed on LeVar. "You did a helluva job. I'm still pissed that you disobeyed my direct order to stay out of harm's way, but you saved Aguilar's life."

Already, Deputy Aguilar stirred and flicked glassy eyes back and forth among the faces in the night.

After radioing for an ambulance, Lambert slapped LeVar's back. "Helluva job. Thomas will be proud of you."

44

After the medical staff hooked Dylan Fournette to an IV and hydrated the rescued child, the boy fell asleep in the hospital bed, curled on his left side as his mother stroked the hair off his forehead.

Thomas rested against the wall with his arms folded, exhaustion threatening to topple him. He wanted sleep more than anything, but his shift wouldn't end until he completed the interview.

"I wanted to tell you everything," said Robyn. "From the night Dylan vanished at the amusement park, I knew you were different and would help me, unlike the police in Illinois. Then Tre sent that message to my phone and threatened to kill Dylan if I talked."

"Did you know Tre was stalking you at the amusement park?"

Robyn paused before answering. "I sensed someone trailing us, though I never glimpsed a face. He must have followed us into the souvenir shop. I felt certain someone was watching, but with all the people crowded together, I chalked it up to paranoia. How long will Tre be in jail?"

Sensing her worry, Thomas pulled a chair beside Robyn and leaned forward with his elbows on his knees. "First-degree kidnapping carries a minimum twenty-year sentence. Throw in assaulting an officer of the law, murdering a nurse, and multiple attempted murder charges, and I'm confident he'll spend the rest of his life in prison. That's what I'll push for with the DA."

Robyn's lip quivered. "So he'll never hurt us again."

"Never. I'll make sure he never gets out." Thomas sat back and crossed one leg over the other, glancing away as he composed his thoughts. "Do you believe Tre Kelly is Dylan's father?"

"It's possible. All this time I assumed Dylan belonged to TJ." She rubbed her eyes. "I can't come to grips with TJ never admitting the truth. He suspected Tre raped me after I passed out. I'll never forgive TJ, even if Dylan turns out to be his."

"A DNA test will confirm who Dylan's father is."

Robyn looked down at Dylan, the child so fragile and innocent as he drew his knees into a fetal position. "I can't accept either man as Dylan's father. Neither deserves my beautiful boy."

Thomas ran through the rest of his questions and left Robyn alone with Dylan. She had a long haul ahead to pull her life together, but at least Tre Kelly would never terrorize her again.

When Thomas entered the hallway, he found Lambert waiting, the deputy just as fatigued as Thomas.

"You look how I feel," Lambert said.

"Right back at you. When this is over, we're both going home and sleeping for twenty-four hours. Any update on Aguilar?"

A wry grin formed on Lambert's face. "She's awake and ordering the doctors around, claiming she's ready to go home."

"Axtell didn't poison her?"

Lambert shook his head. "She hit Aguilar with enough sedative to knock out a bear. Aguilar is groggy, but she's coming around. The doctor wants her in bed for today and tomorrow, but she claims she can return to work. I don't know who will win out, but I'm enjoying the battle."

The tension melted out of Thomas's neck and shoulders. He'd spent the night worrying over his lead deputy, even as he tracked Tre Kelly.

"Fitzgerald is on the second floor," Lambert said, running a hand through his buzzed hair. "Doctor says he has a mild concussion. He'll be out of work for a few weeks and will need physical therapy." Lambert rapped his knuckles against his head. "Lucky for Fitzgerald, he's hard-headed."

Thomas's eyes fell to the tops of his shoes. "Now I need to decide what to do about LeVar. He performed well in the line of duty?"

"Better than I could have. You should have been there, Thomas. LeVar talked Axtell into lowering her weapon. That gave the troopers enough time to converge and take her down."

"I got a text from LeVar an hour ago."

"What did it say?"

"Between referring to me as Shep Dawg five or ten times, he asked about joining the department for the end of summer, then filling in on part-time shifts once or twice a week during the school year."

"Take him up on the offer. He needs to listen to his superiors so he doesn't get his ass shot. But he's way ahead of any recruit I've ever worked beside. We need the help, right?"

"That's the understatement of the century."

"Then stop talking yourself out of it and hire the guy. While you're at it, there's another stack of applications sitting on Maggie's desk. Find that diamond in the rough and hire a full-time deputy."

Thomas slapped his forehead. "Oh, man. I forgot to check on Maggie and the dispatcher."

"They're fine, Thomas. Fortunately, neither ate much of the fruit salad. The hospital wants to keep them through tomorrow morning, but they should be able to go home by lunchtime."

The clock on the wall read one in the morning. Somehow, despite attacks by Tre Kelly and Simone Axtell, everyone Thomas cared about had survived. Before he fell asleep, he'd be sure to give thanks. Someone must have smiled down on Thomas's friends and family tonight.

Before departing, he checked on Fitzgerald and Aguilar. Fitzgerald spoke for five minutes before falling asleep, his head still throbbing from Tre Kelly's sneak attack. Aguilar protested that she was ready to go home and return to work the next day, but Thomas ordered her to take the rest of the week off and not return to the office until the psychologist cleared her for active duty.

"What's wrong with Simone?" Aguilar asked, her fingers kneading the blanket as she sat up in bed. "Is it true her father has been in a wheelchair since she was a child?"

"Yes. The Wolf Lake Consulting team spoke with Simone's parents."

"She made everything up. The molestation, her successful career, traveling the world."

"It seems she created an alternate world for herself and had a mental breakdown."

Aguilar creased her forehead. "But that makes no sense. Simone didn't have a traumatic childhood, and she seemed so normal during college."

"Some delusional disorders are caused by chemical imbalances in the brain, not psychological trauma."

"I hope she finally gets the help she needs."

When the elevator doors opened, Thomas stepped into the hospital lobby. Chelsey was waiting for him, twirling a keyring around her finger, her leather jacket hanging open.

"Chelsey, it's almost two in the morning."

"All the more reason to drive you home."

"But my cruiser is in the parking lot."

Chelsey touched his cheek and smirked. "Do you really think the hospital will ticket the county sheriff? Follow me to my car. This time, you ride shotgun. And no complaining about my driving."

"Yes, ma'am."

Thomas didn't remember the drive to their lakeside A-frame. According to Chelsey, he bobbed in and out of sleep until they arrived.

THE SHERIFF DIDN'T SLEEP for twenty-four consecutive hours as he'd ordered Deputy Lambert to do. But the sun was past its apex when he awoke the next afternoon, and smoke from the barbecue curled through the open bedroom window as he stumbled bleary-eyed to the shower.

Jack and Tigger followed him downstairs, the dog yapping and barking, no doubt excited to see Thomas after two days and nights of nonstop work. Thomas opened the deck door and descended the steps. In the backyard, LeVar grilled a steak and watched the boats float across Wolf Lake.

"Lambert told me what you did last night," Thomas said. LeVar set down the spatula and braced himself for a lecture. "It's not how I would have handled the situation, but you thought on your feet and ensured Aguilar's safety. And no one got hurt. You did well, LeVar. Peacefully deescalating a hostage situation is something even veteran police officers and FBI agents find challenging."

"That means a lot, coming from you."

"I considered your offer of working weekends, and I think it's a terrific idea."

"Seriously? You're giving me the job?"

"Part-time, as you suggested. You'll work a shift or two on the weekends, no overnights, and you'll keep your butt in school. In the meantime, I contacted our mutual acquaintance at the FBI and told her about your first night as deputy and the lives you saved."

"Scarlett Bell?"

"It turns out the BAU has intern programs for minorities."

LeVar narrowed his eyes and flipped the steak. "I want to earn my spot. No special treatment."

"LeVar, everyone gets a break now and then. It's like Andy Warhol's fifteen minutes of fame. Me? I got the LAPD job because a buddy from college knew the chief and put in a good word. When I returned to Wolf Lake, Sheriff Gray hired me because I'd interned under him during high school. It's up to you to take advantage of your opportunities."

"Last night, I got my foot in the door."

Thomas nodded. "Real world experience will beef up your application and get you into the intern program."

"Darren was right about the kidnapping," LeVar said. "It was an inside job."

"Dylan Fournette trusted Tre Kelly because he worked as a park security officer. Nobody questioned Kelly when he emerged from the tunnels and walked Dylan to his vehicle. As far as we can tell, Kelly bribed Ron Faustin to keep him quiet. Faustin allowed Kelly to hide Dylan at his house, so the boy was nearby while Kelly worked."

"Will there be a DNA test?"

"There will," Thomas said, skimming a rock across the water as gentle waves rolled ashore. "I assume the test will prove Tre Kelly raped and impregnated Robyn Fournette."

"That's a terrible burden for Dylan to carry. Who would want Tre Kelly for a parent?"

"Biology doesn't make you a father. Only love does."

Without saying a word, LeVar hugged Thomas. When they parted, LeVar turned away and wiped his eye, pretending the smoke was irritating him.

"Not complaining, but what was that for?"

"For being the only father I've ever had. You're the real deal, Shep Dawg."

Thomas swallowed the lump in his throat. He was relieved when Scout Mourning approached down the concrete pathway, drawn by the savory scent of dinner.

LeVar lifted a hand. "Well, if it isn't our future BAU profiler."

"Stop," Scout said, her face flushing.

"Hey, we might be partners."

"What are you getting on about, LeVar?"

"It seems my friends have been talking to a certain FBI agent and propping me up. So, I'm applying to their intern program."

"No way!" Scout yelled, giving LeVar a high-five.

"Way. You can't get rid of me. I'm like the plague, but prettier. By the way, dinner is almost ready."

Scout bent over the grill and inhaled. "Is that filet mignon?"

"Only the best."

Thomas cleared his throat. "Now that the two of you are together, it's time to set ground rules."

"Raven and Darren already spoke to us," said LeVar, throwing an arm around Scout's shoulder. "We're *friends*. Ain't nothing going on between us. Like she'd be interested in a hard-ened gangster so much older than her, anyhow."

"As if," Scout said, jabbing him in the shoulder.

"We're sorry for creating a false perception, and we promise not to pull the shades or lock the door while we're working inside. But y'all need to pull your heads out of the gutter."

A honk in the driveway brought them around. Chelsey had arrived home from work.

"I appreciate both of you understanding," Thomas said. "But I haven't eaten since this time yesterday, and I could swallow an entire steak."

LeVar warded off Thomas with the spatula. "There's enough food for everyone. Control yourself."

Long into the evening, they enjoyed summer's last stand and roasted marshmallows over the fire. Joined by her mother, Scout danced on legs that refused to ever again be still, and LeVar played hip-hop through a portable speaker, selling the adults on the merits of J Cole and Kendrick Lamar. Thomas held Chelsey close and whispered in her ear, "I'd love to grow old with you, if you'll have me." She answered with a closed-eye smile and a longing sigh.

And Thomas's heart was full.

Thank you for reading!
The Wolf Lake Series continues in the new gripping suspense thriller, The Bone Forest.
Ready to find out what happens next?

Read Book Ten Today.

GET A FREE BOOK!

I'm a pretty nice guy once you look past the grisly images in my head. Most of all, I love connecting with awesome readers like you.

Join my VIP Reader Group and get a FREE serial killer thriller for your Kindle.

Get My Free Book

www.danpadavona.com/thriller-readers-vip-group/

SUPPORT INDIE AUTHORS

Did you enjoy this book? If so, please let other thriller fans know by leaving a short review. Positive reviews help spread the word about independent authors and their novels. Thank you.

ACKNOWLEDGEMENTS

No writer journeys alone. Special thanks are in order to my editor, Kimberly Broderick, for providing invaluable feedback, catching errors, and making my story shine. I also wish to thank my brilliant cover designer, Caroline Teagle Johnson. Your artwork never ceases to amaze me. I owe so much of my success to your hard work.

Proofreader and editor C.B. Moore cleaned up the manuscript and brought my story to a higher level.

Shout outs to my advance readers, Marcia Campbell, Teresa Padavona, and Donna Puscheck, for catching those final pesky typos and plot holes. Most of all, thank you to my readers for your loyalty and support. You changed my life, and I am forever grateful.

ABOUT THE AUTHOR

Dan Padavona is the author of The Wolf Lake series, The Logan and Scarlett series, The Darkwater Cove series, The Scarlett Bell thriller series, *Her Shallow Grave*, The Dark Vanishings series, *Camp Slasher, Quilt, Crawlspace, The Face of Midnight, Storberry, Shadow Witch*, and the horror anthology, *The Island*. He lives in upstate New York with his beautiful wife, Terri, and their children, Joe, and Julia. Dan is a meteorologist with NOAA's National Weather Service. Besides writing, he enjoys visiting amusement parks, beach vacations, Renaissance fairs, gardening, playing with the family dogs, and eating too much ice cream.

Visit Dan at: www.danpadavona.com

Made in the USA
Las Vegas, NV
13 February 2024

85737067R00166